I0614871

Spirit in Tow

by

Terry Segan

The Marni Legend Series, Book 1

Spirit in Tow

Cover Art by *Jennifer Greeff*

The Wild Rose Press, Inc.
PO Box 708
Adams Basin, NY 14410-0708
Visit us at www.thewildrosepress.com

Publishing History
First Edition, 2022
Trade Paperback ISBN 978-1-5092-4360-0
Digital ISBN 978-1-5092-4361-7

The Marni Legend Series, Book 1
Published in the United States of America

The usual cadre of fishermen dotted the docks. If I boldly stepped onto the ship, would they know I didn't belong? Could one be a sentry in disguise? I sauntered past, trying to catch a glimpse of any crew hanging about. The boat was in complete darkness.

Gus waited on my favorite perch. "It's about time you showed up. Why aren't you in all black so nobody can see you? God, you look like an amateur."

"Perhaps because I am an amateur. I'm not the one with a criminal record." I sat beside him.

"Who says I got a record? I ain't never been locked up."

It never occurred to me he'd never been caught. Maybe I should have consulted him—had he bothered to show up earlier. "This way I blend in with the tourists. If anybody comes, they'll think nothing of a woman enjoying the fresh air."

"You got a lot to learn."

Breaking and Entering 101 wasn't a class I wanted to take. "Enough about my lack of burglary skills. Go check the boat and tell me if anybody is aboard."

"Okay, okay. Stop barking orders." He disappeared.

I tapped my foot on the wooden dock, concentrating on the staccato noise. It soothed my racing mind as it conjured all the things that could go wrong. My plan had two parts—break in, and don't get caught. Simple, right?

Dedication

This book is dedicated to my husband, Paul, who equally supports and fears my journey through the world of fiction. And to my daughter, Amber, who constantly cheers me on despite my aversion to current technology. Without her, I'd never know the importance of hashtags and their purpose in life.

Chapter 1

My new pumps clacked an obnoxious beat as I tore down the stairs. The comfy gray loafers at the front of my closet had beckoned me to come to my senses, but visions of Gloria's reprimands kept them out of today's wardrobe selection.

As I bolted onto the sidewalk, my heel wedged in a crack and my body lurched forward. Righting myself, I listed off balance as my right leg now stood three inches shorter than my left. "Crap!"

Two little boys giggled around mouthfuls of black and white cookies. Their mother flashed me a dirty look before nudging the kids to get moving.

I wrestled the triangular chunk of leather out of the crevice, took off both shoes, and ran back upstairs to my apartment above the Italian bakery. Flinging open my closet, I grabbed the flats and could almost hear them cheering as they slipped onto my stockinged feet. They'd fit better with a pair of socks, but the minutes dwindled. Making it outside and down the street, I skidded to a halt, nearly flying out of my new fashion accessories. A twenty-something blond hunk in a blue uniform shirt and jeans leaned against my SUV with his arms crossed.

"How ya doin'?" He gave me the once over from head to toe, then back up where he stopped below the neckline.

I returned the favor and admired his sculpted biceps straining at the seams of the short, rolled up shirt sleeves. His left arm sported a black and red tattoo of a dagger with a green thorny vine wrapped around it. Shaggy hair tickled his forehead as he grinned at me. Looking heavenward, I asked, "You couldn't ever send me a live one of those?"

"Huh?" His gaze shot up too.

"This really isn't a good time." I skirted around him and grabbed for the driver's side door. The back of his shirt read "Jake's Towing Service."

"I didn't choose the timing, lady." He had no trace of the New York accent this time. I added a few IQ points to his score.

He pointed with a thumb over his shoulder at the post by my car. "You should read the parking signs. This side of the street is a no parking zone from eight to ten every Thursday."

"Thanks for the info." I grabbed the parking violation off my windshield and noted the time stamp of nine fifty-eight. Really? I pulled out my phone—ten-oh-five. Three missed calls with voicemails flashed across the screen. I didn't have to check who'd left them. "Look, I'm late for a…a funeral. So, if you don't mind—" I gestured for him to move.

Squinting his dazzling blue eyes as he turned, he said, "I've heard that one before. You'll have to do better."

"I'm not kidding"—I read the embroidered tag on his chest—"Gus." If only they all came with name tags, my life would be easier.

He shrugged. "I gotta take it in. I could lose my job if I don't."

2

"You don't have a tow truck. Are you going to pull it with your bare hands?"

His gaze shot from side to side. "Damn! It was here a minute ago."

"Right. And what year do you think this is?"

"Huh?" His head centered.

This would take more time than I had. "What year is it? It's a simple question."

"It's nineteen ninety-five. Duh!"

With a sigh, I said, "Look, why don't you hop in. I've got someplace to be. We can talk on the way."

He stood his ground.

If I let him go now, who knows when he'd show up next. "Can you please get in?" I batted my eyelashes hoping they wouldn't create a windstorm from the layers of mascara coated on them. The right amount of makeup always eluded me.

Gus looked a couple decades younger than me, so I hoped he wasn't disgusted at my flirty attempt to lure him into the car. I could almost hear the cobweb-covered gears cranking slowly in his head. "I normally don't take rides from strangers, but I'll make an exception for you, beautiful. Hey, what's your name?" *Nope, not offended.*

I hate it when they hit on me, though it's mostly the older men. With him finally in the passenger seat, I shifted my vehicle into gear and hit the gas. Brakes squealed and a horn blasted as I cut off a white, fancy sports car. Drivers of those expensive toys were jerks anyway. Despite it being a couple weeks before Memorial Day, tourists already flooded this seaside village of Northport. With any luck, he didn't live here.

"Did you even look before pulling out?" Gus

reached for the handle above his door, but his fingers went through it.

"Don't worry, you're safe." I palmed the wheel and turned right, then a quick left. "And it's Marni. Marni Legend."

"It's drivers like you, *Marni*, who keep me in business. You're crazy."

Not the first time I'd heard that. "You've got about ten minutes before we get to the church. Let's cut to the chase. You know you're dead, right?"

"Of course, I do. Doesn't mean I wanna re-live another crash."

Now we're getting somewhere. "You died in a crash? You're still in work clothes, so, I'm guessing you were on the job when it happened?"

"You're very calm. I've tried talking to a couple other people, and they either ignored me or told me to go away. Why did you ask what year I thought it was?"

"All my life I've been…visited. Luckily, it runs in the family, though most times it skips a generation. My grandma had this ability and taught me how to handle spirits. As far as the year, many times your kind don't realize time has passed. In your case, it's been twenty-seven years."

"My kind? You make me sound like a leper."

"Oh, don't go all sensitive on me." I swung into the church parking lot and zipped into the nearest open slot. "We're outta time. Find me later, and we'll talk more." Grabbing my purse, I jumped out and sprinted for the entrance.

Gus came along. "Can't I hang around?"

I stopped. "Why would you want to attend a stranger's funeral?"

"It's not like I got somethin' better to do." His accent had returned.

We went into the sanctuary. The casket up front had sprays of flowers arranged on either side, mostly roses and orchids. My sister went a bit overboard fearing people might think Mom didn't have enough friends and family who cared. My eyes watered as the fragrance of the array assaulted my sinuses.

Gus slipped into a seat at the back, but I kept walking to the front pew, and he jumped up and followed. He asked, "How close were you to the deceased?"

"Very." Sliding across the wooden bench, I eased in beside my brother, Calvin. Gus sat next to me.

"You're late," Calvin whispered from the side of his mouth.

"Is Gloria ready to have a cow?" I asked.

"Kittens. I don't think she's reached DEFCON one yet. It was at three when you didn't answer your cell a half an hour ago."

"I had it on vibrate in anticipation of her *what not to wear* suggestions." Leaning over him, I waved at his fiancée. "Hi, Sylvie."

She reached out and squeezed my hand, adding a sad smile. The flouncy sleeves of her gray paisley dress reminded me of something I wore in the seventies as a child. Sylvie appeared to be taking Mom's passing harder than the rest of us. Having no family herself, I knew she'd counted on my mother to help with the wedding plans.

Calvin motioned toward the space to my right. "Did I hear you talking when you came in?"

I nodded. "Say hello to Gus."

Grinning, he asked, "You brought a date to Mom's funeral?"

Gus stared at me his eyes huge. "This is your *motha's* funeral?"

Calvin laughed. "You didn't tell him? Poor guy. How old is this one?"

I wished he could see them like I could instead of only hearing their voices. Nobody in the history of our family ever got the gift halfway like him.

"I'd guess early thirties."

"Hey, lady, I'm only twenty-seven."

"You act more mature." Sometimes I resorted to lying to appease the dead. Turning to my brother, I asked, "Tell me, is she waiting to make her grand entrance so the show can begin?"

Before he could answer, my sister, Gloria, and husband, Robert, slid in on top of Gus, who moved closer to the end. My sister quietly chastised, "It's about time. You're late." She accentuated her comment with a bob of her head, causing her brunette updo to shift precariously up and down. She'd used so much hairspray, the whole nob of hair moved as one.

With a hand on my chest, I asked, "What do you mean? I've been sitting here in silent meditation for fifteen minutes."

"You have not," Gloria rasped. "Where were you?"

I gestured with my arm. "Have you guys met Gus?"

My sister looked at the empty space, then glared at me, face turning red. Having not inherited any of the paranormal skills, she never knew when to believe me. As kids, I would sometimes tell her we had a visitor, when we didn't.

Looking at the floor, she asked, "What are you wearing on your feet?"

Before I could answer, the opening funeral dirge began. If I died first, I'd be leaving a playlist of seventies and eighties hits to keep my mourners awake. As the organ spewed out "Amazing Grace," a large woman in a puce-colored choir robe and more facial hair than a ferret croaked out the first verse. I strained my eyeballs looking for an Adam's apple. Nope—nothing but wrinkles below her double chin.

The service dragged on with every excruciating note possible from an ancient roster of hymns. Gloria stood before the gathering of friends and family and gave a well-crafted eulogy, shedding a few tears at all the critical points. Even Gus's eyes glistened with moisture.

Following the pallbearers as they wheeled the coffin out and whisked it away to the crematorium, I braced for the onslaught of condolences. Gloria and Robert took their posts at the exit like politicians working a crowd. Gus had disappeared. Calvin and Sylvie took their places in the receiving line. My thoughts covered other obligations as my stomach grumbled, reminding me I'd skipped breakfast.

In the reception hall, already filling with mourners, I made a beeline for a table with little pastries and finger sandwiches. As I loaded my plate, a mug of coffee hovered in front of me, held by my ex-husband. "Thanks for coming, Tim. You really didn't have to." I took the cup as he kissed my cheek.

"You know I loved your mom. The least I could do was pay my respects."

"For some odd reason, she always had a soft spot

for you. Even when you divorced me." I noticed his leaner physique. His new workout regimen had paid off.

"What's not to love?" He spread his arms wide. "Besides, she was an amazing lady."

"Did the fetus come with you?"

Tim shook his head, ignoring my shot at his engagement to a younger woman. Maybe I should hook her up with Gus. Wait, that would require a homicide. I hate it when minor details derail a good plan.

"No. With our wedding only six months away, she's busy stomping through Laguna Beach like a giant monster destroying Tokyo. *Everything must be perfect!* Hard to believe she's turned into a creature of my own making. Once I'd asked her opinion, she's never stopped giving it."

"Oh, she's not that bad, Daddy." Ginny walked over and kissed him on the cheek. "Your fiancée is a little high-strung at times, but you can't blame her. She's the daughter of an over-achiever and is now marrying an over-achiever."

"Me? An over-achiever?"

Ginny tilted her head. "How many business meetings are you squeezing in before heading back to the west coast on Saturday?"

Reaching my limit of reunion banter between my ex and our daughter, I excused myself and searched out my brother. I asked, "Have you heard her at all?"

"Nope. Mom went peacefully in her sleep, so I don't expect her to be hanging around. If anything, you would've seen her by now. You've always been more sensitive at picking up troubled strays. Speaking of which, Gus still hanging about?"

"I hope she's not around." I laughed. "If she heard you calling her a troubled stray, she might stay out of spite. As for my burly friend, he split before we left the sanctuary."

"Burly, huh? When are you going to snag yourself a live one and have a life again instead of living vicariously through your novels?"

I smacked him on the arm. "I have a life, thank you very much."

"Well, you better skedaddle. Sylvie has a couple of coworkers she wants to introduce you to. With Mom gone, she's taken up the torch of getting you happily married off again."

"Bold move hooking me up at a funeral." I hugged him. He understood my aversion to these events. Attempting to leave unnoticed, I heard a girlish squeal behind me and felt a little foot stomp on the back of my heel, followed by a push, when my cousin's kids chased each other through the crowd. My shoe slipped off. As I wiggled my foot back inside the loafer, a black pair of stilettoes came toe to toe with me.

I slumped my shoulders and looked up into my sister's face. We were the same height, but three-inch heels gave her the advantage. "Gloria, I was just looking for you to make my goodbyes. Goodbye!" I turned, but not fast enough. Fingers wrapped around my upper arm in a vise-like grip.

She spoke through gritted teeth. "You may not leave until all the guests have gone. What would people think?"

"I stepped out for a smoke?" The glare on her perfectly made-up face telegraphed her favorite emotion—disapproval. "Look, you're so much better at this obligation stuff than I am. Oh, and there's one other important factor."

"Which is?"

"I don't give a rat's *ass* what people think."

Her lips, inches from my face, barely moved. "Keep your voice down."

How does she do that and still be heard? She'd make a great ventriloquist.

"Show some respect for our mother, Marni." The gauntlet was down. She not only threw it to the floor but ground it to bits with her dainty little heel.

"Respect? Like you showed her all these years attempting to move her into a retirement home?" My voice tried to remain quiet, but it rose a decibel. "Don't you talk to me about treating our mother with respect." Playing nice ended, and I needed to go.

Gloria beat me to the punch. She blasted off toward the reception hall.

I gave the princess wave to the back of her head and called, "Tootles, Glo!"

Her back stiffened at the childhood nickname she'd forbidden me to use ever again. Score one for Marni. Now, where'd that gorgeous tow truck driver get to?

Chapter 2

Monday afternoon, we gathered at the military cemetery for the interment. Another place I do my best to avoid—cemeteries. Dad had been in the navy in his twenties, so we'd laid him to rest here almost a decade ago. Mom would be buried in the same grave.

Since the big shindig took place at the church, only immediate family gathered today. The roses didn't make it, but three of the orchid bouquets were marched out for double duty, even with no one to impress this time. Despite their waning scent, they still stung my eyes.

While we waited for the chaplain, an old woman hobbled over and sat next to me. Wearing a black dress with a matching hat covered in netting, she smiled sweetly. As she opened her mouth to speak, I held up my hand. "No, not today. I'm off duty."

Her jaw dropped open, and I thought she might fall off her seat. "But I thought…"

"Stop right there. You thought wrong. Please go back to the counter and take a number," I said quietly.

"Counter? I don't understand."

Calvin turned around and crossed his eyes. Looking at the empty chair, he said, "My apologies, ma'am. Sometimes my sister confuses social skills with bad communication skills. We're here to bury our mother. Please understand, it's nothing personal."

"Oh, I do apologize." She stood. "My condolences."

"Is she gone?"

I nodded.

"Now was that so hard? Sometimes I think you intentionally try to irritate those poor lost souls." He turned back and took hold of Sylvie's hand.

Now was that so hard, I mimicked silently, waggling my head back and forth.

Today his fiancée wore another paisley creation with a crystal hanging from her neck. Add a ring of daisies atop her flaming red hair, and she would've fit right in at Woodstock. Sylvie knew about our gifts and accepted them without a hitch. I wish Tim had been as accepting; we might still be together.

Gloria and Robert walked in with the chaplain and strode to their chairs in the front row. The scowl appeared to be gone from her face. It's amazing what you can do with good makeup these days. Now that the grand duchess had taken her seat, we could begin. We all stared reverently (or pretended to anyway) at the small wooden box containing Mom's ashes. I would miss Mom but having confirmation of spirits going on to a better place, I couldn't be sad over her passing.

The service was brief, and thankfully, music free. If Gloria had dragged that croaking toad out here to sing one more stanza, I'd be searching for cotton to stuff in my ears. Afterward, we all decided to pay our respects at Dad's grave.

As we walked to our cars, Gloria asked, "How do you suppose they dig such a small hole for the box?"

Calvin jumped right in. "With a post-hole digger."

Robert almost cracked and lost his composure, but

years of practicing survival tactics living with Gloria saved him from sudden outbursts. He covered his mouth and coughed, the top of his bald head turning red.

My sister screwed up her face. "No. They wouldn't use such a thing. There must be a small shovel, I'd imagine."

We drove over to Lot 68 and strolled through the neat rows of headstones until we found our father's. As we quietly looked on, rereading the engraving I knew by heart, my brother gently elbowed me. Glancing over my shoulder to where he pointed, I saw a post-hole digger leaning against a tree. I lost it. He joined in.

"What is there to laugh about at this solemn occasion?" Gloria puffed out her chest and squared her shoulders. Her way of dealing with everything had to be in neatly cropped sections filled with good intentions and proper etiquette.

"Inside joke," I sputtered.

The hole to inter Mom had already been dug. At least we missed the excavation portion. My sister might have blown a gasket. Unfortunately, she wasn't done organizing everything.

"Why is Mom being buried at Dad's toes?" Gloria demanded.

The next few minutes held real promise on the entertainment scale. Mom's final resting place lay about five and a half feet away from the marker. Dad's toes could possibly reside there.

"Do you think she requested it?" I swallowed my grin.

Calvin wouldn't look at me. He grasped Sylvie's hand tighter as they both shook, breathing air through their nostrils in bursts.

Gloria glared at me. "She wouldn't have asked to be buried at our father's feet. They should have dug the hole closer to the headstone."

I gestured behind me. "Well, there's the post-hole digger. Maybe Robert can scoop out a better spot?"

Her husband chuckled until Gloria turned toward him with her face turning purple. The tall man silenced his laughter.

A light shower began falling, misting our group. Calvin and Sylvie walked toward the parking area.

Robert grasped his wife's elbow. "Come on, honey. It's mind over matter. Your mother won't know the difference; she's gone. Let's get out of the rain."

She allowed him to escort her back to the car. I caught up with Calvin, who I'd ridden with. We'd agreed to meet at our parents' favorite Italian restaurant—a fitting honor to both.

Our vehicles sat about thirty feet apart beside Lot 68. As we waited for Robert to pull out first and take the lead, the gardener's cart slipped between us toward the gravesites. Sprays of orchids merrily bounced in the back—along with the little box containing Mom's ashes. The passenger door to my brother-in-law's car opened, and my sister put a foot out. Then she pulled it back in, only to put it out again, this time stepping halfway out.

The three of us in Calvin's car rolled with laughter. Finally, she tucked herself back inside and closed the door. They pulled out immediately. I'm sure Robert didn't want to give her a chance to change her mind.

****

Late in the evening, my brother dropped me at my

apartment on Main Street. I trudged up the stairs and unlocked the door. The stress of Gloria's constant need for propriety wore on me more than anything else. Having dealt with the dead all my life, I knew Mom had moved on to another plane and anything else done for her was simply window dressing. Tossing my keys onto a table in the front entry, I went to the kitchen and put my purse on the counter. The dishes in the sink balanced precariously. I'd get to them when I ran out of clean ones.

"So, how was the service?" asked a voice I never expected to hear again. My mother sat at the table wearing her funeral attire.

"Ma, when you died, everything in your life had been resolved. What are you doing here?"

"Well...I got to them pearly gates and stopped. I said, 'Peta, I ain't ready. I got too much to do down there.' "

At which point, I'm sure he sighed with relief and sent her on her way. "I believe the appropriate salutation is *Saint*, and I'm pretty sure Peter has an *r* on the end of his name."

"Don't you give me grief about my accent. I'm a girl from Brooklyn who's proud of her roots. You could take a lesson, here. *And*, for your information, Pete-errr understood completely."

I bet he did. Probably looking for the fool who brought her up this soon. "Ma, what do you have to finish?"

"Are you kidding me? Your brother's wedding for one. I love Sylvie, but all her taste is in her mouth. Their nuptials need to be special, not tacky with sunflowers and beads. And then there's you."

"Me?" If I fled down the fire escape, would she follow?

"Yeah, you need someone in your life. I can help you."

My body collapsed into a chair at the table. "I don't need help."

"You got no husband. No boyfriend. And you live in this dingy apartment. With your income, you could afford a beautiful house."

"I love this apartment. It's right on the main drag and only two blocks from the pier. Besides, it's a very calming atmosphere for me to write my books."

"Those smutty novels? Oh, please, why you ever left Tim…"

Maybe I could point the remote at her and press the mute button. It'd be worth a try.

The talking stopped. It worked! My mother glared at me with her arms crossed—except her lips weren't moving.

"I come back all this way, and you don't even listen to me."

"Sorry you wasted the trip. I've heard it all before, but since you're into repetition, I'll give it to you in bullet points. One, the books I write are called *historical romances*. Two, Timothy dumped *me*, I did *not* leave him. Three, did I hear you mention Gloria's name in your litany of complaints?"

Looking heavenward, she asked, "Where did you learn to be so rude to your motha?" Clasping her hands and putting them in her lap as if garnering all her patience—it wouldn't take long; I think she reached the end of it by the time we'd all hit puberty—she spoke in a controlled voice. "There is bad blood between you and your sister. I can't go on to heaven knowing the two of you have…issues."

Issues. Good word. "We get along fine, as long as we're not within a five-mile radius of each other."

"This isn't a laughing matter. I know you don't always have the same good sense as her, but you need to be the bigga person. Maybe agree with her sometime. Like when you picked this outfit for me. You couldn't settle on something that didn't make me look so fat? I had a beautiful black cocktail dress hanging in my closet since before your father died. I bought it for the cruise we never got to go on." She dropped her chin to her chest.

Had she looked in a mirror over the last ten years? We donated the dress to the local high school for some emaciated waif to wear to prom. All the lard in the world wouldn't have been enough to slide that dress over this woman's body. "We wanted to bury you in an outfit we knew you'd had fond memories wearing. You wore it to our cousin's wedding last year and danced the night away with her new husband's uncle." And Gloria wouldn't hear of anything else except this *proper* black dress. It was a closed casket. We could have dressed her like a circus clown with big red shoes, and nobody would have been the wiser. Except for now, sitting in my kitchen. I laughed at the image.

"How do you find any of this funny?"

Because I see humor in everything. "I'm sorry, Ma."

"And why would you bring up that awful man? He stomped on my feet all night. It's amazing I didn't end up with ten broken toes."

"Look, if I promise to help Sylvie with the

wedding and attempt to draw up a peace treaty between Gloria and me, will you move on? I bet Dad was disappointed you didn't make it."

"Your fatha can wait. He's a man. They're used to it." She swatted the air with her hand. "If I could talk to your sister, I would. But you know she didn't get the gift. Your grandma had been so disappointed about it and your brother, only being able to hear them. He stumped us all. It's up to you to handle this. Now"—she looked around my kitchen—"has your cleaning girl been off the last few weeks?"

I stood and walked out, saying over my shoulder, "Going to bed. Feel free to stay, but I expect you gone in the morning. Your life is over, Ma. Go. Be at peace." Then the rest of us can too.

Chapter 3

On the way to my room, Gus materialized, and I asked, "How long have you been here?"

"Long enough to know I should stay away from your motha. She's a piece of work. Exactly like mine."

I glanced back toward the kitchen making sure she hadn't followed me. "I think they cloned them in Brooklyn. Kinda like a domestic robot, except exuding guilt laced with parental suffering instead of baking skills. Look, I'm beat. Let's meet for coffee in the morning. I'm buying."

"Funny." He smirked. "I got somethin' you need to see. Get your coat."

"I'm exhausted. Can't it wait until tomorrow?"

"They'll be gone in the morning. We gotta go now." He waved an arm toward the door.

"Who?"

He opened and closed his fists. "I'm not sure. It feels like I should know, but I can't remember. You comin' or not?"

The luxury of sleep didn't appear to be an option. As insistent as Gus was, this might be a breakthrough in helping him. "Let me grab a jacket and change into jeans." I walked into the bedroom and closed the door. Pulling my dress over my head as I walked across the room, I tossed it on the floor, kicked off my shoes, and peeled the layer of pantyhose from my legs. Two minutes later, I found Gus waiting in the hallway.

"Wow, I've never known a woman who could change so fast."

"Most can but sometimes choose not to. Let me grab my purse." I hoped Mom would be gone.

Gus stopped me. "You won't need it."

"Driving without your license is frowned upon in all fifty states."

He shook his head. "We're not driving. It's only a short walk down near the pier. Hurry, before they're done."

Glad I'd thrown on sneakers, I snatched up my keys so I could at least lock up. Once outside, Gus and I walked toward the dock, then turned left on the last street before the water. The road sloped upward, and my calves complained at the unwanted workout. "Where are we going?"

"Quiet! You don't want to get caught, do you?"

I whispered, "What are you getting me into?"

"It's around the bend. You'll have to duck into the trees so they can't see you."

I was used to being put in awkward positions, but this sounded dangerous. Following his lead, I skirted between raspberry bushes, feeling their stickers scratch against my pants legs. At least they weren't in season yet, or I'd have red juice stains to scrub out. Glad for the thick denim, I pushed through until I came up behind a Lindon tree with multiple trunks. Male voices spoke, but I couldn't make out what they were saying. Through the darkness, the outline of a detached garage sat about twenty feet away with a large two-story house behind it. Neither building had any lights on. Gus put a finger up to his lips. Edging closer, I stepped on a stick, and it cracked beneath my weight. The talking stopped. I dropped to the ground, allowing the low brush to cloak me. Small rocks and twigs dug into me as I lay in the musty dirt.

"Leave it," a raspy voice said, moving closer. "It's probably a cat or a raccoon."

"We should make sure." A second guy stood on the other side of the tree. The smell of stale cigarettes wafted in my direction.

Pressing myself into the ground, as if I could make myself smaller, I waited to feel a hand on the back of my jacket. A flashlight beam sprayed the foliage, about three feet off the ground.

"Do you want the old lady next door to know we're here? Cut the light, and let's go. There's nothing there!" Raspy Voice said.

The light swung over me one more time before going out. "Maybe you might keep your voice down if you're worried about the neighbors," Stale Cigarettes hissed.

They walked away, still arguing. Once the door on the side of the garage shut with a soft click, I crept backward keeping low. My foot hit pavement, then bumped into something. I froze.

"Are you going to just lie there like a dead squirrel, or are you going to tell me what you're doing?"

The voice belonged to a scrawny old woman in a baggy sweater and red polyester pants. Her lavender perfume smelled better than the murky soil I'd just had my nose in. Even in the darkness, I could make out her tanned, leathery face. If it weren't socially unacceptable, a designer could've used her skin for a handbag. "Have you seen an orange tabby?"

"You're looking for your cat?" her voice cracked.

"I'm watching her for a friend. She slipped out of my apartment, and now Julie is going to *kill* me."

The old woman stood her ground like she'd caught me red-handed stealing her penny jar. "What makes you think she's in my front yard?"

"I…I…thought I saw her run past these bushes. Here kitty, here kitty kitty."

She narrowed her eyes. "What's her name?"

"Huh? I told you her name is Julie."

"The cat's name." She wrapped her sweater tighter as a breeze rose from the ocean.

"Oh, ha ha, sorry, I thought you meant…her name…her name is…Kitty. Yeah, her name is Kitty."

"Maybe we should let the police help you find *Kitty*. If there is a Kitty." She pulled a cell phone out of her pocket. The device had a magnified screen.

Standing, with my hands raised in the air, I said, "That won't be necessary. I'm fine looking for her on my own. In fact, I was just about to give up and try again tomorrow. No need to bother the authorities. I'm sure they have more important things to do."

Holding her finger poised over the keypad, she dropped it to her side. "I better not see you creeping around here again. I'm a light sleeper, you know. The racket you made over by the Fergussons' garage was enough to wake the dead."

Ain't that the truth, lady. Speaking of which, where did my ghostly friend get off to? He made himself scarce when we had company. Backing up a couple of steps, I hurried down the way we'd come. Before I got too far, I risked a glance over my shoulder. Thankfully, the crotchety old lady must've gone back inside her house. The sound of a diesel engine firing up blasted through the air. Was she going to run me down? Wait, the sound came from the property next door. A vehicle turned onto the road, before putting on the headlights and almost blinding me. Racing downhill, I jumped in between two parked cars across from the bar on the corner, aptly named The Corner Bar. The truck drove past, with a two-seat, silver car in tow. I'm not a car nut, but it looked to be an older model—the kind men buy as a mid-life crisis vehicle. My ex had a similar one, equipped with a young bleached-blonde in the passenger seat.

Wasn't it a bit late to be towing a car *out* of someone's driveway? I'd forgotten to bring my phone, but it must be close to eleven. The streetlights were too dim for me to make out the red letters on the door or what the driver looked like as the yellow truck cruised past. Gus might know the men.

Slipping into my apartment, I peeked through the kitchen doorway. The only thing I saw were dirty dishes and a couple of take-out containers on the counter. I stepped into the room, set my phone on the counter, and slid the window closed. Relieved at being alone, I shed my clothes in a trail down the hallway, pulled on my pajamas, and crawled into bed. "Oh, crap!" I got back up, retrieved my phone where I'd left it in the kitchen, double-checked the lock on the front door, then slid under the covers.

****

The alarm on my phone went off at six. Even though I worked from home, I kept a routine during the week. It helped me stay focused, especially when I had a publishing deadline. Since I'd gotten home late and

23

had company, I'd forgotten to set up my coffee pot the night before. Throwing on a sweatshirt to battle the cool spring air, I wandered into the kitchen.

"How ya doin'?"

"Gus, it's too early."

"You invited me for coffee. At least I can watch you drink it." He leaned back in the chair, hands cupped behind his head.

As I filled the filter with grounds of my favorite dark roast and poured water into the unit, I hit the "strong" button before turning it on. Letting it drip into the pot, I said, "I'll be right back." Slipping into a pair of flip-flops, I unbolted the door.

"Where are you goin' in your pajamas? I know you told me it's been twenty-seven years since I...left. Are street clothes now optional?"

"Just chill!" Shuffling to the ground floor and outside, I looked through the bakery window and saw Bart sliding trays of freshly baked bread onto the shelves behind the counter.

He turned and smiled at me, wiped his pudgy hands on his apron, then grabbed a small white bag and threw in two rolls. When he unlocked the front door and handed it to me, their warmth radiated through the paper. The aromas of rye bread, chocolate, and sugar escaped outside. "Thanks, Bart, you're a prince. Say 'Hi' to Sally for me."

"You're welcome, sweetie. My condolences again about your mom."

"I think she was ready." At least I hoped she'd come around to my way of thinking. When it's time, it's time. "Thanks for coming to the funeral. See you tomorrow." I jiggled the bag.

Back at the table in my apartment, I slathered butter onto the gooey insides of my breakfast.

"You're killin' me, you know that? Oh wait, I'm already dead." If Gus could have salivated, I believe he would have. "How can you eat in front of me? It's torture. I lived in this area when Mr. Fugacci ran the place downstairs."

"He left it to his son, Bart, along with all of his recipes. Did you ever taste the almond horns?" I bit into my roll.

"Now that's just cruel. Why don't you bring in a box of Napoleons and scarf them down in front of me too?"

Laughing, I said, "I'm sorry, Gus, but there have to be perks to living over this place. Free bread and pastries are one of them. Now, to business. What went on last night besides my being busted by an ancient member of the local neighborhood watch?"

He knitted his brows. "I knew those guys. Can't remember their names as I never got properly introduced, if you know my meaning. They did some jobs with me."

I sipped my coffee. "What *kind* of jobs? Moving furniture? Invading small countries?"

"You know, the kind where you get paid in cash and don't ask a lot of questions."

"Were they stealing that car last night?"

"Of course, they were. What did you think?"

I slammed my hands onto the table. "You *knew* they were car thieves, yet you had me go anyway! What were you thinking?"

He didn't answer for a few moments. "You're right. I shoulda warned you. But then you wouldn't've helped me."

"What makes you think I'll help you now? Those guys are criminals! They could be dangerous. They could have guns. You can't be hurt, remember? Things flying at you, oh say, bullets, can't hurt you. Me? I'm thinking it could go horribly wrong."

"What else am I supposed to do?" He bolted up and paced. "Nobody else has been willing to help me."

My appetite disappeared, and I pushed the food away. Never had I been put in danger before. All my other *cases* had been harmless regrets. Most of them I'd been able to fix without too much meddling in the lives of the living. This had a very different feel to it. It wouldn't take a detective to leap to my next conclusion. "If you did *jobs* with those clowns, exactly what did they entail?"

"Whatta ya mean?"

Placing my arms on the table and leaning in, I asked, "Were you a car thief?"

"It wasn't like I did it a lot. Only to make extra cash here and there. Nobody ever got hurt."

"Are you forgetting you're dead? Maybe you were doing a *job* when the accident happened. Or maybe you didn't die in an accident at all. Gus, I'm not sure I can help you."

"Fine. See ya!" He disappeared.

I shouted at the air around me. "Don't be like this. If there's something I can do that doesn't involve creeping around at night spying on felons, I'm there for you. This situation may be more than I can handle. Gus, please, let's talk about it."

Silence. He'd gone—at least for now. They always came back once they'd gotten a foot in the door.

Chapter 4

Not having a good excuse to bow out, I showed up for dinner at Gloria's on Saturday with a bottle of chardonnay and a chocolate meltaway cake. It had been five days since Mom had made herself known then disappeared, and I hoped to keep the record going.

My thirteen-year-old nephew greeted me at the door and took custody of the dessert. He kissed me on the cheek and mumbled something. It resembled English, possibly a greeting. He obviously inherited his mother's ability to speak without moving his lips, except he needed to polish his diction.

I followed him through the house and a set of sliding glass doors onto a large wooden deck running the length of the house. My brother and Sylvie relaxed on a cushioned wicker couch at the far end. Each held a koozie-covered bottle, which they raised in acknowledgement toward me.

Gloria walked over and accepted the wine. "I'll put this in the fridge for another time. You must've forgotten we're having steak for dinner. Red wine goes best with red meat."

Don't worry, I'll chug it down before Robert finishes overcooking the meal. I took it back. "I thought white would be refreshing since it's been so warm. Mind if I pour myself a glass?" Or three or four? "Would anyone else like some?" With no takers, I went inside and filled a stemless wine glass nearly to the rim. As I returned to the patio, my sister scowled at the beverage in my hand. There's my favorite look again. I'd have to remember to buy her a bucket of cover-up for Christmas as her face seemed to have a chronic condition of dissension.

Robert worked the gas barbecue with a pair of tongs in one hand and a beer in the other. Meat always smelled delicious while he had it on the grill, but I knew the result would be less than palatable. Peering inside, I noted the usual London broil he always made for a crowd. "Looks delicious," I lied.

"Thanks. I think I've perfected the seasoning. Let me know what you think after you taste it."

"Absolutely." Then we can re-sole our shoes with the leftovers.

He flipped the plank of meat. "How's your current book going? What era is your heroine pining away in this time?"

"It takes place in the Yukon during the Klondike Gold Rush around the late eighteen-nineties. I'm thinking of calling it *Treasures of the Yukon*. What do you think?"

"Catchy. You must spend more time researching than you do writing. The historic details you include are amazing."

"You've read my books?" Looking over my shoulder, I spied my sister talking with Sylvie and lowered my voice. "Does Gloria know?"

He laughed. "Who do you think bought them? We've got all twelve. She's never told you how proud she is of you as a published author, has she?"

I shook my head.

"I know you two have your differences, but you need to bury the hatchet at some point, preferably not in each other's back." He smirked.

"Have you been talking to our mother?"

"Funny." He moved the steak around the grill. "Hey, wait. Have you?" Gloria had filled her husband in on our family's quirks when they'd first met over thirty years ago.

I sipped my wine, gave him a sly grin, then wandered over to my siblings. The wicker chair crackled as I sat and attempted polite small talk. "Will the boys be joining us for dinner, Gloria?"

"They're eating in the den so they can watch the ball game. I thought it best since we have family business to discuss." She leaned back, sipping a glass of red wine, probably the merlot I saw on the counter. Thank goodness she had the appropriate wine and wouldn't offend the barbecue gods.

"You didn't mention anything when you invited me. What's there to talk about?" As if I didn't already know. This evening would go downhill fast, bypassing annoying and hurdling straight for disastrous.

"Yeah," Calvin chimed in. "Me neither. What gives?"

Gloria cleared her throat. "I think it's best we wait until everyone is gathered at the table. It'll be easier to talk."

Sylvie stood and took Calvin's empty. "Would you like another, honey?"

"Please." He nodded.

"Anyone else need a refill while I'm up? Gloria, more merlot? Marni, another bottle...I mean glass?" She gave an impish grin. She may come across as spacey at times, yet I knew her to be highly perceptive with a constant aura of calm about her. I wished that would've been the gift Grandma passed on to us. My life would be less chaotic.

"Thanks, Sylvie, I'm good." I'd probably be leaving sooner than later and needed to be sober enough to drive.

Gloria refused the offer as well, then remained quiet.

I decided against sharing our mother's visit just yet. Right now, the living needed more attention. "How about giving us the highlights?"

Robert sat beside his wife and patted her on the leg. "Maybe we should talk about it now, honey. The steak needs ten more minutes anyway."

"How I wish I could knock back a brew." Gus leaned over my brother-in-law, reaching for the bottle he could never again hold.

Calvin looked at our brother-in-law, then to me.

"You disappear for almost a week, and now you decide to show up? Your timing sucks, Gus."

"Well, it wouldn't be the first time. Put down the glass, we gotta go." He walked around the couch. "Is that your sister? Damn, she's hot…for an older lady anyways."

Calvin laughed. I ignored them both.

Gloria glared at me. "What's going on?"

"You know, Gloria, Marni has a guest," Calvin explained. "The same one from Mom's funeral. Should we set an extra plate at the table?"

"Thanks, dude, but Marni and I have someplace to be."

I didn't budge, not being interested in witnessing

another theft. Danger and intrigue didn't belong on my resume. "Come by my apartment tonight, Gus, and you can tell me then."

Sylvie returned with two more beers. I regretted not asking for a refill; it sounded like I'd be needing one. She walked through Gus, handed Calvin his, then slid onto the cushion.

"Ooohhh, baby, do that again!" Gus waggled his shoulders and eyebrows. "I love it when they walk through me."

"Gus, I can't see you but can certainly hear you. That's my fiancée you're talking about."

"Oh, sorry, man. Look, tell your sister we gotta boogie."

"Please make him go away!" Gloria's body became rigid. "Whatever his problems are, you can take care of them later. We have important things to talk about."

Smoke wafted from the other side of the deck with the acrid smell of something burning.

"Oh, damn!" Robert jumped up and ran to rescue dinner. He flipped open the lid, and a huge white cloud billowed out. With tongs, he fished the charcoal-crusted slab away from the fire and dropped it onto a platter. Hanging his head, he put it on the table. "Who wants hot dogs?"

Saved from another meal of beef jerky. I refrained from doing a victory dance.

"Marni, please. This is important," Gus said.

I didn't know whether to believe him or not. If I didn't go, he'd probably hang around making me crazy. Dealing with both my sister *and* current rescue project didn't enthuse me. Standing, I said my goodbyes. Gloria protested, and I left mid-tirade with Gus in tow.

"This better be good."

"You could've gotten a dog to go," he offered.

Passing through the kitchen, I took one last sip of wine and set it down. I held my hand in his face. "Don't talk to me until we're in the car."

"What? What'd I say?"

Once behind the wheel, I took a deep breath and asked, "Where are we going?"

"Do you know where Wanachee Bluff is?"

Of course, I knew. We used to swim there as kids. It would take almost an hour to drive from my sister's place. "What's out there?"

"It's the last place I remember being."

While he'd made progress, I didn't understand his urgency and told him as much. Despite being saved from Gloria's *family business*, it might've been easier getting the discussion over with instead of dragging out whatever drama she'd had planned. I'm sure it had something to do with the disposal of Mom's house. Maybe she knew a buyer, so we didn't have to bother putting it on the market. At least I could delude myself with the thought of it being something simple.

"Any idea what you would've been doing at the bluff?" I glanced at Gus. His not wearing a seat belt felt strange even though I knew it didn't matter.

"Yeah, I think I was answerin' a call. Somebody had a dead battery or somethin' because they couldn't get it started. Now I think about it, the whole thing seemed kinda weird."

I stopped for a red light at an empty intersection. "What would be weird about calling for a tow truck when your car won't start?"

"Because it was already dark, and the parking lot

should've been closed for hours. They shut down at dusk." He turned toward me in the seat. "Can't you go any faster? You drive like an old lady goin' to church."

The light turned green, and I accelerated to forty, five miles above the speed limit. I'd traveled these back roads since my teenage years, and the local cops would let you scoot by going slightly over but no faster. The last thing I needed was another moving violation on my license.

We passed Jamestown Road, about a half a mile from Wanachee. Gus yelled, "Stop."

I slammed on the brakes, and the car skidded to a halt. "What?" I shrieked, almost as loud.

He tried bracing himself on the dashboard without success, but his body didn't budge from the seat anyway. "Geez, lady, it's a good thing nobody was behind us."

Glaring, I said, "You screamed. I thought there was a squirrel in the road or a small child. Why are we stopped?"

"We need to go down there." He jerked his thumb toward the street behind us.

"You said we needed to go to Wanachee Bluff. The only way in or out is the road we're on." I motioned to the street ahead of us.

"I felt something pulling me in this direction. Look, back up. If there's nothin' to see, we can come back this way and go to the bluff."

Backing over the freshly made tire marks, I drove east on Jamestown Road. Ten minutes later we passed the old psychiatric hospital. The facility had closed over twenty years earlier, and the vacant red brick buildings stood in eerie silence. Spread across the grassy lawns towered the three main buildings, each ten stories tall. They dwarfed the three outer structures which consisted of two floors, and the gardener's shed at the back of the property. I'd heard a few movies had been filmed on the grounds about a decade ago, some horror trilogy. Not something I'd want to see, but the teenagers flocked to the theaters to be scared silly. If only they could see life through my eyes, they'd truly know terror.

At the far edge of the property, the road ended at a chained entry with a sign reading, "Private—NO TRESPASSING." Beyond, it curved toward the shoreline, probably a service entrance to the facility.

"We'll have to turn around," I said to my passenger, only to find myself alone. "Gus? Where'd you go?" Silence filled the car. Great, he'd led me to a creepy part of Long Island right at dusk. I waited for the undead to crawl out of the shadows. We wouldn't make it to Wanachee before it closed. "Gus, this isn't funny. Why are we here?"

Tapping on my window made me shriek. A policeman stood there signaling for me to roll it down. Glancing in my rearview mirror, I saw his patrol car parked behind me. I hadn't noticed him drive up, but then I'd been focused elsewhere. Heeding his request, my brain scrambled for an excuse as to why I'd be on this road. Somehow the lost kitty scenario wouldn't sound convincing. *Damn it, Gus!*

"Good evening, ma'am. May I ask what you're doing here?"

"What I'm doing here?" Good stall tactic. He'd probably never heard that one before.

His voice remained steady. "Yes, ma'am. The road

continues onto private property, and this facility is closed to the public."

Putting on my sweetest smile, I batted my eyelids. "Isn't this the way to the bluff, Officer..." I looked at his badge. I really loved people with labels. "Talbott."

"No, ma'am." He placed a hand on his holster. Not the reaction I'd hoped for.

"Oh, wow. I must've gotten turned around."

His hand remained planted. "A lot of people find this place fascinating and drive out to see it in the dark. You look a bit...ah...mature for the usual crowd."

Did he just call me old? I'd have to work on my doe-eyed innocent look. Right after I located Gus and strangled him. With the polite smile still pasted to my face, I said, "No, Officer Talbott. I didn't intentionally want to come here." At least I told the truth.

He stared down at me, his lips a straight line.

Not good at the waiting game, I asked, "May I go, please? It's getting dark, and you know how most of these back roads don't have streetlights." The corners of my mouth, still in an upward position, were starting to tire.

"Don't let me catch you around here again, or I'll have to cite you for trespassing. The parking lot at the bluff will be closed by now, so you'd best head home."

I took his words as an order to turn my vehicle around and get the hell out of the area. You don't have to tell me twice! Shifting my car into reverse, I stepped on the gas and glanced in the mirror in time to brake before slamming into his cruiser.

"Ma'am!"

I shrugged. "Oops. Why don't I make a U-turn instead?" For good measure I added a wink.

He stepped well out of the way and watched me make a three-point turn, which became a five-point turn on the narrow lane. His image remained in my rearview mirror, still staring, as I drove the way I'd come. Reaching the intersection, I almost turned right toward the bluff but decided not to attract any more attention in case he followed me. If I tried to go there now, it would be trespassing, and I could be cited, or worse, arrested. Wouldn't incarceration be an interesting tidbit to add to the bio on my next book?

Turning left, I got about a mile before the car died, and I rolled to a stop on the shoulder. And the hits just keep on coming! I tried to restart it, but the engine wouldn't turn over. Hitting my flashers, I dug out the auto club card from my purse. After navigating the automated system, I got through to a live person who told me a truck would arrive in about forty-five minutes. Swell. Maybe before then my new buddy, Officer Talbott, would come by, and we could reminisce about old times.

Five minutes later, the glare of headlights filled my rearview. Terrific, now I'm psychic as well as spirt-sensitive. Can this night get any better? I waited for him to reach my open window glad I hadn't closed it when I drove away the first time. As his footsteps approached, I said, "Hello, again, Officer Tal…." I squinted up at a face with a much better tan and softer eyes. While this man also wore a shirt with his name on it, I began to see a trend. He wore work clothes and not a police uniform.

"Well, I'll be damned," a male voice beside me said.

"Gus!" The name escaped my lips before I could stop it. Sometimes this happened, and it would be easy enough to explain away in most circumstances. This wasn't one of them.

The man introduced himself. "I'm Jake. You called for service?"

He acted as if he hadn't heard my outburst, which saved me from coming up with another lame reason for my actions. I made a mental note to compose a list of viable excuses for the next time I found myself in an awkward situation.

"Yes. You startled me. The auto club said it would take forty-five minutes. Thanks for putting it into hyperdrive."

Jake laughed. "I happened to be out here at a friend's when the call came in. My shop is outside Northport."

"Lucky me!" I admired how well he filled out his shirt, complete with bulging muscles. His cropped salt and pepper hair accented his dark eyes. This guy looked a few years older than me, so I hoped to get through the rest of the night without being thought of as *old*.

"Try turning the key," he suggested.

Wow, why didn't I think of that? The engine made a feeble clicking sound. Nothing more.

"It's the alternator," Gus said. "Even a monkey like him could figure it out."

Resisting the urge to turn toward my passenger, who wasn't really there, I asked Jake, "Do you think it could be the alternator?"

"You know somethin' about cars, do you?" Did I detect a hint of sarcasm?

"Not really, but this has happened before." Beside me, Gus stifled a laugh. "Stop it," I whispered from the corner of my mouth.

"What did you say?" Jake asked.

My face hurt from all the good will I'd had to force this evening. "I said it just stopped in the roadway. Can you fix it?"

"Pop the hood. Let me check a couple a things." He walked to the front as I pulled the lever to unhook it.

The back of his shirt read Jake's Towing. So, he had his name on both sides of the uniform. I asked Gus, "Was he your boss?"

"You could say that." He faked a cough then crossed his arms and glared at the man in front of my car.

"What are you mad about? Is he the reason we came out here?"

He shook his head. "We need to get into one of those buildings back at the psych hospital."

"What?!"

"I didn't say anything." Jake stood outside my window again. "But it looks like the belt is loose. Gimme a minute, and I can tighten it. The battery might need a jump, but it should start then."

My face flushed. I finally get a live guy in a well put together package, and he probably thinks I'm a lunatic. "Okay." I admired his backside in my side view mirror as he walked away. "I'll wait here." Despite the growing darkness, the color of his truck stood out— yellow. Please don't let it be the same one.

Snapping fingers appeared in front of my face. "Marni, focus will you. We need to go back to the hospital."

"First off, I practically had a police escort out of there. Not that you would know because you vanished. Second, there is no way I'm going anywhere near those grounds again, let alone inside one of the dilapidated old buildings. If you want to go exploring, be my guest. Let me know if you find anything."

"I don't think I'll find anything else. Are you having other problems with your car?" Jake asked returning with a toolbox and portable battery charger. He moved to the engine. After ten minutes of grunting and metal clashing, he poked his head around. "Turn the key."

The car chugged but didn't start.

"Give it a few minutes," Jake said.

I couldn't see him behind the raised hood, so assumed he hooked the battery to the charger. After waiting on his direction, Jake yelled for me to try the ignition again.

The car started.

"Hey, the jerk fixed it. You need to ask him about me. Maybe he could tell you how I died or where."

Gus finally had a good idea, well, at least part of a good idea. "I can't just blurt it out. How do I explain knowing you?" The car hood slammed shut and so did my mouth before saying anything more to my ghostly sidekick.

My new mechanic mumbled something about getting paperwork, so I fished a tip from my wallet and got out of the car. I enjoyed the smell of lilacs as they scented the crisp spring air. Summer, my favorite season, wasn't too far around the corner. When Jake returned carrying a clipboard, my mind raced, trying to find a way to get him to talk about his old employee. His eyes, I think they were smoldering, gave me the once-over. At least Jake had enough class to stop at my face and not below the neckline. *This might work out better than expected, if I don't botch it.* Despite being single for six years, my flirting skills could be bested by a five-year-old on the playground.

"Can I have your card, please?" He held out his hand.

"Oh, right. It's in the car," I leaned in through the window and stretched for my purse, realizing too late the denim covered view I flashed at him. A muffled laugh came from behind me. Heat rose in my face. Fumbling with my bag as I turned around, I couldn't find my auto club card. "I had it when I called." I looked at him then remembered. "Oh, it's in the cup holder." This time I opened the door to retrieve it.

As he wrote my information on the form, he asked the obvious. "So, your name is Marni Legend, and you live in my neck of the woods?"

Wait, was he *hitting on* me? "Guilty on both counts, your honor."

"You're funny. How'd you like to have dinner sometime?" He handed back my card.

All means of speech left me. My traitorous vocal cords refused to participate.

"If you need time to think about it…"

"Yes!" The word pushed forth like a tornado.

Jake weathered the blast and held his footing. "Yes, you need more time, or yes, you'll meet me for dinner?" This man probably wasn't used to women saying "no," or even having to think about a night out with him.

"Dinner. Yes. That would be nice." I progressed from five-year-old to pre-pubescent teen. Maybe by the time the night arrived, I would have achieved adulthood.

"Great." His dazzling smile mesmerized me. "Gimme your number, and I'll call this week. Maybe we could get together on Friday?"

Beside me, Gus sneered. "You're not gonna go out with this clown, are you? Just ask him about me and be done with the guy."

I gritted my teeth. "Friday works for me. I guess I'll talk to you soon, Jake. And thanks for fixing my car."

"My pleasure. Glad I was on duty tonight." He motioned as if firing a six shooter from the hip.

He put my number in his phone and said he'd text, so I'd have his. During our exchange, I heard a disgruntled Gus voicing his indignation. It took all my self-control not to tell him to bug off.

Almost forgetting, I held out a folded bill. "This is for you."

He looked at it, then held up his phone. "Believe me, your number is worth more than any tip. See you around, Marni Legend."

Very smooth. I got into my car, which I'd left running, and shifted it into gear. Once out of earshot, I let Gus have it. "What the hell is wrong with you? First you want me to talk to him, and now you don't."

"He was right there. You couldn't ask him a couple a questions?"

"Listen up, bub. I've been at this a lot longer than you. People tend to get skittish when asked questions about friends or acquaintances who died years ago. There needs to be a bit of finesse when I tell them why I want to know. Not everyone is as accepting as my brother and me about your hanging around. Besides, maybe I'd like to go out with a living guy for a change."

"You know he only wants to get into your pants."

"Maybe I want him to get into my pants!" Was that a grimace on his face? I'd give him a lecture on dating mature women, but the point would be lost. "What do you have against him anyway? Or do you feel threatened I find him attractive?"

"Listen, lady, I do just *fine*, thank you very much! Or I did anyways. I had a woman for every day of the week and two on Sunday. Threatened by an old guy like him?"

"Old? He looks about my age. I am not *old*. Maybe you should find somebody else to help you." I slowed for the red light at the corner of Main Street, then rolled through turning right. At my building I flipped an illegal U-turn and slammed against the curb in front of the bakery. My front seat no longer had a rider. Good. All I wanted was to forage in the fridge for something passing for dinner and collapse into bed.

Not happening. My mother waited at the kitchen table.

"Did you have a nice dinner at Gloria's?"

Losing my appetite, I switched off the light and went to bed. Nobody deserved this.

Chapter 5

Much to my surprise, Jake called and suggested we have dinner at Chorizo Mexican Restaurant. I'd eaten there a couple of times. Not the best in town, but it would do, and I could walk the few blocks. He garnered points when he wanted to meet at the restaurant instead of picking me up. I didn't like depending on him for transportation in case the night went south.

When Friday arrived, my mother showed up as I debated wardrobe choices—big surprise. "Cleaning out your closet?" She motioned to the pile of clothes on the bed. "You need to get rid of those things. They are *so* outdated."

Snagging a blue dress with small pink flowers from a hanger, I held it against me and looked in the mirror. Casual, yet feminine. I didn't want to overdo it especially being the first date I'd had in months. Ignoring my mother, I changed then went to the bathroom for makeup.

"The Catholic church on Maple Street takes donations. You should drop those off and buy some new things. Maybe you and your sister could spend a day shopping. She always has such good taste in putting together outfits."

I'd rather don a straitjacket and howl at the moon. Brushing on mascara, I tried not to turn my lashes into solid sheets of black goo. "I'm not cleaning, Mom, I've got a date." Finishing with a tube of mauve lipstick, I viewed my perfume selections and picked something fresh and light.

"And that's what you're wearing? Who is it? Anybody I know?" Mom's voice chittered on like a baboon at feeding time.

"No, Ma, nobody you know. I met him last weekend." Back in the bedroom, I studied the mess on my bed and decided to pick it up later—which probably meant swiping it onto the floor. Sometimes living alone had its perks.

"What does he do for a living? Is he as successful as Timothy? I still don't understand why you left such a good man." She perched beside the stack of discards with her hand to her cheek.

Oh, good, this conversation because the first eighty times we'd had it wasn't enough. Her denial over *his* wanting the divorce irritated the heck out of me. Pulling a new pair of pumps with kitten heels from a box, I slipped them on and did a once-over in the full-length mirror. "He's a local business owner."

"That sounds promising. What kind of business?"

I never liked the game twenty questions, and this felt more like an interrogation. All she needed was a trench coat and a heat lamp. "Jake owns a towing company."

"Oh." Her face pinched. "What's his last name? If he's local, maybe I knew the family."

It never occurred to me to ask him. "He doesn't have one. He's like one of those celebrities who only goes by one name." I went to the kitchen for my purse. The gray leather didn't quite match, but it would have to do. Besides, we'd be eating dinner at a local

44

restaurant not attending a corporate gala.

My mother followed, firing off questions like mortars. "What do you mean he doesn't have a last name? How do you know he isn't an ax murderer?"

"I perused the local post office and didn't see his face on any of the wanted posters. Look, as enjoyable as our little mother-daughter chats are, I need to go. Make sure you lock up on your way out." With keys in hand, I locked the door behind me. To my relief, I made it to the street without an escort.

I window shopped along Main Street, enjoying the cessation of chatter. Sauntering ensured I wouldn't arrive a sweaty mess. A block away, my solitude ended.

"That's what you're wearin'? All you need is a walker and support hose."

Now Gus and my mother played tag team. I checked his hand for a baton. "Thanks for the encouragement, now go. A date consists of two people, and you aren't one of them."

"At least he won't want to bang you after seein' you in this outfit."

I glared. "Fashion has changed in the last twenty-five years, and so have women. Not all of us wear skintight spandex hoping to get lucky on the first date." A couple passing by stared at me having a conversation with myself. I looked back. "I'm practicing for an audition. What do you think?"

They kept walking.

"Look, all I'm sayin' is he might have looser lips if you dressed a bit..." He looked me up and down and made a thrusting motion with his pelvis while rocking his arms back and forth. "Ya know, sexy. Why didn't you wear the black dress you had on at the funeral?

Now *that* was hot!"

Great, I had to endure my mother's opinions, now I'm getting fashion tips from a cretin with his name forever on his shirt. "This isn't only a fact-finding mission. Maybe I'd like to see him more than once."

He motioned with his thumb. "That jerk? You need higher standards, Marni."

Look who's talking. "I'm doing this solo and will fill you in on anything I find out." Looking up, I saw Jake standing by the door of Chorizo sporting a grin and well-fitting jeans, paired with a burgundy polo. Below the sleeve I noticed his tattoo—the same dagger with a thorny vine wrapped around it—like Gus's except this one was blue and black with the green vine.

"Were you having a conversation with yourself?" He tilted his head and squinted his eyes.

"Yeah. I do that a lot. It's part of my charm." I smiled. "Have you been waiting long?"

"Nope, just got here. You look great, by the way." He held the door for me.

The hostess looked over my head, which wasn't hard to do at her gargantuan height, and smiled. "Hi, Jake. Here for dinner?" She flipped her long blonde tresses back over each shoulder.

"Oh, hey, Penny, I didn't know you worked here. Yeah, you gotta table for two out on the patio? Ya know, that corner one I like?" He winked at her.

Her bright pink lips flattened as her eyes narrowed. It took all my self-control not to shield my face from the impending claws. As she searched the seating chart, her nails drummed on the wooden podium. "I'll see what's available." The temperature dropped several degrees. Without looking our way, she picked up two menus and said, "Follow me," as if it were an assault rather than a request.

As she led us outside to a garden-like setting, her four-inch heels sounded like bullet strikes on the ceramic tiles. The requested booth had a semi-circular bench and sat against a back wall. Lattice work woven with vines flanked two sides blocking out most of the other diners. I could see why Jake had requested this one and wondered if a plaque bearing his name had been welded to the underside. A picture formed in my mind about my knight in shining armor—the metal started to tarnish and grow thin. He motioned for me to slide in first, while Penny slapped down a menu with more force than necessary. She tossed his across the table and mumbled, "Enjoy your meal," never once making eye contact. Good thing she wouldn't be our server, otherwise the food might come with a dose of arsenic.

"Friend of yours?" The question didn't need to be asked, but I wanted to see what he'd say.

"I know Penny from the neighborhood. We might've gone out a time or two but nothin' serious. You grow up around here?"

Nice diversion. "In Smithtown, but I moved to California in my early twenties. I've been back almost two years."

Our waiter came and filled the water glasses. "Good to see you, Señor Jake. And with such a beautiful lady."

"*Hola, Pedro*. This is Marni."

"Ah, *mucho gusto*." He gave a slight bow.

"*Mucho gusto*." I hoped that ended the Spanish lesson. Beyond ordering a couple of drinks and asking where to find the bathroom, I'd expended my vocabulary.

Thankfully, he continued in English. "May I take your drink order? Our house margarita is on special tonight."

I'd always been more of a wine drinker and said as much. Hard liquor, especially tequila, and my sensibilities never played well together. Despite pressure from both Pedro and Jake to give it a try, I stuck to my guns and insisted on a glass of the house red. Besides, I owed it to Gus to stay coherent and see what information I could glean from his old boss. If my date turned out to be worth a second outing, then it would be all about me.

Jake ordered the margarita and said he'd drink one for me. What a guy. While we perused the menu, he inched toward the back of the booth. "Why don't you slide a little closer, baby? You're so far away."

Boy, he didn't waste any time. While my libido needed to be put back into service, sex on the first date had never been my style. Not that I really had a *style*, though I preferred first base before going for the whole enchilada. Guess I did know more Spanish than I thought.

Placing my elbows on the table and resting my chin on my hands, I said, "But then I couldn't gaze into your…" Damn this dim candlelight. What color were his eyes again? Taking a guess, I crossed my fingers. "I couldn't gaze into your dreamy brown eyes."

A grin spread across his face as he conceded round one, or so I thought. "Okay, I get it. You're shy."

My jaw dropped toward the table. I gave up being demure over two decades ago. Before I could respond,

Gus beat me to the punch.

"You are definitely not shy, lady." He sat between us.

"What?!" Maybe, that came out a bit too loud. At least I didn't blurt out expletives attached to Gus's name. Recovering, I added, "No. I like to get to know a guy before we rub shoulders and play footsie under the table."

Without missing a beat, Jake said, "So, I guess this condom in my wallet won't get any use tonight, will it?"

"Nope, but the credit card will. I haven't eaten all day. Are we having appetizers or going straight for the entrée?"

"Wow, Marni, you really are rusty at dating," Gus chimed in. "No guy likes to be told he's buying dinner and not getting any."

My date sat back and waited while Pedro delivered our drinks. Lifting his glass, Jake toasted, "To finally meeting a mature woman who is *not* a bimbo." We clinked glasses while I tried to figure out if I'd been dissed or complimented. I hoped for the latter.

We agreed an appetizer would be a mistake with Mexican food; we'd waddle out of there. I ordered chicken fajitas, and he chose a beef tostada with beans and rice. After the waiter left, and unfortunately Gus had not, I excused myself and went to the lady's room. Once in there, I checked under the stalls and didn't see feet. "Gus, get in here now."

He appeared with his hands over his eyes. "This is the chick's room. I can't be in here. What would guys think?"

"What guys? Do you have a ghostly entourage you

need to impress?"

He glowered. "So, when are you gonna quit sippin' wine and ask him about me?"

"You need to leave. Like I told you, I've been doing this for years, and asking questions about the deceased requires tact. People can get sketchy if they don't understand my motives."

The door opened and two women walked in. I turned on the tap and washed my hands. They each entered a stall and I whispered, "Let me handle this. Unless you can give me any clues to go on, you need to go!"

"Ya know, the redhead in the end is kinda cute. Maybe I should hang around here." He twisted his neck looking around me.

"Get out." A toilet flushed. "I can't do this with you sitting between us."

The brunette came out of the stall and raised her eyebrows at me. I smiled and reached into my purse for a lipstick. Smearing it over my lips, I flashed my eyes at Gus and nodded toward the door. The woman glanced toward me, then away. Why couldn't I have one normal night?

Back at the table, Jake sat engrossed in his phone. "Do you need to make a call?"

"Nah. Just checking for messages. Owning the shop, I'm never off duty. What do you do for a living?"

Besides enjoying a healthy divorce settlement from my ex-husband? "I'm a writer."

"You mean, like for a newspaper? Would I have seen any of your stuff?"

"I doubt you've read my work. I write books. Historical Romances. They tend to be more popular with women than men."

He bobbed his head. "I've never met anyone who'd written a book. Are you any good?"

Gus materialized again. "Enough about you. Ask him about me."

Clearing my throat, I kept my annoyance at bay. "My agent seems to think so. Twelve of my novels have been published. How long have you owned the towing company?"

"Now we're getting somewhere." Gus rubbed his hands together, while I resigned myself to having a chaperone all evening.

Before he could answer, our dinner arrived. The aroma of spices mixed with flame-broiled meat made my stomach growl as the waiter set the plates in front of us. Another server refilled our water glasses.

Once alone, Jake answered. "Back in ninety-two, I bought out Petey, the previous owner. He could be a schmuck sometimes, but he gave me a good deal since he wanted to retire and had no kids. You got kids?"

"Two. They're both grown and on their own. Tim, Jr., works with his dad in Laguna Beach, and Ginny is a flight attendant for Coastal Airlines based out of Portland. You?"

"Uh-uh. Been a happy bachelor all my life." Then he laced his hands behind his head, like a proud rooster. Red flags raised and alarms screamed in my head. I'd dated a few of these before. Fifty-something and never been married usually meant a guy had only one focus in life—himself. Maybe I should change my first date rule and enjoy the ride, then walk away. His voice intruded. "How long you been divorced?"

Back to me again. This game of ping pong might

run its course early and fizzle. His history needed to come out in more than small dribbles, otherwise we'd be through with dessert before getting past childhood. "Six years. I don't like to talk about." The line worked with most people. If I could wrap up Gus's info, I might be able to enjoy the rest of the night. "That's an interesting tattoo." I put my hand on his bicep. "Does it have any meaning?"

He flexed, and I pulled away. "It used to, but not anymore."

Gus's face screwed up. "You bastard! Tell her about it."

As if Jake heard him, he added, "We did it on a dare from a couple of buddies." He grinned. "Boy, was the old man pissed! But we were over twenty-one, so he couldn't do anything about it anyways."

"Liar! Tell her why we did it." Gus's irritation festered.

Trying to ignore the outbursts, I asked, "We? Did you and a friend get them together?"

He slammed back his margarita and signaled Pedro to bring another one. "You need more wine?"

Probably, but I nursed the last half of my glass and shook my head. Instead of continuing, he shoveled food into his mouth. After three mouthfuls, I nudged. "So, you and a buddy got the same tattoo?"

"Nah. Me and my younger brother, Gus. Like I said, it don't mean anything now."

I thought I'd imagined what I'd heard. Glaring at our spectator, I waited for Jake to look down at his plate and mouthed the word, *Brother*!" Studying the two men's faces, I saw the family resemblance. The corporeal one had crow's feet at the corners of his eyes and a fuller face, while the spirit had stopped aging, yet the similarities were there. Now they could pass for father and son. Keeping my voice steady, I asked, "Aren't you close anymore?"

He put his fork down. "Considering the bastard stole fifty grand from me and disappeared, I would say 'no.' If I ever do find the little weasel, I'll beat him senseless!"

Gus bolted up and took a swing at his brother, which went straight through his target's head. "You filthy liar! I didn't take nothin' from you!"

My head snapped back in surprise, and Jake jumped in. "I'm sorry. I didn't mean to be so loud. It's a sore subject with me. Because of him, I had to take on a partner to keep my business."

"I heard enough from this bum." Gus left.

Thankful Jake thought I reacted to his outburst, I said, "No, I should be the one to apologize. I didn't mean to bring up bad memories." Pay dirt. "You must've come out of it, since yours is the only name on the back of your work shirt."

"Let's say I still have a *silent* partner and leave it at that. I do okay now."

"You never heard from your brother after he took the money?"

"Hey, you wanna have a drink somewhere else? I ain't a wine drinker, but I hear Ozzie's Bar down the block has a good selection."

Just when I'd thought he'd slipped into the Cro-Magnon category, he pulled himself out of the mud, despite ignoring my last question. While those bells in my head issued a subtle warning, I decided to live dangerously and not end the evening yet. Ozzie's had become one of my favorite local bars, and I knew the wine list well. Not wanting to burst his bubble, I didn't say so. Jake paid the bill, left our waiter a generous tip, and we walked toward the entry. Penny's laser beams drilled holes in my skull as we passed her podium. I made a mental note to avoid this place for a while.

Ozzie's had been a staple on Main Street since the nineteen-fifties. The décor had changed a couple of times over the years, but the dark mahogany bar running the length of one wall had been in the original establishment. The same family owned it today. Sometimes on the weekends they had live music. Tonight, a lone performer, channeling a singer from the sixties, graced the small stage. With his warm hand on the small of my back, Jake guided me to two stools on the end farthest from the entertainer. Making it easier to talk without the music in our ears meant he hadn't shut down completely.

Derby and Selene worked the bar tonight. Without asking, Derby set a glass of zinfandel in front of me. "Hey, Marni, we just got this in from Panache Winery in eastern Suffolk County. It's got the same profile as the zin you like from Paso Robles. Let me know what you think." He offered a hand to my date. "Jake, good to see you, man. What're you havin'?"

"I might be working later, so keep it light. Lemme have whatever you got on tap."

"Coming up!" Derby went to the fridge, pulled out an icy glass and filled it. He set the brew in front of Jake then went off to help other customers.

He tilted his head. "I guess you come here sometimes?"

"Occasionally. You were right about them having

good wines." I lifted my glass in a toast. "To a fun evening."

He hefted his mug and clinked my wine glass. "And it ain't over yet." He winked.

Please don't tell me I'm in for a wrestling match. I wavered on whether we should see each other again. Since I hadn't gotten enough information about him and Gus, I might need to soldier on another night. "Did you say you might have to work tonight?"

"Yeah, but not 'til later. Don't worry—it won't spoil any of our plans." He sounded evasive. And what plans? Dinner ended and a nightcap sat before us. God, I wish I were better at dating.

Conversation led to comparing dance clubs we'd frequented around Long Island as teens. It turned out he was five years older than me, but we knew all of the usual places. Roller rinks had been a huge fad too, and he'd gone to them also. Before our drinks ran out, I tried to steer the conversation back to Gus. "Do you have any other siblings?"

The light in his eyes faded. "No." He looked across the bar. "Only Gus. Why do you wanna know so much about my family?"

Telling him because his family had joined us for dinner wouldn't have been a good answer. Why couldn't Gus be looking for a lost will or have an unresolved apology? I'd never had a case as tough as his.

Before I could answer, Jake received a text. He glanced at his phone and cussed. "I'm really sorry, but I gotta go. Are you okay to get home on your own?"

"Sure…I'll cover the drinks. You get going." Too bad the date would end on this note. *Guess I'll have to do research on my own.* "Thank you for dinner."

He took my hand and gazed into my eyes. "No. Thank *you*." Before I knew what was happening, he kissed me. "You doin' anything next Tuesday?"

Wow! So this wasn't the brush off. I almost had myself convinced he'd messaged a buddy to text and save him from a disastrous night.

"If you're a writer, then you're available during the day, right?"

I nodded, still a bit stunned.

"How about we pack a picnic and get in some beach time? I could pick you up about ten."

Before I could think, I heard my voice agreeing. "Sounds like fun. Which beach?"

"Wanachee Bluff."

I gulped.

Chapter 6

Wandering home, I felt unsettled. Our date went okay, but something about Jake bothered me, and I couldn't put my finger on it. I had more questions now than when the evening began. He acted almost clandestine about having a *silent* partner. What's next? Meetings with a secret handshake? Did Jake have anything to do with the car thefts his brother had been involved with? If so, was he still involved? Was it his tow truck I saw pulling the Fergussons' car? Dating someone who could go up the river for grand theft larceny had never been on my bucket list.

Before realizing it, I arrived at my front door but didn't feel like going in. The thought of enduring another cozy chat with Mom inspired me to keep walking until I hit the dock. As I breathed in the faint clammy scent of the tide, I passed fishermen with their poles in the water. The sound of waves lapping against the pylons and anchored boats in the bay echoed throughout the harbor. I went to the end of the wooden planks and dropped onto a bench. As I stared out to sea, someone sat down beside me. I assumed it was Gus and didn't look up.

"You could almost pass for a law-abiding citizen this evening."

I knew that voice. Last time I'd heard it, she sounded a lot more accusatory. Beside me sat the sentry from last week. At least this time I wasn't scurrying through her bushes and trespassing. "I clean up pretty good when I need to."

"Ever find Kitty?"

"Nah, I think she decided to hitchhike to Mexico."

She proffered a hand. "I'm Darla. Darla Billingsly."

I scrunched my face. "Are you gathering intel for your report?"

The old woman laughed, which stretched out the wrinkles on her face. Almost. "How about we start over?"

Grasping her hand, I said, "Legend. Marni Legend."

"Well, Legend, Marni Legend, it's a pleasure to meet you. I've noticed you around town and am curious why you were crawling around my front yard. I'd like your take on what happened. Did you know the Fergussons', my neighbor's, car got stolen that night?"

"I did see a yellow tow truck hauling a small silver car. You sure they weren't repossessing it?"

Darla sputtered. "Quite. The car has been in the Fergusson family for years, and I'm sure it was paid for long ago. They're what you'd call 'old money' and pay cash for everything. What were you doing there? *Please* tell me you weren't the lookout."

This woman thought I could be a hardened criminal. With a little work, I might pull off being the toughest lady at the community rec center. "No, I wasn't the lookout. You could say I'd gotten inside information from a friend to check the place out. He didn't say anything about a crime being committed though."

She tilted her head. "Who gave you this tip?"

"Darla, you wouldn't believe me if I told you. You seem like a nuts and bolts type of person, and my source isn't your ordinary type."

"Nuts and bolts—great description! I do like things to be straightforward without a bunch of bullshit."

I burst out laughing. "My, my, missy, you do use some colorful language."

We watched a nearby fisherman fighting with his line until he hauled in a large, flapping thing with fins. It seemed like an awful lot of trouble to secure dinner. I preferred mine to come filleted with a choice of seasonings. No telling what kind he reeled in, but that's why God created menus.

"What *type* is your source?"

She did catch the reference. Most times I don't share my gifts with the living not involved in a case, but occasionally I come across someone with an open mind. Darla struck me as one of them. If she didn't believe me, she already thought I was a criminal, so what's a little lunacy thrown in? I fixed my gaze straight into her eyes. "A ghost. And no, I don't know who stole it. When they came out, I threw myself down and prayed for invisibility. I couldn't see their faces with my nose in the dirt."

"Thought you meant some kind of spirit." She didn't even flinch.

"Can you see—" I began.

"No. But I've met folks before who could right here on Long Island. With so much history, I guess it would be hard not to bump into a lost soul or two. I'd heard enough to believe 'em."

My new best friend, Darla, might know Gus's

family. "Darla, how long have you lived in Northport?"

"All my life. I grew up in the house you were sneaking around." Her voice had a happy lilt, acknowledging I'd wormed my way into her good graces. "Got married in the backyard and raised three kids. They've all scattered, like rats on a sinking ship, and the husband…well…Drake's been gone two years."

"I'm sorry. So, it's only you now?"

"Yup. What's your story?" She settled back against the hard wood.

Oh, lord, we'd be here 'til dawn if I gave her the full run down. Maybe if I told the condensed version, we'd have time for her to give me history on my young tow truck driver and current paramour. Her kids might've even known Gus and Jake growing up. I gave her the short version of growing up a few towns over, moving to Cali, marriage, divorce, and the move back. As I wrapped it up with whipped cream and a cherry on top, intentionally omitting my date tonight, we had gained another pair of listening ears. Gus leaned against a post holding up the small roof above us. "Did you know most of the kids who grew up around here?"

"Depends. Like I said, I've been here forever."

"How old are your children now?"

She thought a moment. "My Randall is fifty-six. The girls are fifty-two and fifty-three—Adriana and Justine. They were so close they might as well have been twins. Those two loved to dress alike when they were younger." Thinking of my own mother, I wondered if Darla's kids missed her as much as she missed them.

"Did they know a couple of brothers, Gus and

Jake? Jake owns the tow truck company in town."

Gus moved closer and studied the old woman's face. "Mrs. Billingsly? Damn, she got old. She looks like the crypt keeper. All the woman needs is a black robe and one of those blade thingies on a pole."

I covered my mouth, stifling a chuckle. He wasn't far from the truth. Darla had to be pushing eighty.

"I knew those boys. Augustus and Jacob Zuckerman. Both were nothing but trouble! Regular hoodlums."

Having met both brothers, I'd have to agree with her assessment. Neither would have passed for a choir boy—or whatever they called them in the synagogue. With a name like Zuckerman and living on Long Island, they had to have grown up Jewish. And Gus's real name was Augustus? I planned to have hours of fun with that one.

"Yup," Gus confirmed, "she's Mrs. Billingsly all right. The old bat. She never liked me. Always gave me crap whenever I took out her daughter. And you can forget that whole Augustus thing. I quit using it in the third grade." He crossed his arms and returned to his stance against the pole.

"My Adriana went with Gus in high school. He broke her heart when she found out he'd been two-timing her with two other girls. I hated seeing my baby hurt but was certainly glad when she cut that thug out of her life." She wrapped her sweater tighter as a soft breeze came up off the water.

"You were no picnic either, lady. If I still had..." I glared at Gus, and he shut up. Running into Darla might be more useful in finding answers than Jake had been. If only my young sidekick would be quiet long enough for me to have a conversation. Maybe I should try the mute button on the remote with him. It didn't work on Mom, but you never know.

"Did your daughter stay in touch with him after high school?"

She shook her head. "I don't believe she did, but you know kids. Parents are the last to know about most things in their lives. She probably ran into him occasionally after college when she moved back home for a few years."

"Did she get a job someplace else? It sounds like none of your children live here anymore."

Darla shivered. "Not exactly. A close friend of hers had been murdered. You know the old Beach Street Psych Center?"

I nodded.

"Her body had been found in the basement of one of the buildings. She'd been driving around in her father's fancy convertible, which they never found. The police assumed whoever did it killed her and stole the car. Adriana was devastated, especially since the girl had invited her to go out dancing, and my daughter canceled at the last minute. A boy from her college called and invited her to dinner. They're husband and wife now. She was wracked with guilt when she'd found out what happened to Dominique. Always felt her friend would be alive had she stuck to the original plan."

"Wow. Your daughter couldn't have known. Besides, had she gone with Dominique she might have been killed too. What was Dominique's last name?"

Darla turned toward me. "Now why would you want to know? And why are you asking about the

Zuckerman brothers? The younger one has been gone for years."

Because Gus led me to the old psych center, I feared car theft wasn't his only crime. "Occupational hazard. I do a lot of research." I loved it when I could stick close to the truth.

"Just what is it you do for a living?"

"I'm a writer. Do you read historical romances?"

Recognition lit in her eyes. "Now I know why your face looks familiar. The local library has a display of your books. I've read a couple. Very engaging, except for the racy parts. I skip over those."

Racy? Not one of my novels is a bodice ripper. If her standards are that high, she probably thinks young adult books should be X-rated. "The library told me they were featuring local authors this month and would be displaying a few of mine. I haven't gotten over there yet to see it."

"Are you going to tell me who the spirit is you're helping?"

"Can I ask you to be patient? It might sway your answers."

She studied me with her face taut. "I'll let you off the hook for now. What other answers do you need?"

"Did the police ever catch the murderer?"

"No, but when they'd found Dominique's body, Augustus had disappeared, and he became what they called 'a person of interest.' The man had been seen around town with her from time to time. A friend of Dominique's remembered passing her car around eleven that night and a blond-haired man rode in the passenger seat, but she wasn't sure if it was the Zuckerman boy. Word had it Augustus embezzled money from his brother and took off for greener pastures at the same time as the murder."

"You bitch!" Gus stomped his foot, yet only I could hear him yelling as I watched out of the corner of my eye. The whole foot stomping thing would never be real again either. "I didn't take nothin' from nobody. And I didn't kill nobody either." I waited for his head to spin around and maybe his voice to dissolve into tongues. Would've been entertaining.

"Do you think he did it?"

"Which one—the murder or take the money?" Darla asked.

"Both."

She gazed at the water. I got the feeling she'd thought a lot about this as the years passed. "I believe he stole the money from his brother. Truth be told, as badass—excuse my French—as the boy had been, I don't believe Augustus killed that girl. The violence of what had happened to her..." Her voice caught, and her eyes moistened.

I placed a hand on her arm. "How did she die?"

Taking me by surprise, Darla bolted to her feet. "I can't talk about this anymore. I need to get home." She hurried down the pier and onto the street.

Her reaction stunned me into silence, and all I could do was watch her leave. I turned to question Gus and found myself alone. Why did he always disappear when it was his turn to fill in the gaps?

Chapter 7

Monday morning came, and I hadn't seen hide nor hair of Gus—or my mother, but I didn't want to jinx myself by thinking about her. After Gus's outbursts to Darla's accusations on the pier, he'd probably gone off to sulk. I needed to ask him about the girl who'd been murdered, since it sounded like he knew her. Perhaps he and Dominique had been more than just friends?

Drinking my coffee and munching a freshly baked roll, I popped open my laptop. Since my source refused to appear, I'd have to do my own research. There had to be articles on the murder. The timing of Gus's disappearance and demise were too coincidental. Darla never told me the last name of the victim, but it wouldn't be difficult to find.

After ten minutes of searching, I found an article from the Long Island Newspaper dated July 25, 1995. The headline read *Body Found in Beach Street Basement* and it went on to say:

The naked body of a young woman has been discovered in the basement of Building 3 at the Beach Street Psychiatric Hospital. The victim, identified as 26-year-old Dominique Perez, had bruises about her face and upper body. It appeared she had been raped then strangled.

The facility, going through a phased shut down, has not utilized Buildings 2 and 3 for the past two years. Two of the staff facilities are also closed. All patients reside in Building 1. Maintenance workers discovered the body while checking on the source of a strange odor emanating from a basement window. It appeared the attack took place elsewhere, and she had been dumped through the broken window of the unused building.

Ms. Perez had been reported missing by her family on Sunday, July 16, when she did not return home after going out to meet friends the previous evening. She was last seen leaving a Northport establishment, Ozzie's Bar, alone at approximately ten o'clock. The victim had been driving her parents' maroon convertible, which has not been located. Authorities speculate she may have been the target of car thieves.

The rest of the article provided details about the family and where her body would be laid to rest. I continued searching in hopes the perpetrators had been caught but found nothing more, leading me to believe the case had never been solved.

Every ounce of my common sense, which many times eluded me, screamed I should walk away from this one. While I didn't want to be haunted by Gus the rest of my life, nosing around could result in my own life being cut short by a few decades. If the police couldn't find a connection between Dominique's murder and the Zuckerman brothers, how could I solve the case?

I decided to do a search for Gus on the internet. Typing in *Augustus Zuckerman*, all I found was a small blurb from July 31, 1995, about his being a *person of interest* in the case of an unsolved murder. No mention of his being located or questioned. While his brother, and apparently many of the locals, believed he took off with a load of cash, maybe he never got to spend the money. If his plan had been to get away, somehow it backfired, and he wound up dead.

Unable to do anything further on my current mystery until speaking with Gus, I decided to visit the library and check out the local authors' display. The director had been after me a couple of months ago to do a reading or a talk, and I'd never gotten back with him. If he was available today, he could give me a better idea of what he wanted and when.

The theme from a murder scene in my favorite horror movie bounced off the walls of my kitchen. Only one person in my contacts had the honor of that ringtone. I'd avoided Gloria all week. She'd already left a dozen messages. Thirteen might make the phone explode.

Bracing for an attack, I accepted the call. "Hi, Gloria."

"Where have you been? I've left several messages. Even Calvin hasn't been able to reach you." I'd spoken to Calvin and knew our sister was on the warpath to get this *family business* wrapped up. Sounded like he didn't report back to the commander to say he'd made contact. Smart man.

I thought of Christmas trees and puppies to force some cheer into my voice. "Oh, really? Maybe my service is being flakey. What's up?"

"I find it hard to believe you didn't get any of my messages." Her voice remained even. Had she reverted to speaking without moving her lips? It wasn't as effective when you couldn't see the performance in person.

"Anyway, besides the discussion you ran out on at my place, we have other issues to sort through." Truly an understatement.

Withholding a sigh, I asked, "What else is going on?"

Gloria did not contain her exasperation and let out a long breath. "The cemetery called me."

Oh, no. "You didn't make them move the hole they dug for Mom's burial, did you? The interment is over and done with."

"Hardly, but I wish the location of Mom's final resting place was our only problem. The crematorium believes the box of ashes we buried may not be our mother's."

I tried hard to mask any humor in my voice. I failed. "You have *got* to be kidding me," I sputtered. "That's hysterical."

"How can you find this funny? Don't you understand what this means? They may have *lost* our mother."

Believe me, she's not lost. "What happens now?"

"The crematorium wants to meet with us to discuss how to correct the error. We have an appointment with the manager at two o'clock this afternoon. Calvin will be there. I expect you to be there as well. *On time*."

My hand swung up in a mock salute even though she couldn't see me. "Okay. Text me the address." No escaping this one. Honestly, it had the potential to be an amusing afternoon. With nothing better to do today, I was all for it.

My sister hung up without another word. Almost immediately, my phone chimed with a text from her.

****

An hour later I'd gotten in a shower and set off to the library. After a short stroll, I went up the cement steps of the ancient building. Originally built in the eighteen-hundreds, scaffolding had become a constant feature of the outer décor with workmen making renovations. At least the plumbing and electric had been updated within the last decade. It wouldn't do to have something short out and destroy the books and ancient artifacts displayed.

Speaking of ancient artifacts, Mrs. Barton worked the front desk. I believe she'd been *renovated* in the last decade as well. Her science-fiction high cheek bones stretched the skin so tightly across her face it looked more like a skull. I wondered if the cosmetic reconstruction made it difficult to open her mouth.

Watching me over the top of her reading glasses, she didn't smile when I approached the counter— probably another casualty of the face lifts. "May I help you, Ms. Legend?"

"I wondered if Mr. Tavish would be available?"

"Mr. Tavish retired last month. His replacement, Mr. Kramer, is due to arrive in about twenty minutes, if you would care to wait."

While her words conveyed he could see me, the condescension in her voice signaled it would be an imposition. Perhaps I should have had my secretary call ahead for an appointment. Oh, wait, I don't have a secretary. "Yes, I'll wait. Thank you."

"Very well." The aura of old-time school marm surrounded her. Perhaps retirement would be around the corner for her too, and they could bring in some new blood for the next eighty-year run. Mr. Tavish must've been close to ninety.

I wandered over to the local author display of my books and those of four others. Two were best-selling fiction writers I didn't realize came from around here. Alongside my most recent three novels stood a horrible publicity shot taken a couple of years ago. *Mental note to self: have my agent set up a photo shoot.* The brief bio on me left out my current marital status. No need to spray too much personal information over the good folks of Northport. I was thankful I'd made the decision to publish under my maiden name, which I took back after the divorce.

"Marni, it's good to see you after all of these years," a male voice spoke from behind my shoulder.

Turning, I found a pleasant surprise standing before me. Like mine, a few new lines crinkled at the corners of his eyes and mouth, but he still had a full head of sandy-blond hair. "KK, how are you? I didn't realize you were back on Long Island. How've you been?"

He laughed. "Nobody's called me KK since high school. I go by Kendall now."

"You're Mr. Kramer? As in the new library director?" We'd lost touch after I married Tim and moved to California. I'd heard he'd gotten married. His empty ring finger indicated otherwise.

"Like you, I'd gone off into the world but have returned to my roots. I saw your mom's obit in the newspaper. My condolences."

"Thank you. It was sudden, but she's at peace now. Well, sort of." Wherever she may be buried.

"Mrs. B said you wanted to talk with the director. Shall we go to my office?" He gestured toward the private area off one of the side wings.

I leaned in and glanced back and forth before asking, "Does she really allow you to call her Mrs. B?"

He shrugged. "I never asked permission. After correcting me a few times, she gave up. Score one for the new guy."

His office had very little clutter and smelled of lemony wood polish. The pictures on the credenza were of young couples with babies and toddlers. Probably his kids. There weren't any of a woman who could be around our age. I sat in a chair opposite his desk and waited for him to get settled.

"I didn't realize Mr. Tavish had retired. He'd contacted me about doing a talk here some time. Did he leave any notes?"

Kendall opened a drawer and pulled out a file. "Actually, he did. Old Mr. T retired sooner than planned due to health reasons. Lucky for me. This is the perfect gig."

Good thing we were on a first name basis, otherwise I'd be Ms. L. "Have you been home long?"

"I moved back four years ago and took a job at a library over on the south shore. When this position became available, I jumped on it."

"Sounds like a great opportunity. I would think there'd have been a lot of competition."

"Not many wanted it. This library is a bit antiquated for most. The newer facilities are larger, have more computers and meeting rooms. I liked the idea of working in a sleepy corner of the Island, plus it's closer to where I live. My house is a short eight-minute commute, and that's only if I hit all red lights. How long have you been back?"

He'd said *my* house not *our* house. "Two years

ago." Let's get the history lesson out of the way and move on. "Tim and I divorced, so I saw no reason to stay on the west coast. Besides, I've missed this area."

"Sorry to hear that." His tone held no sympathy. "My story kinda sounds the same. Carina and I split almost five years ago. Not to air my dirty laundry, but I caught her sneaking around with a younger man."

"Pool boy?"

He chuckled. "Close. He was a valet at our favorite restaurant. The divorce got nasty, and I moved back here the second it ended."

"At least Tim waited until the ink dried on the decree before taking up with an uptown twinkie. We're still amicable, yet he was the one who wanted out." Kendall didn't know about my special abilities. Teenagers could be merciless when it came to anyone different, and I hadn't wanted to deal with being a freak *and* having acne.

"Congratulations on a wonderful career as a writer. Twelve books is impressive."

A tingle went down my spine. He'd followed my career. "Thanks. My next is scheduled to launch this October, so I've been plugging away at the computer."

"Well then, let's get down to business. The library is planning a series of author talks, but the program has been pushed back until the fall. Right now, our focus is on the summer reading programs we're kicking off the end of May." He leaned forward, placing his hands on the desktop. "You planning to be around come September?"

Did his voice have a tinge of hopefulness? This was shaping up to be a great morning. "Yes, I'm not going anywhere."

Kendall nodded. "Good." He opened the folder on his desk and wrote a couple of notes. "We can hammer down the details when it gets closer, if that works for you." He looked up, "Why don't you give me your number so I can contact you when we have definite dates?" After I rattled it off, he asked, "Do you live nearby?"

Was this his way of angling for my address too? "Remember Fugacci's Bakery on Main Street?"

"You live in the bakery?"

"With as much as I eat from there, I probably should. My apartment is above it. There's two bedrooms; one I use as an office. The location is great, and I'm not ready for another house yet. The tiny living suits me for now."

"I love that Italian bakery. They make great black and white cookies. Maybe one morning I could swing by, pick up coffee and pastries, and we could take them over to the dock. The bench on the end still one of your favorite spots?"

"It is." Was he reminiscing or revving up for a second chance?

"Are you free Thursday morning? Say about eight?"

Of course, but I still made a show of checking the calendar on my phone. I had to play a little hard to get before tripping farther down memory lane. "It's in my calendar."

"Great. I'll see you then, Marni." Damn, he'd always had a dynamite smile.

I took that as my cue to leave and stood. "This meeting turned out to be a nice surprise. See you Thursday."

Kendall walked me to the door. He smelled of the same fresh-scented aftershave he'd used back in high school. For a moment I feared he would hug me. What would Mrs. B say? Luckily, he only waved and sent me on my way. Now, if only the meeting at the crematorium this afternoon would go as well. I had my doubts.

Chapter 8

The GPS spouted directions as I got closer to Roseview Crematorium. It took over twenty-five minutes to get there. Guess I should have checked the distance when Gloria first sent the address. Both Calvin's blue pickup and her white luxury sedan were in the parking lot. Of course, they would be—the clock on my dashboard read two twelve.

I hurried up the steps to the reception desk inside the lobby and was greeted by a young woman with bright red talons sprouting from her fingertips. If I had nails like that, I would have to wear foam casings on the tips to keep from hurting myself. She directed me down a hallway to the manager's office. The door stood open, and I joined my siblings at a small conference table.

Gloria glared at me, then turned to two men sitting across from us. "*Now*, we may begin. I appreciate your patience, gentlemen."

No point in apologizing. My sister would have already made an excuse. Both men wore black tailored suits with crisp white shirts. The only difference between their *uniforms* was one wore a blue tie and the other a silvery-gray. Blue Tie clasped his hands together, the knuckles turning white. Silvery-Gray eased back with one elbow leaning on the arm rest of his chair. His well-rehearsed composure smacked of seniority.

Blue Tie led off. "My name is Charles Dilboy, and I'm the General Manager of this facility." He gestured to the man beside him. "This is Cavanaugh Grayson, the District Manager. We appreciate you making time to meet with us today."

We all nodded in unison like a bunch of robots and waited for Dilboy to continue. "As I'm sure the cemetery manager mentioned, we're afraid there may have been a slight…ahhh…mix-up with the cremains of your loved one." A bead of sweat rolled down his balding temple.

Grayson took over. "Unfortunately…"

Bad choice of words. As a writer, I know dialogue. Starting a sentence with that word creates angst and unrest, as displayed by Gloria with the way she leaned in hanging on the man's every word. The corners of her mouth pointed down.

He continued. "…we had a new employee in training the day your…Mrs. Legend came into our care. Four recently departed had been on the schedule, your mother being one of them. One of the families requested the token be verified before burial."

"Token?" Gloria challenged.

"It's a metallic coin stamped with an identification number which accompanies the deceased throughout the cremation process. It is used to ensure the correct remains are delivered to its final resting place. Rarely do we need to check this since there should have been accompanying paperwork." Grayson cleared his throat. "While we are still trying to figure out what happened, the bottom line is the cremains from the one family were not those of their loved one."

Calvin stifled a laugh. "You're saying our mother might not be who we buried with our dad?"

Dilboy raised his hands off the table. "Not necessarily. It's possible one or two of the cremains were delivered correctly. We've attempted to contact the other two families and alert them to the...possibility." He patted his forehead with a handkerchief.

"Cut to the chase, gentlemen." I'd heard enough finessing about the situation and knew exactly what they were asking. While it would have been fun to force them into making the request, I felt Dilboy needed to be put out of his misery before he had a stroke. "You want to dig up the box with our mother's ashes and check the ID coin, right?"

"Over my dead body is anyone digging me up! You boys can go desecrate someone else's tomb. What am I, the lost ark?"

Calvin shot a look at me. Though he didn't need confirmation, I gave the slightest of nods and motioned with my eyes at the space between Grayson and Dilboy.

"Marni," Mom demanded, "you tell them they can't do this. Let them sift through someone else's dust." She put a hand to her chest. "Oh, my God. You don't think I got buried in a Jewish cemetery, do you? I've always been a good Catholic girl. I don't deserve this."

If she weren't already dead, I'm sure this would have done her in. I'd wait until later to tell her the Jewish faith doesn't allow cremation. It might be fun stringing her along for a while. Yes, I have an evil streak. I raised my fingers off the table and gently waved her off. She crossed her arms over her bosom and stood her ground.

Gloria had the same stubborn set to her jaw. "What have the other families said to your request?"

"One hasn't responded back. They took their father's remains to France so he could be buried in the family plot there. The family who first discovered they had the incorrect ashes had been given the remains of the man destined for a French burial. It might be more difficult to get permission to ah…exhume his ashes. The other family had their loved one interred at the military cemetery, the same as yours. I was hoping…"

My sister cut him off. "Please check the remains of the other burials first." She stood and gathered her purse.

"I understand how upsetting this can be." Grayson spoke, his voice soft and even. "Please consider signing the papers to have Mrs. Legend's remains verified."

Always the diplomat of the family, Calvin stood. "We need to discuss this matter in private. You understand?" As kids I referred to him as a kiss-ass.

"Calvin, there is nothing to talk about," Mom fired off. "These idiots, *Gorilla* and *Dingbat*, are not removing me from my final resting place. *End* of discussion." Having laid down her ultimatum, she evaporated.

My brother watched me raise my right hand and rub the thumb over my four fingers. This signaled to him our visitor had left. Without further acknowledgement to Gorilla and Dingbat—*good one Mom*—we followed Gloria down the hall and outside.

"So much for Mom being at peace," Calvin said.

Gloria didn't pick up on his meaning. "She will remain at peace. I refuse to sign those papers and have her dug up like an autumn potato."

"No, Gloria, he meant Mom was in the room with us. She stood between the ding-a-ling twins voicing her displeasure at being exhumed. When we left, so did she…for now."

"You think she'll be back?" she asked.

Confession time. "Actually, she's been back since after the interment."

Calvin bugged out his eyes. "Why didn't you say anything?"

"Because I kept hoping she'd go away. She's got nothing unresolved, and there is no good reason for her to be hanging around."

"Well, she's got a reason now," Gloria said. "Look, I have to get home. Can we please all get together and resolve this? I'm free for lunch tomorrow. How about you two?"

"Where do you want to meet? I'll be at the new construction site until noon."

Sheepishly, I chimed in. "Can't…I've got a date."

Calvin flattened himself against the wall while Gloria crossed her arms. Perhaps I should introduce myself. Hello, I'm the sibling who has a life.

"You do not." Gloria stated. "Why are you so stubborn about getting things resolved?"

"Yes, I do. We're going for a picnic on the beach."

"A little beach blanket bingo?" Calvin arched his brows.

I smacked him on the arm. "How about we meet at the diner in Crandall Ridge for lunch on Wednesday? That'll be convenient for all of us. Deal?"

They both agreed, and we went our separate ways. I didn't want to return home, afraid Mom would continue her rant. She'd become partial to my kitchen, and it surprised me when she appeared at the meeting today. In the end, I went home. With a deadline for my thirteenth novel approaching, I needed to bang away at the keyboard. Maybe I could incorporate this new mess into one of the chapters. Nah, who would believe it?

Back at my vacant apartment, emphasis on vacant, I settled down to work. The irony of my love life taking off during the thirteenth romance novel didn't elude me. The harbingers didn't bode well, but I chose to muddle through. Not only did I have the one hunky paramour, but I acquired a second with the reintroduction of Kendall into my life. He didn't waste time asking me out.

Honestly, I viewed seeing Jake as a chance to resolve Gus's issues rather than a dating option. Kendall, on the other hand, had long-term potential. People always liked to quote the cliché, "You can never look back." I disagreed and thought repeating history had possibilities.

Chapter 9

Tuesday morning, I sat in the kitchen enjoying my usual fare. A creature of habit, I rarely cooked breakfast. Too many carbohydrate-filled options beckoned from below. I never asked Jake if I should bring anything and assumed he'd provide lunch. Just in case, I chilled a bottle of cabernet. Reds aren't supposed to be put in the fridge, as Gloria had once spouted at me, but by the time we got to drink it, the bottle would be at the right temperature.

I got in a solid chapter before the clock read nine-thirty. Changing into a bathing suit, covered by shorts and a tee shirt, I found a cooler for the wine and added a six-pack of beer I'd picked up. Not knowing what he normally drank, I'd gotten a pilsner produced by a local brewery.

By nine fifty-five, I waited on the sidewalk in front of my door. Funny, I could make it on time for a date but not anything my sister planned. Okay, that was intentional. Someday I'd grow up. Maybe. At ten on the dot, a black diesel pickup pulled up, and Jake hopped out. He walked around the truck, gave me a quick kiss on the cheek and said, "Your chariot awaits." Opening my door, he pointed to the cooler. "What's in there?"

"A cabernet and a six-pack of beer. Oh, and glasses. I'm not drinking wine from a red plastic cup."

"Fair enough. I brought enough food to feed a

small country, plus beer and wine. I think we'll be good. Do you like fishing?"

Fishing? No! "I love to fish. Haven't done it in years so I'm a bit rusty. You'll have to teach me." Not touching any damn worms either.

It took twenty minutes to reach Wanachee Bluff. Jake pulled into a spot near the stairs. He came around and helped me out of the passenger seat. I needed a parachute to reach the ground from the cab of his big diesel. With my small cooler slung over my shoulder, he reached into the bed of the truck and retrieved a larger cooler, blanket, two fishing rods, and a bucket full of gear.

We trudged down the switchback of wooden stairs to the sand. Not many people came this time of year. The real season began at the end of the month. Other fishermen dotted the sand. With my new discoveries causing me to doubt on which side of the law Jake resided, I was glad we weren't alone.

He spread the blanket near the shore's edge and set everything on top. It was high tide, and the waterline wouldn't get any closer. I dropped my bag then removed my sneakers and wriggled my toes in the sand. "What are we fishing for?"

"This time of year, flounder, cod, mackerel mostly, sometimes bass. You never know. Just cast your rod out and see what you get."

He could have been describing my dating life over the last few years. It hadn't been great—until now—and I'd reeled in some doozies. Jury's still out on whether it had improved. "Don't we need a license to do this?"

"I got an annual one, but the town constable never

comes down here. Besides, I know the guy, and he won't hassle you."

Eyeing the container of nightcrawlers he pulled from the cooler, I pointed. "I do have to make one teeny little confession."

He looked at his hand.

"I hate touching worms. This is a deal breaker. Will you bait my hook?"

Laughing, he said, "I didn't take you for the squeamish type. But I will do that for you." He gave a slight bow.

"You are a true prince, sir."

"Have you ever ocean fished before?"

Busted. "No. I prefer my fish to come filleted, preferably on fine china." He hung his head. "But I'm willing to try. This was a great idea." I picked up one of the poles. "Shall we?"

He smiled. "Worms are on me. Let's see what we can catch."

Jake taught me to cast and what to do when I snagged one, which I did. I had to admit, this whole fishing thing was more fun than I'd imagined. He might have created a monster, except for the baiting my own hook ordeal.

Come lunch time, he had to wrestle the pole from my grip. After an enjoyable morning, it felt awkward bringing up his brother. While we fished, there hadn't been much conversation. Sitting on the blanket with a deli-made pastrami sandwich, potato salad, and wine, I needed to get something accomplished today other than perfecting my casting skills. I regretted Gus's not appearing before my seeing his brother again. Not knowing his connection to the dead girl made this doubly hard.

Not exactly mealtime conversation, but I decided to tell Jake about the mix-up at the crematorium. Maybe if I talked about my siblings, he would feel comfortable sharing a little about his brother.

"Will you let them dig her up?" he asked.

"Not if my sister has anything to say about it. We're all getting together at lunch tomorrow for the debate."

He swallowed the bite in his mouth. "Debate? Sounds like you don't all agree."

"It isn't so much we don't agree; my sister likes to make a big deal about family decisions. If it will give the other families peace of mind to know Grannie or Uncle Phil got planted in the right spot, I don't see the harm in it. I've always believed wherever someone is buried, they're not actually there anyway. Headstones and gravesites are places for the living to go to mourn and remember. Calvin, my brother, will go along with whatever Gloria and I agree on."

"Will you go with her decision?" Jake sipped one of the pilsners I'd brought. My psychic powers must be improving as he'd said it was one of his favorites.

I crinkled my nose. "Depends on how feisty I'm feeling tomorrow. I'll probably give her a hard time but, in the end, let her handle it."

"So, you would *intentionally* give her a hard time?" Another laugh.

"Didn't you ever antagonize your brother, what was his name, just for the fun of it?" Smooth segue. I dabbed at the juice dribbling from the corner of my mouth. This pastrami tasted amazing.

A grin spread across his face. "Gus. His name was

Gus."

I did a double take. After gulping my wine, I asked, "*Was* Gus?"

"Huh?"

"You said his name *was* Gus. Don't you think he's alive anymore?"

"Good catch," said Gus. "Marni, you should be writing crime novels not that romance crap."

And just like that we acquired a third wheel. I ignored him and focused on the conversation with his brother. Gus knew I could see and hear him. I wouldn't risk acknowledging him and tipping Jake off.

The grin left Jake's face. "Oh…well…he's been gone so long, I guess I think of him in the past. He isn't in my present."

Nice recovery. "Makes sense. So, did you ever poke at him like I do Gloria?"

"Of course! We were brothers." His lips curved up again. "We were always daring each other to do things. Sometimes it got pretty wild. Like the tattoo. My friend dared me, and I turned around and dared Gus to get one too. It was cool doing that with my brother. Like we had a special bond besides just being brothers. You know what I mean? After we both went through the design books, we picked the same one, so we got them in different colors. And we both agreed the old man would blow a gasket!"

Gus laughed at the last part. "We weren't far off. He told us we were grounded, but we lived in our own place then."

"What did your dad do when he saw them?"

Jake snorted and shook his head. "The old man was ready to spit nails. He wanted to ground us, but we didn't live at home anymore."

This made me laugh because my mother would have had the same reaction. Though, I couldn't picture Gloria and I bonding over matching tattoos. Maybe I should dare her?

"Me and my brother rented a house together. Not too far from here. It was the year before I bought the towing company. Petey still owned it, and we worked for him."

"Besides, the…you know…stealing the money thing…" I refused to look at Gus. His silence encouraged me to think he would quit storming about like an ignored two-year-old. "Do you miss him?"

Jake held a second beer up to his mouth, then rested it back on the blanket. "Why you so interested in my brother?"

I'd prepared for this question. "Because family is very important to me. Despite endlessly tormenting my sister, I love her. We'll always be family, and whoever I'm with needs to feel the same." If that wasn't a beauty pageant finalist's answer, I don't know what is— besides wanting world peace. Gus gave me a round of applause.

Jake took a long swig of his beer. "That's really nice. You are a *nice* person, Marni Legend. Except for the annoying your sister thing, but that's funny."

We packed up our picnic, grabbed the fishing gear and bucket with today's catch, then walked to the stairs for our trek up. I noticed Gus had made himself scarce. By the time we'd reached the top, I huffed and puffed like I'd run a marathon. My date hadn't broken a sweat. So unfair.

I casually glanced at my armpits making sure I

didn't have huge sweat stains. The sports tee shirt did its job and wicked away the moisture as promised on the tag.

Jake tossed everything into the back of the truck and put his hand on my door. Before opening it, he said, "Since you're so into family…"

Uh-oh, maybe I overdid it a tad.

"…I have a favor to ask."

Tilting my head, I nodded for him to continue, hoping he knew I was beyond child-bearing years.

"You see, I told my mom I had another date with you. She wants to meet you." Hope shone in his eyes.

"Don't you think it's a bit early for parent meeting? I mean, I've only been back in the dating game a few years, but I thought parental involvement happened a few months down the road. You haven't even met my goldfish yet." I backpedaled, wondering how to slow this train down. Those sweat stains might have appeared anyway.

He roared. "You got a great sense of humor. When I told my mother your name, she recognized it. She's read a few of your books and wants to meet you. Maybe get you to autograph a couple, if you're okay with that?"

"Ahhhhh, now I feel dumb." I looked at my shoes, then back up. "Not that I don't think you're a good guy, and maybe, who knows, this could…okay, I'm going to stop talking now before my foot needs to be surgically removed from my mouth. Yes. I would love to meet your mother and autograph her books."

Before I knew what was happening, his lips were on mine, and his arms slowly wrapped around my waist pulling me closer. Another proven method to get me to stop talking.

When he pulled back, he asked, "You got a goldfish?"

I shook my head. "I can't keep plants alive. You think anyone would allow me to have live animals?"

He opened the door and helped me into the truck. On the drive back he suggested I come to his place for dinner, and he'd barbecue our catch. Relieved he didn't want me to clean or descale or whatever it was you did to prepare fresh fish, I consented. What else had I agreed to by going to his place on our second date? Technically this could be considered the third date, since there would be a time lapse and wardrobe change. There must be a self-help book out there for navigating this stuff.

Chapter 10

We settled on six o'clock for dinner. Hopping in the shower to wash off the beach, I heard my phone chime while I toweled off. Dressing in a clean pair of shorts and shirt, I checked the text. Jake had an emergency at work and had to cancel. He promised to make it up to me. Awww, isn't that sweet—not! At least I wouldn't need to struggle with the curling iron tonight. Women who can curl their own hair must be contortionists.

I ran a comb through my wet mop and let it air dry. Convincing myself the evening on my own would be for the best, I grabbed a diet soda and settled into the office chair. My head brimmed with chapters, and I decided to make headway on my novel.

Something out of the corner of my eye moved causing me to jump. Gus perched on the edge of my desk. "Can you please announce yourself when you appear!"

"So, the bum ditched ya?" He slapped his knee.

"Adults prefer to call it 'rescheduling.' Your brother had to deal with something at work."

"Sure, he did." Why did he have to look so smug?

"Were you and Dominique an item?"

"An item? Like was we engaged or somethin'?" He jumped off the desk and paced the floor. No guilt there.

"Don't avoid the question. Were you seeing her?"

Gus stopped. "Not exactly. Dom was what you would call a free spirit."

"I get it. You were screwing around with her but no commitment."

He grinned. "Like what you're doing with my brother? I saw you in the parking lot at the bluff. You weren't exactly shaking hands."

I scowled. "Were you with Dominique the night of her murder?"

His face darkened. "I didn't kill her."

"I didn't say you did. I asked if you'd been driving around town with her. According to Mrs. Billingsly, a blond-haired man rode in the convertible with her."

"Nah. Funny thing is I don't remember her gettin' killed. I woulda seen it in the newspaper, right? I was probably workin' that night. Jake could verify it if he kept call records. Besides, I told you Dom did whatever she pleased with whoever she pleased. She had daddy's money, which she loved to rub in my face. Only one thing she needed from me, and it wasn't a steady gig."

"If you don't remember her death, how do you know you weren't the guy in the car with her?"

"I don't, but I think Dom had another guy on the side. She quit being as friendly, if you get my meaning."

Crossing my legs, I leaned back into my chair. I'm sure he wasn't the only fair-haired guy in town, but the timing was too much of a coincidence. Since he wore his work shirt, it would've made sense he'd been on shift when he died, and his body never found. "Do you know who he was?"

"Nope, but Dom quit showing up at the usual places."

I didn't get it. Gus was a handsome guy, not big on brains, but I doubted he had trouble getting women. "If she treated you so badly, why did you keep seeing her?"

"Because she was great in the sack! I tell you, that girl had flexibility. She could—"

My hands flew up. "Whoa! Please stop. Those aren't details I need to figure this out. Keep those fond memories to yourself."

"You asked, lady."

No, I don't remember ever asking *for any of this.* "Can you remember anything else helpful? Like where or how you died?"

He slid his back down the wall until he sat on the floor. Everything I'd been doing would lead us to his body. Did he think about that? What if he felt pulled to Wanachee Bluff because he fell, and the ocean washed him away? Or had gotten pushed? Either of those possibilities resulted in a missing body if the tide took him.

"Marni, is it normal for…our *kind*…to not remember stuff?" Gus ran his fingers through his hair. Maybe he believed finding out the truth would make things worse. What could be worse than dead?

"Yes. I've helped many spirits who didn't even know they'd died. Sometimes their memory gets blocked. The only way to resolve it is to show them proof, like a headstone with their name on it or a newspaper article."

"Does it usually happen when the person got offed?" His wise guy lingo became annoying at times.

"No. Most who've come to me died of natural causes or in an accident." Of all the individuals I'd helped over the years, none were as difficult as Gus's case. I'd discovered the more violent the means of death, the bigger the memory gap. This wasn't something he needed to know yet. The young hoodlum had grown on me, and I wanted to put his spirit to rest. I couldn't do that if he kept getting angry and vanishing.

He jumped up and paced again. On the third lap he asked, "Do you think I got murdered?"

Since his brain made the leap, I didn't want to lie. "I believe you died violently. Whether by someone else's hand or an accident, I couldn't tell you. Not yet. Jake wants me to meet your mother. Do you think she might know anything?"

"Mom?" He screwed up his face. "Ain't it a bit soon to be meeting parents?" I doubted he ever got as far himself.

"That's exactly what I asked your brother. Your mom is a fan of mine and wants to meet me and get her books autographed."

"We didn't live with her no more. I don't know how she could know what happened to me. Jake was her favorite anyway. She probably thinks the same as everybody else—I stole money from him and bolted."

"You can't know for sure." I turned off my laptop. There wouldn't be any work getting done tonight. Since my evening plans fell through, I decided to dine at Maestro's, a small Italian restaurant not far from Ozzie's. I went into the bedroom to find a pair of jeans. He followed. "Gus, I need to change. Do you mind?"

He leaned on the door jamb smacking his lips. "Not at all."

"I'm not amused. I'm hungry. We've done all we can today. Why don't you go off to wherever it is you go when you're not hounding me?" I pulled pants off a hanger.

"All right. I can take a hint. But I'm going with you when you go to Mom's."

"Deal. And Gus…" When I looked back, the doorway stood empty.

****

Out of character for a Tuesday night, the restaurant hummed with activity. A din of silverware clattering against plates mixed with soft jazz piping through the sound system. Aromas of roasted garlic and fresh basil tortured my empty stomach. I preferred a spot at the bar, but all the stools were packed with bodies. The head waiter led me to a small table in the back where he left me with a wine list and a menu. Their cellar had a rotating selection of labels, and I enjoyed trying new ones. A practiced hand at eating solo, I came armed with my tablet to catch up on emails.

A server filled my water glass while I asked her opinion about a California zinfandel featured on their list. With her recommendation, I ordered it to go with my lasagna and salad.

Over the next forty-five minutes I waded through emails while stuffing myself with the best pasta in town. The unique spicy bite of the sauce gave the dish a little heat without scorching my taste buds. Seated with my back to the wall, I participated in a favorite sport— people watching. My mind created scenarios as I speculated on the dynamics of the other diners. Parents and kids were a no-brainer. Couples made for the best fodder to the imagination. The nervous, overly polite ones were new to being together. The couple next to me would fit this category. Long-timers had a comfortable air and conversation flowed, like the two sitting across from me.

Usually at the bar, small groups of women enjoyed a girls' night out while couples smoldered in lustful encounters. By the hoots and yells coming from the crowd tonight, I assumed they watched sports on the television screens overhead. The exception being the redhead closest to the front, leaning into the man next to her. He faced me, but I couldn't see him since her poof of curls blocked him out. Didn't big hair go out in the eighties?

I paid my bill and maneuvered around tables toward the front of the restaurant. My gaze landed on the couple at the bar. From this angle I could see the man's face. I could see Jake's face. Emergency at work my ass. *Sorry, babe, I got a hotter number on the other line.* If he looked my way, he'd see steam spouting from my ears.

Forcing my fists to unclench—it took a few tries—I decided not to cause a scene. It wasn't as if we were a couple. While I hated being lied to, the best thing would be to slip out without his seeing me, which would be easy if his attention remained consumed by his companion. Gus would be my priority with Jake from here on out.

I marched for the door. My feet chose to mutiny and walked me over to where he sat. I leaned in between the two. "Try the fish. I hear it's delicious!"

Jake stared at me while his date slurred, "Who the fuck are you?"

"Nobody. Enjoy your evening." Not giving him a chance to say a word, I left. He had the good sense not to follow.

Behind me I heard him say, "Don't worry about her. You want another gin and tonic?"

Once out on the sidewalk, my bravado waned. While it felt good calling him out on canceling under false pretense, I hoped this didn't blow chances of getting more information. Damn it! Why'd he have to be at Maestro's?

Instead of going home to fume, I hit Ozzie's for a drink. I took the only seat available next to two older gentlemen drinking cognac from snifters.

Derby came over and placed a glass of red wine before me. "New red blend out of Paso Robles."

The well-dressed man next to me nodded his head. "You must rate high. I didn't hear you order."

"Maybe you should check the batteries in your hearing aid." I don't know where those words came from, but I thought his buddy might tumble off his chair from laughing.

My bar mate stuck out his hand. "Jason Dilboy. You certainly have a quick wit, young lady."

"Marni Legend. A pleasure." I returned the gesture. "You know I was kidding, right? Derby knows my tastes and is always introducing me to new flavors. Is your friend okay, or do we need to put a net under him in case he falls?"

Now it was Jason's turn to laugh. "He'll recover." He signaled Derby. "Put her wine on my tab please."

"That's not necessary, Jason."

"I insist. It isn't every night we have the company of a stunning young woman."

"Then I won't insult you by declining." I lifted my drink in a toast. "To new friends."

He raised his snifter, and we clinked glasses.

His buddy did the same, reaching in front of Jason. "Wesley Brandt. Nice to meet you. Local or visiting?"

"Careful with this one." Jason winked. "He's a player."

"Don't worry, I can hold my own. And I don't take guff from anyone. In answer to your question, I'm local."

"Bravo!" Jason raised his glass again. Not sure if he toasted my holding my own or being local, but the two were so charming, I counted myself lucky to have landed next to them. Good conversation with total strangers was exactly what I needed right now.

"How about you two. Local?"

"I am. Wesley here lives in Bangor, Maine. We served together in the Korean War. Last of our platoon we are." His eyes clouded for a moment, then brightened again. "Our buddies are gone, but that's the way of things, isn't it? Life goes on, and we'll celebrate 'til the end."

Wow. I hoped to have his attitude when I reached eighty-something. He's got a great outlook. "Thank you for your service."

Jason nodded. "Why is a beautiful lady like yourself here alone?"

I raised my eyebrows. "I guess at your age you can ask any question you like and get away with it."

He grinned. "Severe old age gets you a lot of hall passes."

I loved this man's candor. "I'm a writer. Can I use that line some time?"

"It's yours. Now answer my question," Jason persisted.

Okay, you asked for it. "Short version, I got

married at twenty-two, divorced at forty-two, and moved back home to Long Island two years ago. This afternoon I had a fishing date, with a promise to barbecue our catch. We caught fish, then he canceled dinner. I ate at Maestro's, only to see him at the bar with another woman. My way of thinking believes it was a scam to get dinner for this other woman. What are your thoughts?"

Jason stared a moment. Then his contagious laugh erupted. When he could breathe again, he commented, "You got dumped, yet you still have a great sense of humor about it. All I can say is both the ex-husband and the date are idiots."

"Thank you for saying so. I'd have to agree. Now, as wonderful as the company is, I need to head home. I'm glad I decided on one more drink tonight. You gentlemen are refreshing." I offered my hand, and Jason brought it to his lips. They don't make them like that anymore.

"The pleasure was all mine, Marni. Maybe we'll run into each other again sometime."

If he's local, I don't see how it could be avoided. Maybe I can play yenta and hook him up with Darla. "I'm sure we will. Thank you for redeeming my evening." I waved to his buddy then walked home. Checking my phone, I noticed Jake had left a message thirty minutes prior. It could wait until morning.

Chapter 11

Coffee, lots of coffee, and breakfast fortified me enough to read Jake's text. He apologized and insisted the situation wasn't what I thought. After the emergency at work, he'd stopped in at Maestro's for a drink. An old friend from the neighborhood, Genevieve, happened to be there and invited him to join her. His neighborhood must've been populated with all women, and I'd only met two so far—Penny and Genevieve. He wanted to make it up to me with dinner tonight. I deleted the text.

At eleven-thirty I drove to the Crandall Ridge Diner to meet with Gloria and Calvin. Parking in front, I read the sign in the window touting "Under New Managment." I prayed they could cook better than they spelled.

For once, I was the first to get there. Must mark this occasion on the calendar. Inside, it smelled of stale bacon grease and another odor I couldn't identify. We might all get to go on a wild ride of indigestion or ptomaine poisoning. When my siblings arrived and we'd all ordered, I looked at Gloria. "Let's get down to it. What do you think?"

"I think we should let the other families dig up their deceased first. What if we did bury the correct ashes? Don't you think Mom would be mad if we dug her up for no reason?"

Calvin bugged his eyes at me and nodded. Why did I always have to be the bad guy? "Yes, she would, considering she'd already voiced her opinion on the subject. You may not have heard her, but Calvin and I did."

"She really appeared at the meeting, didn't she?" Gloria asked.

"Yes," Calvin confirmed. "And she wasn't happy about being exhumed."

The server came and tossed out our plates with the efficiency of a Vegas dealer. I had to stop my sandwich from sliding off onto my lap. Good thing I didn't ask for hot coffee. "Can I get you anything else?" she asked.

With no requests, the girl hurried on. I noticed only two servers working the entire restaurant. New management must be all about pinching pennies and spreading staff as thin as possible. I peeked under the top slice of bread on my sandwich and found a couple greasy slices of corned beef swimming in a sea of sauerkraut, except it smelled more like Korean kimchee—the stink I couldn't identify earlier. And the brown goo slathered on the bread didn't look like thousand island dressing. Pushing the Reuben aside, I voiced my opinion on the subject at hand. "What harm would it do? Don't you want to know for sure Mom's final resting place is with Dad?"

"Absolutely not!"

Resting my head against the wall behind me, I didn't rule out indigestion, despite not eating. "Ma, give it a rest. You're dead. Do you really give a crap if we poke around in your ashes?" I looked at the bench next to Gloria.

"You're making this up," Gloria accused.

"She's not." Calvin assured her. "Ma, please, wouldn't you want us to check?"

She hugged her chest. "I'd feel violated."

"What did she say?" Gloria splayed her fingers on either side of her salad.

It was like being at the circus, and all the performers were blood relatives. I lifted my arm into the air. "Everyone who thinks the *living* should decide this matter, raise your hand."

"Don't you disrespect me, young lady," Mom scolded. "Your sister is on my side." She forgot to add, "the perfect one who does everything right."

"Ma, you don't have a say in this." I ate a potato chip, the safest thing on my plate.

"Stop it." Gloria deployed her signature speech abilities—talking without moving her lips.

The waitress made another pass. "Everything good here?" Her brown ponytail bobbed with the question.

If we refrained from ingesting the food, we'd all survive. "I'm good, thanks."

"Can I get more iced tea, please?" Calvin asked.

"Of course." She took his glass. We remained silent until after she'd returned with the refill.

As my siblings ate, my mother scowled with her arms crossed, and I tried to bury my food with a napkin in hopes of smothering the stench.

Gloria spoke first. "I think we need to respect Mom's wishes and not sign the authorization papers."

Kiss up. I decided to concede this one to my sister and quit fighting. Only one of us needed to give permission, and I could go behind Gloria's back if necessary. I had other problems to solve. "Okay. We don't sign for now and see what happens with the others. But if the family of the dude being buried in France doesn't go along with it, we may have to give in."

Calvin agreed. "I can live with that. Gloria?"

She nibbled her lettuce longer than necessary. What a drama queen. I knew she was hell-bent on leaving whatever ashes we buried in place—even if it would be at Dad's toes. I still chuckled silently over the scenario. "Agreed. We only give permission if necessary."

"Finally, a voice of reason." Mom said. She evaporated, and I gave Calvin the all-clear sign.

"She's gone," I said for Gloria's benefit. "She gave her stamp of approval. Do you want to contact Dilboy?"

"I'll take care of it." Gloria forked more salad into her mouth.

I drank my iced tea and let the matter go. "What's the family business you wanted to delve into? We might as well get everything done."

Gloria looked at me sideways, as if trying to assess my reaction. I'd seen it too many times before to misread her intentions. "I wanted to talk about Mom's house. Are you sure she isn't here?"

I nodded.

"I would have liked her opinion as I'm sure she'd agree but will move forward. Robert and I have been talking."

In Gloria-speak, her last sentence was code for, *you're not going to like what I'm about to say*. With great difficulty, I held my tongue.

"We believe it would be more profitable as a rental instead of selling." She paused for effect. "Robert knows a realtor who handles property management. We've already spoken with her, and she agreed. It could be quite lucrative, and she has a tenant lined up for us. We'd all stand to profit."

If the reek of the sandwich didn't make me queasy, the thought of going into business with my sister had me looking around for the rest room.

"Calvin, what do you think?" she asked.

He cleared his throat. "Honestly," he stalled, "I'd never thought about being a landlord. It could involve more work than we bargained for, sis." Diplomatic response.

Gloria set her jaw, bracing for my answer. Time to lob one over the fence and be done with this cozy little luncheon. "Not interested in being a slum lord. If you want to buy me out and wing it on your own, that'd be up to you. Get an appraisal and write me a check." I flagged our waitress to bring the bill.

"Why do you have to be so negative?"

"I'm not. I am *positive* I don't want to own rental property." The server came, and I handed her my credit card.

"Let me pay for my lunch." Gloria reached for her purse.

"It's on me."

Out of character, Calvin outright sided with me. "Sylvie and I have enough going on. I have to agree with Marni on this and will pass."

"Fine." She bolted up and stormed out of the restaurant.

Calvin nudged me in the shoulder with his. "I guess the meeting is adjourned."

"Awwww. I didn't get to slam the gavel." I stuck

out my lower lip. "Thanks for the united front. Do you think she and Robert are having money problems?"

"Doubtful. Robert's a financial consultant with several high-profile clients. You know Gloria; she's always looking to make more. Maybe they want a new wing built on the house. I'm glad you weren't interested either. Being a landlord can be a headache, even with a manager handling the direct contact. In my business, I've run into several people wanting to tweak a house enough to make it rentable. Many bite off more than they can chew."

"We both know our sister." I slid out of the booth and followed my brother outside. "This is only round one of the house disposal discussion."

****

Over the course of the afternoon Jake sent two more texts. Both contained apologies and asked me to dinner. I ignored them. There couldn't be any reason for him to want to see me, given the company he kept last night. His persistence confused me, unless it was a blow to his ego to lose. I didn't imagine many women said "no" to him, especially in my age range. He'd just have to tap his cache of "friends from the neighborhood," for his next candidate.

Arriving home, I found a small vase holding a bouquet of flowers in the doorway. *You've got to be kidding me.* What's next, carrier pigeon? I picked them up and glanced at the card. "Marni, Nice running into you again. See you tomorrow. KK."

With everything going on, I'd almost forgotten about our breakfast date on Thursday. He probably thought there was more than one apartment upstairs, so decided to leave them down here. My resolve had been weakening to give Jake another try. This reinforced my decision to let him go for now. I would figure out a way to help Gus, without being romantically tied to his brother.

From behind, I heard a familiar voice. "I'll have to quit sending texts and step up my game."

Turning, with the vase in one hand and my keyring in the other, I resisted slipping the keys between my fingers in a defensive move. "Jake, leave it alone for a while. You don't owe me anything. I can see you're more of a player than a companion. Don't worry about it."

I moved to open the door to the stairway and felt a hand on my shoulder. "Please, Marni. You seem like a nice lady, and I want to get to know you. You're the first woman in a long time who excites me."

Could it be because you've screwed every other female within a five-mile radius and need a new pool to draw from? "Let's take a break and maybe we could try again another time. I'm not going to dinner with you tonight. Thank you for the invitation."

He laughed. "You're mad at me but can still say 'thank you.' I don't think I've met anyone with your kinda class. You're different—and I'm not giving up. Especially now it looks like I have competition."

I wasn't a kewpie doll at a carnival attraction. This man needed someone who could strut in four-inch heels without falling on her face and achieve a pout in less than eight seconds. "I'll see you around."

"It don't seem right, but is there any way you could find time to meet my mother? I told her you agreed, and she was so excited." His eyes softened. "Please, Marni. Just coffee at her place. It would mean a lot to her."

Low blow pulling the mother card. My mind conjured a sweet old lady, who didn't have much to do with her days but sit around and read. I couldn't turn him down. "Okay, you got me. When?"

A grin spread across his face. "Thank you. Thank you so much. You don't know what this means to her. And to me."

Since lunch wasn't palatable, my hunger raged, and all I could think of was getting inside and raiding the refrigerator. Did I have any groceries? "Jake, when?"

"Is Friday at ten good? My mom brews great coffee. She'll be so excited!"

"Text me the address. I'll be there."

He shoved his hands into the front pockets of his jeans and bounced on his heels. It looked out of character for a man his age, yet he appeared genuinely pleased. "Thanks." He leaned over and brushed his lips across my cheek. "See ya Friday."

Rid of my stalker, I went upstairs and put the vase on my kitchen table. I knew meeting his mother was a lame attempt to get me to go out with him again. Though, I had promised before the aborted dinner fiasco happened. How did I end up with such a busy social life in the last week?

Not finding anything in my refrigerator that wasn't moldy or out-of-date, I settled for peanut butter and crackers. I really needed to go grocery shopping.

****

Who the hell was banging on my door? I reached for my phone and realized I'd overslept. It was ten minutes after eight. Crap! Diving out of bed, I made sure I wore pajamas. Running down the hall, I checked the peephole, then unlocked the door.

105

"Hey, sleepy-head, ready for breakfast?" Kendall held a drink carrier with three cups. From the aromatic fumes, I knew he had dark-roasted java from downstairs. Bart had the magic touch when it came to brewing delicious coffee in a commercial urn. The other hand grasped a white bag. "Bart told me which door to find you behind."

"I am *so* sorry! How long were you knocking?"

"Only a few minutes. Maybe ten or twelve." He shot me a crooked grin.

I pointed toward the kitchen. "Have a seat. I'll be changed in a heartbeat. Is someone else joining us?" I gestured toward the carrier.

He pulled a paper cup from where it nestled. "Nope. If I remember correctly, you drink more than one. Why don't you start on your first?"

Why did I stop seeing this man? "You are a godsend." I took it and did a quick face wash, then changed into jeans and a long-sleeved tee. With my hair brushed into submission, I dabbed on a little makeup and had my sneakers laced in record time.

On my way through the entry, I grabbed my keys and called, "Just waiting on you."

He carried the rest of our breakfast and followed me to the street. We strolled the couple blocks to the pier. Unlike the other night, the street bustled with pedestrians this time of day.

"I can't believe I slept this late."

"You must've been burning the midnight oil. I hope you're hungry. On today's menu," he faked a French accent, "we have a selection of pastries."

"Starving! Thanks for the beautiful flowers too." My favorite bench on the end of the pier sat empty, and we settled down with the bag between us. "What did you bring?" My mouth watered as the scent of almond paste wafted from the open package.

He tore the bag to form a flat placemat for an almond horn with the ends dipped in chocolate, an almond paste Danish, and a Napoleon. Picking up a plastic knife, he sliced each one in half. "I know it's been a few years, but I'm assuming you still like almond paste?"

"Like I'd ever lose my taste for it!" I scooped up half the horn and bit into the chocolate end. "Mmmmmm."

Kendall sipped his coffee and ate the other half. We watched a large luxury boat drift in beside the dock. One of the crew hopped off and secured the bow to a stanchion then did the same with the stern. It looked to be about forty feet long.

"Awwww, ain't this a cozy tea party?" Gus leaned between us from behind the bench.

I needed to start posting office hours. Clenching my lips together, I jerked my head in a "scram" gesture. He remained in place, but Kendall caught the motion.

"What's over there?" He looked off toward the park running parallel to this section of the pier.

Pointing at a grassy area, I said, "I thought I saw a squirrel. It must've scampered off. You know how annoying those pesky critters can be to the picnickers." I looked Gus in the eye then turned back to the harbor. "You didn't tell me where you'd moved to when you left the Island."

"Boston first, where I completed my master's degree. That's how I'd met Carina, my wife. Ex-wife now. She also attended the university and worked on her Master of Fine Arts Degree. I say *worked on* because she never completed it. After we got married, I found Carina never completed much of anything she started. I landed a job in a publishing house in Cleveland, and we picked up roots and moved. She never forgave me for dragging her away from her beloved Boston, where she grew up."

"You ogre." I picked up a fork and dug into the Napoleon. Gus knelt in front of me pretending to bite the piece as it traveled to my mouth. I glared at my obnoxious ghost then redirected my attention to Kendall. "Did you consider moving back to Massachusetts?"

Kendall held his cup with both hands and watched a skiff motor by. "She did. All the time. Shortly after we bought a house, she got pregnant with the first of our three kids. I made good money, but it went a lot farther in Ohio than it would back in Beantown. As penance, her mother visited often and tried to pressure me into moving the family back east."

"I bet you enjoyed every minute of those conversations." I laughed. "Did her father get in on the act?"

"He would visit occasionally, but I knew he was on my side. For survival's sake he never admitted it out loud in front of his wife."

"This guy is borrring." Gus leaned against a pylon across from where we sat. "My brother's a jerk, but at least he's fun to be around." I found sometimes if I ignored the spirits, they would go away. Gus could be slow on the uptake, but he might take a hint.

A seagull landed a couple of feet from our bench. He hopped closer, and I shooed him away with a wave in Gus's direction too. I had no intention of sharing my breakfast with anyone but KK. The bird soared up and over the end of the dock. Thankfully, we had a roof over our bench, otherwise I think he would have left us a parting gift. My ghostly friend didn't scare as easily and remained on the boardwalk. I jabbed another piece of food and made a show of wrapping my lips around it. He flipped me off.

"Did Carina ever come around to your way of thinking?"

"Not really. We had several good years. The last few we co-existed until the boys were in college—back in Boston. If she'd gotten a job instead of staying at home once the kids were older, she might have felt differently. Our daughter had two years left of high school when Carina decided she needed an extracurricular activity to occupy her time."

I picked up my second cup of coffee. "Enter the restaurant valet?"

"Freddy. Freddy the valet. He grew up with our oldest son."

"Ouch! She must've perfected her cougar growl."

Kendall grimaced. "You could say that."

"I wouldn't mind being somebody's *extracurricular activity*. It's been a long time since I...you know...got it on with a hot chick." Why couldn't I have gotten one who was house broken? Gus and his twenty-seven-year-old libido needed to be wrapped up and sent on their way soon. If he didn't, I was pretty sure I wouldn't be *getting it on* without interruption.

"After catching her in our bedroom with her new toy, I admitted defeat. We divorced, sold the house, divided our assets, and she moved back into Mommy's mansion with Katy, our daughter. She accepted a lump sum payout instead of alimony."

It might have been easier for me to move on had I caught Tim in bed with another woman. Divorcing me because of my paranormal gift left me making excuses to everyone of how we'd grown apart. "I'm sorry it worked out like it did. Are you close with your kids?"

"For the most part. I talk to the boys at least a couple times a week. They never blamed me for their mother's unhappiness. Katy was more immature and sided with her mom. We never told her about the valet. I guess that made me look like the bad guy, but she was too young for us to share."

"Marni, how much longer is this gonna take? I remembered somthin', and we need to go for a drive."

"She'll come around." I glanced at Gus. "Some things take time."

KK enjoyed the remaining pastry. "What's your story? I know you met Tim right before I moved, and he whisked you away to the west coast. How did the saga continue?"

Did I hear regret in his voice? We'd both agreed to go our separate ways as romance got too difficult with our differing college plans. "After we had Ginny and Tim, Jr., I wanted to go back to work. Tim wanted me to stay home with the kids, and we compromised. I'd always wanted to write and used my history degree as a springboard into the historical romances I cranked out. As much as I'd like to say my talent got me an agent, she happened to be an acquaintance of my husband at the time. He arranged the introduction, but she loved my books, and it's been *history* ever since."

Kendall groaned.

"Okay, bad cliché. I do love to write, though."

He tilted his head at me. "You're avoiding the ending."

I hung my head and launched into my prepared excuse. "We grew apart and decided to call it quits. I stuck around the west coast for a few years hoping we could rekindle what we'd lost. He decided to rekindle the spark with someone else—fifteen years his junior, blonde, with more plastic parts than a toy doll."

"No jealousy there." He poked my shoulder.

Gus rubbed his hands together. "Maybe you could give me her address. I'd be happy to take her off old Timmy's hands." *Settle down, horn dog.* Later I'd have to remind him he's dead.

"Nobody likes being replaced with a younger model."

"Ain't that the truth!" Kendall punctuated with his fork in the air.

"I survived it, and since I missed the east coast, decided to return. In time I'll probably move into a house."

"Why not your mother's?"

I chuckled. "That's a loaded question. My siblings and I are in dispute over what to do with it. Calvin and I want to sell it, and Gloria has this money-making scheme to rent it out. Besides, I want someplace closer to the water. Mom's place is almost half an hour away." I stood holding my coffee and walked to the edge staring off toward the horizon.

The silence between us stretched on yet didn't feel awkward. When I brought the cup to my lips, Gus yelled, "Marni, look out!"

My gaze shot upward as a seagull made a kamikaze run straight at me. Instinctively stepping to the side, I fell with my arms windmilling, and my coffee flying through the air. Freezing cold water engulfed my body as I sputtered for breath. I thrashed about until my feet hit bottom and launched myself upwards. Breaking free of the surface, I coughed and spat. Something splashed in front of me sending more water into my face and blurring my vision. My eyes burned from the salt. Is someone attempting a rescue or trying to send me back under?

"Grab the ring, lady!"

As my sight cleared, I saw an orange life preserver bobbing a foot away. I grabbed hold and was immediately pulled across the surface. The crewman who'd tied up the boat stood on the deck winding in the rope attached to the ring. Kendall jumped down beside him and moved toward the stern. Reaching the ladder on the side, I let go of the preserver, started to climb, then got hauled up onto the deck. My chest heaved, while Kendall cleared hair from my face.

"Marni, are you okay?" I loved the concern in his eyes.

Catching my breath, I said, "Damn!"

"Don't worry, you'll dry."

"It's not that." I grasped his hands, and he pulled me upright. "I spilled my coffee."

Both he and the deckhand snickered. The crewman handed me a towel, and I wrapped it around my body.

"What's going on here? This ain't a ferry service." An overweight guy with thinning brown hair and a beer in his hand walked from the front of the yacht. The neon green of his Bermuda shorts hurt my eyes worse than the sting of the ocean water. His banana-colored polo looked one cookie away from bursting at the seams and spraying shreds of polyester across the deck.

My body shivered. Not from the cold but from his voice. His raspy voice. Now here I stood dripping on his boat.

"It's okay, boss. This lady fell off the dock, and I pulled her in," my rescuer said.

"Well, she looks good to me now. Don't you have work to finish in the galley?"

I'm fine, thanks for asking. Maybe he'd like me to swab the deck before I left. "Thank you for your help. You're a real hero. We'll get out of your way."

Kendall thanked him also, ignored tubby with his brew, and helped me off the boat. We'd only taken a couple steps away when Raspy Voice called, "Hey, you stealin' that towel?"

I peeled it off my body, wadded up the dripping terry cloth, and lobbed it onto the boat. It landed with a splat at his sandaled feet. I'd aimed for his head.

With his arm around me, Kendall led me off the dock. "Can you believe that guy? You got fished out of the water, and all he cared about was getting his flunky back to work."

"What a jerk. He looked like he escaped from a cruise in the Caribbean with those clothes. Probably doubled as the ship's beacon." While I made light of the situation, my muscles remained rigid after coming face to face with the other night's felon. Had Stale Cigarette guy been part of the boat crew too?

My date offered to fetch me another coffee while I went upstairs to clean up. Thanking him for an exciting morning, I suggested he get to work before Mrs. B sent out a search party. I imagined she didn't stand for tardiness, even from the director.

I trudged up the stairs, my shoes squishing on every step, while my wet shirt and pants clung to my body like a sausage casing. Expecting Gus to be waiting in the kitchen, I peeked through the doorway and found it empty. I went straight to the bathroom, stepped into the tub, and peeled off my clothes, which now had a fishy smell. They might as well get a rinse too while I washed the saltwater off myself.

As the steamy drops cascaded over my hair and down my back, I remembered Gus saying he needed to tell me something. Did he know Raspy Voice owned the boat, or had it been an acquisition after Gus had departed this world? Seeing the car thief frightened me, especially in his current fashion choices, but I needed to get back there and snoop around.

Chapter 12

Having made the trek to the grocery store, I filled my kitchen with the smell of fresh basil and tomato sauce as it simmered on the stove. I put together a salad and smothered it with Caesar dressing. Dishing the portobello mushroom-filled ravioli into a bowl, I covered it with marinara, grated parmesan on top, and dug in.

Gus sat opposite me. "Ya know, even though she wasn't Italian, my mom always made her own sauce. The stuff out of a jar don't compare."

"I'm seeing her tomorrow; maybe we can swap recipes." I continued enjoying my store-bought substitute. "Now, if you're done channeling your inner chef, can you tell me what you remembered when you interrupted my date at the dock?"

He burst out laughing. "I almost forgot about that. You were hysterical the way you jumped into the water."

"For your information, I fell. I didn't jump. Did you notice who owned the boat that dragged me out of the drink, or were you too busy rolling around holding your sides?"

"Yeah. It's kinda funny he showed up right when I thought of the names of the two guys who stole the car last week. The fat guy is Murphy. The scrawny short one is Diggs."

"So, Murphy, with his horrible fashion sense, was the one on the boat. I didn't get a look at either of the guys when I crawled around in the bushes but knew his voice immediately. What does Diggs look like? The crewman who helped me looked too young to fit the other guy I heard."

Gus crossed his legs and leaned back. "He's short and skinny with brown hair down to his shoulders. Now it has streaks of gray. Wears it in a ponytail like an old hippie."

"Definitely not the other one on the boat. Do you know their last names?"

"We was never that friendly. Like I said, we did a couple a jobs together."

I finished my dinner and dumped the dishes in the sink without rinsing them. Since I hadn't cooked in almost a week, this began the new pile. Strange how these things no longer bothered me since moving back east. When I had a house to run, I kept it sparkling without a speck of dust anywhere. I guess moving here changed my perspective on what mattered. Certainly, a clean kitchen didn't make the list.

"Do you remember Murphy owning a boat when you were…coworkers?"

"Nah, he didn't have the bread for somethin' like that. He drove a muscle car, so he could pick up chicks. Guess he saved his pennies from all them heists."

"Do you think they would keep any kind of evidence on the boat, maybe something incriminating we could tie to your past? My gut tells me you were murdered. There might be a ledger of who bought the stolen cars, possibly what happened to Dominique's car."

He leaned his elbows on the table. "I hate to believe it, but you might be right about what happened to me. But why would my brotha say I stole money unless someone else took it and convinced him it was me?"

"The fact you disappeared probably convinced him." My phone chirped at receiving a text from Jake. He sent his mother's address and a happy face. The man didn't strike me as the emoji type. If this was him upping his game, he'd have to try harder. "Gus, before I went for my swim, you said we needed to drive somewhere. Where?"

"Back out by the bluff."

"You didn't say anything about the place when I went there with Jake. What do you think we'll find?"

He stood. "Not at the bluff. Near there. I remembered where the house was me and Jake shared when I died. There might be a clue. Grab your car keys."

"Uh uh. I am not going back there tonight. It'll be dark soon. Didn't you say you rented anyway? Someone else probably lives there now. I doubt they'd appreciate my knocking on their door asking to look around. Let's wait until after I talk with your mother. She might say something that will click with you. Besides, I have another mission tonight closer to home."

"You goin' on another date with Mr. Cheapskate that can't buy you a real breakfast?" He snorted.

Again, with the dating tips, as if he were a shining example of what to look for in a man. He needed to stay out of my love life. "For your information, I'm going back to the scene of the crime."

He crinkled his brow. "Back where those guys stole the car?"

"No, where I took the plunge and wound up on their boat. How hard would it be to slip inside the cabin and look around if nobody is there? I'll wait until after dark and stroll down as if I'm out enjoying the harbor. What I need from you is to go on board and make sure the coast is clear."

His eyes widened, and his jaw dropped toward the floor. Had I impressed him with my plan? "Listen to you, talking like a real detective. Do you really want to be messing with these guys? It would be safer to break into the rental house."

Okay, *impressed* might be too strong of a word. "Thanks for the vote of confidence. Right now, the boat is our best connection, and it's sitting in the harbor two blocks away. If the house is near the bluff and hospital, the last thing I need is another encounter with Officer Talbott, especially if I'm trespassing. Finding me in the area after dark twice wouldn't look like a coincidence."

"But there's something at the house I need to see. I say we drive."

"Gus, this isn't a democracy. You've been overruled. Now will you help me check out the boat, or are you going to leave me hanging? If we wait too long, it might motor off somewhere else, and we'll have blown our chance."

We faced off from opposite sides of the kitchen like wrestlers about to mix it up. Lucky for me this round was a battle of wits, and Gus lacked the ammo.

"You win. But if we find nothin', you have to take me to the house."

"I'll agree to taking a drive over there, but only in

the light of day, and after I visit with your mother. Those are my terms." I spread my arms wide. "Take 'em or leave 'em."

"Guess I have no choice. See ya later."

****

By nine o'clock I couldn't wait any longer and left before I lost my nerve. I called Gus's name before going. He didn't show. If he refused to appear by the time I got to the yacht, this would be the shortest mission ever. Rather than attempting stealth mode and dressing like a ninja, I wore jeans and a light blue sweater. Tension in my shoulders shot off the charts, and I had to force myself to move at a casual pace.

The usual cadre of fishermen dotted the docks. If I boldly stepped onto the ship, would they know I didn't belong? Could one be a sentry in disguise? I sauntered past, trying to catch a glimpse of any crew hanging about. The boat was in complete darkness.

Gus waited on my favorite perch. "It's about time you showed up. Why aren't you in all black so nobody can see you? God, you look like an amateur."

"Perhaps because I *am* an amateur. I'm not the one with a criminal record." I sat beside him.

"Who says I got a record? I ain't never been locked up."

It never occurred to me he'd never been caught. Maybe I should have consulted him—had he bothered to show up earlier. "This way I blend in with the tourists. If anybody comes, they'll think nothing of a woman enjoying the fresh air."

"You got a lot to learn."

Breaking and Entering 101 wasn't a class I wanted to take. "Enough about my lack of burglary skills. Go check the boat and tell me if anybody is aboard."

"Okay, okay. Stop barking orders." He disappeared.

I tapped my foot on the wooden dock, concentrating on the staccato noise. It soothed my racing mind as it conjured all the things that could go wrong. My plan had two parts—break in, and don't get caught. Simple, right? It felt like an eternity before he returned. I jumped as he materialized beside me. "What's wrong with casually walking up so I can see you coming?"

"Because it's fun watching your reaction."

Guess I'm not the only one with a mean streak. "So? Anybody home?"

"It's empty. All the lights are out. You brought a flashlight, right?"

I shook my head.

"Are you kidding me? How're you gonna find any clues if you can't see?" He paced to the edge of the pier and back. "I can't believe you didn't bring somethin'. How about matches or a lighter?"

What a great idea. And when he startles me and I drop the lighter, I could torch the boat with me in it. "I'll turn on a light. You keep lookout and tell me if Murphy comes back. If you see him, zap in, and I'll douse the light and scram."

"Zap in? What am I, a lightning bolt?" He held his hands up in the air.

My exasperation slipped out in the form of a heavy sigh. "You know what I mean. Just get in position." Going to the stern, I looked both ways, then stepped down onto the deck. The tide was out, so the boat sat lower than the dock compared to where it had been this morning. My sneakers squeaked as I walked. To my ears they thundered, but I knew my nerves escalated the sound. The quiet voices of the fishermen farther up the dock carried over the lapping of water against the sides of the vessel.

I tried the back hatch leading below. It opened easily. *Shouldn't it be locked*? I descended the four steps to the main sitting area. Having never been on a luxury cruiser before, I didn't know what to expect. The smell of bleach assaulted my nose. Peering through the darkness, I made out couches on either side. Running my hand along the cushions of one, I moved forward and banged into a coffee table. Crap! Getting around it, I continued down the walkway. An island separated the left section from the galley and on the right sat a table with built-in benches. Past that I moved down a hallway with a door on either side and one straight ahead. I assumed it to be the master chamber. If there were any records to find, it would probably be in there.

Creeping forward, I eased open the door and stepped inside. My fingers felt along the wall until they found a toggle switch. On the verge of pressing it, I realized someone snored directly ahead of me. So much for the boat being empty. I whipped around and fumbled for the doorknob.

"Murphy, is that you? I told you not to wake me up unless you had a problem." The voice sounded aged and cracked.

I opened the door and bolted, forgetting to close it behind me. A light in the bedroom flipped on, and I turned, sweat forming on my forehead. He couldn't see me since I remained in the darkness of the hallway, but what if someone came out of the other bedrooms? The man sat up. I froze as I recognized him from Ozzie's the other night—Jason Dilboy. Could this be his boat? Deciding the question could be debated from a safer distance, like two streets away, I ran for the stern where I came in.

Gus stood in the exit waving me off. "Murphy and Diggs are coming. You gotta hide."

"I can't," I hissed, hoping it didn't sound like a shout. "Somebody was asleep in the master bedroom. I thought you checked the boat?"

"All the lights were off. How could I know there was a guy sleeping? It ain't even ten o'clock yet. Who goes to bed this early?" Gus whispered too.

With my hands on my face, I shook my head. How had he avoided arrest during his car-thieving career? "Where am I going to hide? The boat isn't *that* big." Approaching voices grew louder. Without a doubt, they belonged to Murphy (aka Raspy Voice) and Diggs (aka Stale Cigarettes). I shot through Gus and out onto the deck. The footsteps drew closer. Crouching down, I slipped around the far side of the boat so they couldn't see me from the dock. Why didn't I wear all black?

A light inside the main area went on, and Jason went past the window. The boat dipped toward the dock then back as the two men boarded near the front. The occupant inside moved toward the hatchway I'd exited through. I was trapped and couldn't go forward or back. Murphy and Diggs talked on the bow, barring my escape to the dock.

With only one option available, I gritted my teeth and braced for the shock. Dropping to the deck, I slid my legs over the side and gently lowered myself into the icy water, stifling a gasp. I couldn't believe this was happening twice in one day—fully clothed and immersed in the harbor. Instead of the thugs going to the back of the boat, I heard Jason's voice move forward. I treaded water as quietly as possible, praying the lapping of the waves covered my splashing. Reversing direction, I swam along the hull toward the stern. If I got around the backside without them finding me, I could duck under the pier and swim for the park. Under cover of darkness, I'd slip out of the water and make a run for it. As I made it around the stern, I hesitated before moving those last couple of feet between the boat and the boardwalk. Moonlight shone bright as a searchlight on my escape path. What if they saw me? Garnering my nerves, I glanced up and read the name of the boat. "Holy shit," escaped my lips. In black letters, it said *Dominique's Dream*.

I dreaded my next maneuver. Taking a deep breath, I dove into the murky depths and swam for shore. Darkness obscured my vision, and I prayed I wouldn't run into a pylon on my way beneath the boardwalk. My lungs burned as I ran out of air, but I kept swimming. Upon reaching the shallows, my hands clawed through the spongy bottom, pulling myself farther away from the dock. Poking my head out of the water, I looked toward the boat. Flashlight beams sprayed back and forth off the rear of the yacht. I crawled onto solid ground and hid behind the trunk of a large oak a few feet from shore. The lights hit either side of me then withdrew. Where was Gus?

As I leaned against the tree catching my breath while my teeth chattered, leaves rustled to my left.

"Out for an evening swim?" Darla asked.

Neighborhood watch was on the job again. She had

to have seen where I came from. To my astonishment, she held out her sweater.

"You'd better put this on before you freeze to death," she said quietly.

Too cold to protest, I stood and wrapped it around my shivering body.

She motioned for me to follow her. "Let's get out of here. You and I need to talk, and I don't believe this is the place for a chat, given the stir you've caused on that yacht over there."

We walked to the edge of the park and up the street to her house. She unlocked her door, and in the entry said, "Wait here."

Hoping she wasn't calling the police, I did as I was told until she returned with a towel, sweatpants, and a shirt. "Take off your shoes. There's a guest bathroom." She pointed to the nearest door. "Go change, and I'll make us tea." She started toward the back of the house and stopped. "You drink tea, don't you?"

I nodded and went to get dried and changed. On the way out of the bathroom, I dropped my wet clothes on the tiles next to my sneakers. Carrying her sweater, I found Darla in the kitchen setting out two mugs with a tea bag in each. "Thanks for the rescue. Are the cops on their way?"

"Not yet. Convince me why I shouldn't make the call." Damn, she was tough. No wonder her kids scattered when they had the chance.

"I'm trying to solve a murder. Well, I guess it would be two murders now."

The kettle whistled, and she turned off the burner. "Dominique's being one."

"Yes. When I saw the name on the boat, it startled

me. Jason Dilboy had been in the master chamber, so I guess he's the owner. The other two men are the ones who stole your neighbor's car, but I can't prove it. What connection did Jason have to Dominique, or is the name on the stern a coincidence?"

She sipped her tea, studying me with a piercing gaze. "You know him?"

"We met a couple days ago at a bar. He and a buddy sat next to me, and we chatted."

"Dominique was his great-niece. His niece married Oscar Perez, and Dominique had been their only child. Jason doted on the girl and was devastated when her body turned up at the old hospital."

"I didn't ask him, but my siblings and I are dealing with a man at the Roseview Crematorium named Charles Dilboy. Any relation?"

She laughed. "You certainly have been getting around. Jason is his grandfather. Charles took over the place when his own father retired. They used to own it outright, but it got bought by a larger corporation about ten years ago. They allowed Charles to stay on as manager, probably part of the deal. For a time, there'd been rumors of shady business deals going on around the place a couple decades ago. Might've been the reason they had to sell."

This town seemed to be shrinking by the moment. How many people could be connected to this mess?

As if coming to a decision, Darla squared her shoulders. "Now, are you going to tell me what's going on? Is it Dominique's tortured soul you're trying to save?"

"No. It's Gus Zuckerman."

She sat back. "After all these years, he's come back

125

to the scene of the crime. Where did he go when he took the money? Did he kill that girl?"

"I didn't kill nobody." Gus spat. He hadn't been there a moment ago.

Looking at the chair between us, I found no point in pretending to my host. "You be quiet and let me explain a few things to her. I believe she's on our side."

She looked at the empty chair, then arched her brows at me.

No stopping now. "Darla, he never left town. Gus died in nineteen-ninety-five. And he never stole the money from his brother like everyone believes. Though he is the reason I ended up in the drink tonight because of his lack of surveillance skills." I glared at him.

They both laughed, then Darla said, "Well then, Gus, you know what I think of you regarding Adriana." Her tone turned serious. "But I'm real sorry you died so young. I guess this means you were murdered. How awful."

This woman didn't let anything get past her. I made a mental note not to doubt her perception. "The problem is, he doesn't remember what happened to him. It's common for someone who…dies violently. He's slowly getting his memory back, but not enough to lead me to where his body lies or how he got killed. One thing for sure is he's adamant about not stealing money from his brother. Do you remember who spread the word about that?"

She screwed up her face. "No. You know how it is in a tight-knit community. Rumors run rampant, and you can't pinpoint the source. This explains why the police never brought him in for questioning about the girl's death. Does he know anything about what happened to her?"

I shook my head. "He didn't know she was dead until you mentioned it on the pier the other night. Which means they either died at the same time, or she died after him. Either way, he doesn't know."

"If what you tell me is true about the memory loss, what if he killed her and can't remember?"

"That's a good question, which I can't answer. I'm tired and better head home. Nothing will get solved tonight. Do you have a plastic bag I can put my wet stuff in?"

Darla got up and retrieved a grocery bag from a broom closet.

We went to the front door, where my wet clothes sat in a puddle, and I stowed them in the sack. "Thanks for the assist. I'll return your clothes in a day or two."

"I expect them to be washed. No bleach, please." Her stern look softened. "And Marni, be careful. Do you think Jake started the rumor about his brother stealing the money, but he'd already been dead by then?"

I bit my upper lip and shrugged. The thought had crossed my mind, but I'd shelved the idea after meeting Jake. Hearing someone else voice the concern aloud made me rethink my security of going anywhere with him alone.

Chapter 13

I stopped at the curb in front of a white painted residence with decorative blue shutters. These ranch-style houses dominated the middle-class neighborhoods of Long Island. The dormer window on the right had the curtains pulled back, but the screens obscured a clear view of the living room inside. The only thing missing was the white picket fence.

Jake's truck sat in the driveway behind a small blue car with a broken mirror. Rows of marigolds stood at attention on either side of the walkway, while rose bushes lined the front of the house emitting their delicate scent. When I reached the stoop, the outer door swung open.

"Come on in, Marni," Jake said.

Upon entering, I heard a raucous voice from another room. "Is she here yet? She's ten minutes late! I hope she's not one of those snobby celebrities."

His eyes bugged as he mouthed the word *sorry*.

I whispered, "Should I ring the bell and start over?"

"Nah." He turned his head. "Ma, she's here."

Heavy footsteps pounded down the hall followed by the appearance of a large woman with mounds of jet-black hair. Her loose tunic-style blouse covered a host of bulges, making it difficult to distinguish where her breasts stopped and stomach began. The swirls of dark and light gray paisley reminded me of the wild prints Sylvie wore, except in Mrs. Zuckerman's case, it did nothing to mask the bulk beneath. So much for my notion of Jake's mother being a little old gray-haired lady. She had to be in her seventies, so the jet-black hair and bushy eyebrows, dyed to match, didn't fit with her wrinkled complexion. What happened to aging gracefully?

"Ma, this is Marni Legend. Marni, this is my mom, Anita Zuckerman."

I extended my hand. "What a pleasure to meet you, Mrs. Zuckerman. Thank you so much for inviting me over."

She grasped my hand with both of hers. "The pleasure is all mine. And *please*, call me Anita. Won't you sit down?" She gestured toward a beige couch, a throw-back from the seventies, with clear vinyl covering the cushions.

Before sitting, I handed her a white box from Fugacci's, tied with red and white string. "I hope you like rugalach."

She put a hand to her cheek and accepted the gift with the other. "How thoughtful of you. I love rugalach. Jake, isn't that thoughtful of her?"

"That's real nice, Ma."

"I usually make my own," she continued, "but I'm sure these will be fine."

Now I knew why Gus hid in the shadows whenever my mother showed up.

The plastic on the sofa burped as I sat and eased back. Glad I wore pants and not shorts, so I wouldn't leave behind a layer of skin. "What a lovely home you have, Anita. Have you lived here long?" Oh, lord, I sounded like a goody two-shoes buttering up the teacher.

Anita handed the pastries to Jake and backed onto a lounger. "All my married life. My husband, Howard, God rest his soul, bought this house as a wedding present for me." She gazed at a picture on the mantel, one with a much younger, *and thinner*, version of herself standing next to a lanky young man in a suit and tie. They were on a beach with a Ferris wheel behind them on the boardwalk. "Jake, bring the tray from the kitchen with the coffee pot and *homemade* cakes. And be careful you don't drop it! My good cups are on it."

The way Jake hustled off to the kitchen I could tell Anita wasn't used to being denied any demands. The house smelled of pinewood furniture polish and flowery carpet freshener. If she were like my mother, this woman didn't trust anyone to do it as well as she could, but I couldn't imagine her squeezing around the furniture with a dust rag or dragging a vacuum.

Jake returned carrying a large tray with a glistening silver urn, three china cups, and a variety of breakfast cake slices on a matching platter. Small plates, forks and cloth napkins lined one side. *She didn't have time to fold them into swans?* The cups rattled as he set the overloaded thing on the coffee table, eliciting a gasp from his mother.

He perched on the couch beside me, and we stared at the tray. Anita gestured with her head toward the setting, but her son's hands remained in his lap. What a contradiction from the confident guy who'd blown off rocket-heeled Penny at the restaurant with me on his arm.

I picked up the pot and asked, "Shall I pour?" If we

waited for Anita to struggle her way out of the recliner, it would be lunch time before her feet found the floor.

Her face flushed. "That won't be necessary. Jake can do it." She evil eyed him.

"Oh, it's no trouble. How do you take yours?" I filled all three cups, leaving room for milk in two of them. From writer to barista in thirty seconds.

"Two sugars, please, and cream. I like real cream in my coffee, none of that awful fake stuff. Don't you agree? Oh, and a slice of all three cakes please." She settled back, waiting to be served. "Two of them are a new recipe, so I want a smattering of every flavor."

Smattering? Each slab could feed a family of four.

"Ma, is that you?" Gus squinted from where he sat on the other side of me. "Boy, did you get fat. You look like Aunt Ella after her round-the-world cruise."

Clearing my throat to cover my amusement, I turned to Jake. "Cream and sugar?"

"You get yours, Marni. I got mine."

Gus leaned in. "I'd say the cinnamon streusel is your safest bet. Mom was a great cook, but most of her baking tasted like sawdust or lard. The chocolate one looks more like lard."

With the serving knife hovering over the brown cake, I shifted and followed Gus's suggestion. His mother might have improved over the past couple of decades, but I didn't want to risk having to choke down something inedible. She'd probably take a contract out on me for not finishing. I toyed with cutting the piece in half but saw no way around insulting Anita if I did.

Jake dug in with gusto after doctoring his coffee.

Over the next few moments, the only sounds were slurps and chewing. Feeding time at the zoo would have been more sophisticated. I struggled for a topic conducive to her mentioning her younger son. This would be easier if her living son wasn't present. I inwardly cringed at the thought of being force-fed a new flavor of streusel if I had to make a second visit. The current one could double as a door stop.

In between mouthfuls, Anita broke the ice. "When is your next book coming out? Can I get an advanced copy?"

"Ma, she can't do that." Jake looked at me. "Can you?"

"Well…"

"What's the good of knowing a famous author if you can't get a preview? Right?" She raised her brows at me. I hadn't realized what close pals we'd become in the brief moments since arriving and choking down her latest kitchen experiment.

I sipped my coffee. Then sipped again. "Unfortunately, I'm under contract not to give advance copies. You understand, don't you, Anita? Legally, I could get in trouble." Maybe the talk of illegal activities would spur talk about Gus?

"Oh, sure. I get it." Her lips pouted. Should I offer a tourniquet for the gut wound she'd just received? "Can you at least tell me what it's about?"

It wouldn't hurt to toss a few crumbs her way. "It takes place in the Canadian Yukon during the gold rush of the eighteen-nineties. My heroine, a recent widow, must work her deceased husband's prospecting claim, or she'll lose everything. What do you think?"

"Borrring!" Gus chimed in. "Forget about the dumb books. Ask her about me." He channeled his inner three-year-old. Me, me, me, me, me.

Anita's face revealed no emotion at the description. "My favorite is the one in New Orleans. Did you really meet a Gypsy Princess to do your research? Did she tell your fortune?"

If only I could tell her the truth. My research came from a lost soul, not a flesh and blood person. "As a matter of fact, I did. She said I would meet a rich, handsome man and have lots of babies."

"Well, you've already met the handsome man." She stabbed another piece with her fork before using it to point at Jake. "You, being a famous author, shouldn't need a man to pay your bills. And no offense, but aren't you a bit past your prime to be having kids? Lemme have another piece of Chocolate Dream Cake." She held her plate out to her son. Jake must not have clued her in on our current dating status—non-existent.

"Ma," he slapped another healthy serving down and handed it back to her. "I think Marni was kidding."

I grinned. "Yes, he's right. While I did see a fortune teller when visiting the city, she didn't tell me anything prophetic."

Anita screwed up her face. "*You* she called pathetic? Oh, honey, you've still got a lotta good years left. Maybe wear a bit more makeup and lose a couple pounds. What does she know?"

I prayed my mother didn't follow me here. Tactless advice in stereo didn't appeal to me. One thing was for sure: both boys got their smarts from their mother. No wonder poppa moved on first. I set my empty dishes on the tray. "Thank you, Anita. Both the coffee and treats were delicious!" Maybe she had antacids in her medicine cabinet. "May I use your bathroom?"

"Of course. It's the second door past the kitchen."

She pointed down the hall. As I walked away, she yelled, "The air freshener is under the sink."

"Ma!" Jake hissed.

"You wouldn't want her to be embarrassed if she had to, you know…"

I did *not* want to hear the rest of that conversation. Closing the bathroom door behind me, I leaned against it. "Gus," I whispered. "Gus, I know you can hear me. Get in here now."

"Why you always gotta talk to me in the bathroom?" He sat on the edge of the tub.

"What am I supposed to do? Excuse myself so I can talk to her dead son out on the front lawn?"

He opened his mouth to answer.

I held up my hand. "Shush. That was a rhetorical question."

His brows knitted.

"Look it up. I'm sure there's a dictionary buried in this house somewhere, though it's probably still wrapped in the plastic it came in."

"You be nice to my mom."

"Look, I will do my best to turn the conversation to you. With your brother here, I need to be careful. He's already suspicious about my questions, and I don't want to tip him off and have him shut down. The best thing right now is for you to zip it when I go back out there. Capisce?"

"Got it. You love to boss people around, don't you? No wonder your husband dumped you."

Glaring at him with laser precision, I enunciated, "That will be the last time you *ever* mention my ex, or you're on your own. Agreed?" His kind was the reason Tim and I split. Having it rubbed in by a ghost irritated the hell out of me. "Now, get out. I have to pee."

Alone, I took care of business and hurried back to the living room. I heard Jake in the kitchen, unloading the tray. With Anita still ensconced in her throne, I walked to the mantel and picked up the picture she'd indicated earlier. "Is this you and your husband?"

"We were so young. The year before we had Jake, he took me to Coney Island. We didn't have a lot of money back then, you know, with buying the house and everything." The smile on her face was the first genuine one I'd seen. "So, we split a hot dog and root beer. Then later he took me on the roller coaster, and I threw it all up." She giggled. "Look how handsome my Howard was then. Even at seventy, the man had every woman in the room looking at him when we walked by."

Her description piqued my imagination. "I haven't written any books about Brooklyn in the mid-nineteen-hundreds. Might be a good backdrop for a story."

"Does that mean I'd get paid for helping and have my name on the front cover? My friends would be so jealous!" Her eyes brightened.

Of course! Then we could go on tour together promoting our book. Picking up another picture, I did a double take. Two blond men flanked a young Hispanic woman whom I recognized from my research on the internet. Both guys looked like Gus. Taking it to her, I asked, "Are these your children? Jake told me he had a younger brother. Were there two other sons?"

Anita took the picture from my hands, not answering for a long moment. Shaking her head, she pointed. "No. This one here, on the left, is my baby, Gus."

I glanced sideways to where he sat on the couch, his hands curled around the edge of the cushion, as if he were gripping it.

"Where is he now?"

Her smile vanished. "He left. Just up and left, and I haven't heard from him in years. Is that any way to treat your mother?"

I placed a hand on her shoulder. "Who are the other two in the picture?"

"The one on the right is Jake."

"What?"

She laughed at my surprise. "You would think they was twins? Gus dared his brother to dye his hair blond. They were always doing stupid things like that. Have you seen the tattoo on Jakes's arm? He got it on a dare. Gus too." She looked back at the picture. "The girl, Dominique, she was a…friend, I guess you could say. Between you and me she was what the kids called a *slut*. I heard she *dated* a lot, if you know what I mean. For some reason Gus loved her. Her father was a rich guy who owned a chain of grocery stores. Always, her nose in the air, that one. Yet Gus couldn't talk about any girl but her. She used to joke about being in business with my boys, that's why she hung around them so much. I never knew what she meant."

"Marni, she's lying. I didn't love her." Gus dove off the couch. "We rolled around in the sack. Nothin' more."

"Ma, what are you talking about. We was never in business with her." Jake came into the room and took the picture out of her hands, returning it to the ledge over the fireplace.

Anita sank deeper into her seat. A crane might be

required for her removal later. "I never liked her but felt bad when someone killed her. It happened only a few days after that picture was taken. She probably ended up teasing the wrong man."

Now I needed to drag out an award-winning performance. "She was murdered? How awful. What happened? Did they catch who did it?"

"Ma, why'd you bring that up? Marni, forget about it. That stuff's ancient history." Jake paced.

"I miss him, Jake." Her eyes watered. "If he could pay you back the money, maybe he could come home."

"He's not coming home, Ma. The bum took off and doesn't care about us. Give it a rest, will ya?"

Working her way toward the edge of the lounger—this took a few moments accompanied by several grunts—Anita inched off until she could stand upright. "Don't say that! Someday he'll come back to me. You'll see."

"She thinks I stole the money too. My own motha'. I'm outta here."

The discussion spiraled downward. I needed a hasty exit myself. "Did you have books you wanted me to sign for you?"

Her face brightened at the reminder. "Yes, I've got five. Jake, get them from my nightstand. There should be a pen in the kitchen." Her authoritative tone returned, as if she'd flipped a switch and the saga of her missing son and the murdered slut never took place. "My mahjongg group will be *so* jealous when they see these. Can you sign it, 'To my dear friend, Anita?' "

Once the books were autographed and another round of thanks doled out, Jake walked me to the curb. My plan of a clean escape before he could solicit another date faded.

I chirped the alarm on my SUV, and he opened the door for me. Tossing my purse onto the passenger seat, I was almost home free, until I felt a hand on my arm. Should have known it wouldn't be so easy. Turning to look at him, I lied. "What a wonderful woman your mother is. Thanks for introducing me."

"No, no, thank you, Marni. I appreciate you taking the time. Look, I know things didn't go right with us. But I got this buddy, see, and he has this boat. Well, it's more like a yacht. Anyways, I would like it if you would go with me on Sunday. He invited me to go out into the Long Island Sound, maybe do some swimming, and he said I could bring a guest. What do you say? It won't even have to be like a date because there'll be other people."

Every fiber in me wanted to scream *no*. With all the coincidences adding up, I knew which boat we'd be on. My obligation to Gus prevailed. Against my better judgement the words, "I would love to," escaped my mouth.

He grinned. "Really? That's great. I'll pick you up at ten."

"Can't wait." I lied again. The fibs rolled along with a life of their own. Jumping into the car, I drove around the corner and pulled over to the side. My hands gripped the wheel. Sunday I'd be spending the day with Jake (a possible criminal), Jason (the grieving great-uncle), and probably the two car thieves from the other night. And we'd be somewhere out on the ocean far from shore. Could this be what happened to Gus?

Chapter 14

A little before nine on Sunday morning, I put Darla's freshly laundered clothes in a bag and walked to her place. She answered the door wearing a smile. I almost didn't recognize her.

"Just in time for coffee. Come in." She took the clothes and led me toward the back of the house.

I'd already had two cups at home but didn't want to turn down the invitation. It would make it easier to chat at a kitchen table rather than standing awkwardly in the doorway. A plate of half-eaten eggs and bacon sat on the table. "I didn't mean to interrupt your breakfast."

"Nonsense. You're not interrupting anything. How do you take your coffee?" She poured me a large mug. Had to like a woman who drank coffee by the vat like I did.

"Black, thanks." Smells of the rich blend steamed off the top of the warm cup. Since we'd become partners in crime, I didn't think she'd object to the favor I needed.

Darla beat me to the punch. "Off to do more sleuthing today?"

She made it sound like a normal day. Lately, I guess you could say that about my life. "You're not going to believe where I got invited."

Taking a bite of egg, she chewed and swallowed

before answering. "A talk show?" Her pleasant attitude frightened me a little.

"Jake, you know Gus's brother, invited me to join him on Jason's boat. At least I think it's *Dominique's Dream*. All he said was it's a yacht owned by a friend. How many people could he know who have an expensive toy like that?"

"So, is there romance budding?"

"Somehow, I don't believe Jake understands the term." We laughed. "I had fun on our couple of dates, but he really isn't the long-term relationship type. And we keep running into *old friends from the neighborhood*, which translates to *women he's dated*. The other factor about his *old friends* is they've more boobs and big hair than I could ever pull off. Makes me wonder why he's bothering with me."

She sipped her coffee. "Maybe he's trying to upgrade his style?"

"Whatever he's doing, I have to go along with it for now to help Gus."

Her jaw tightened. "Are you sure you'll be safe? If the boat is populated with the cast of characters you've come across so far, you might be putting yourself in danger if they suspect your motives."

I'd lost count of how many times the thought crossed my mind since accepting the invite. Of course, with my habit of running toward red flags rather than away, I knew I wouldn't cancel today. "My fingers and toes are crossed. Can I ask a favor?"

"I'm all ears." She perked up.

"Would you be my safety buddy?"

The confusion in her eyes told me she had no idea what I'd asked. I guess she'd never indulged in online dating. Don't they have senior sites like oldfolks.com or something? I never tried them myself, but in California, several girlfriends had used me as a safe contact, being I had no social life to speak of. "Can we set up a contact plan? I'll text when I get to the boat and when I return. If I don't show up or respond in a normal timeframe, you call out the Coast Guard."

Darla sipped her coffee and remained quiet. This was asking a lot from a virtual stranger, but heck, she'd aided and abetted when I escaped the other night. She got her phone off the counter. "I guess we better swap numbers."

My shoulders relaxed knowing somebody would be listening. I could have enlisted Calvin, but he would protest my plan. He rarely dug in and stood his ground, but his sister intentionally putting herself in danger would qualify as one of those times. We entered each other's cell numbers and sent a text to make sure they were correct.

"What time are you heading out?"

"Jake is picking me up in twenty minutes, so I better get home."

At the front door, with her hand on the knob, she said, "Maybe you should send me a note mid-day. If you run into trouble when you get there, it would be hours before I called in the troops."

"You're good at this." I tucked my cell into my back pocket. "I'll send word about noon."

Still hesitating before opening the door, she added, "Marni, please be careful. I realize you're used to residing just this side of crazy, but I believe parts of your common sense have taken a time out. I'd like to think there will be other mornings we'll have coffee and a chat."

Next, we'd be getting friendship rings and piercing our navels. What would the other locals think? "I will. I'm probably blowing the situation out of proportion and going overkill by dragging you into it. See you later."

Her door didn't click shut until I reached the end of the driveway. Checking the time on my phone, I hustled down the hill and around the corner in case Jake showed up early. Not seeing his truck anywhere, I swung open the door and tore up the stairs, nearly knocking him over on the second step. He caught me before I fell backward.

"Hey. I was thinking you changed your mind when you didn't answer."

My face flushed as if he'd found me doing something deceitful. Wait a minute, I was, in a way. "Oh, I had a quick errand to run. You're early." With his arms around me, I placed my hands on his chest so he wouldn't pull me any closer. "Let me run upstairs and get my bag."

Earning my release, I pushed past, and he followed.

"I never been upstairs in any of these old buildings. How many apartments are up here?"

"Just the one." I unlocked the bolt on the first door and headed directly to the bedroom where I'd left my beach bag stuffed with a wallet, sweatshirt, and bathing suit. Footsteps followed me, and I turned. "I'll be right out."

He took the hint and went back to the entry. I'm sure I dashed his hopes of a morning tumble. With the day ahead of us, I knew there'd be other opportunities to fend off his affections. To think only a week ago I'd been excited to see him. Guess I got blinded by the packaging.

"Where'd you park? I didn't see your truck out front." The hallway stood empty, and I found him in the kitchen looking out the window. Better there than observing the mess in the sink. I hadn't anticipated company other than his brother, who stood beside Jake.

"Nice. You can see the water from here," Jake said.

"Wow, Einstein. Like you never would've guessed." Gus walked toward me. "Do you really think that old lady is the best you can do for backup? She might keel over with a stroke or somethin' before she can dial the phone."

I put my finger to my lips, wondering why he hadn't shown himself. If he knew I'd gone to Darla's, he must have followed me there.

Jake turned around as I whipped my hand away from my mouth. "Something wrong?"

"No, no. I had a fly on my hand." I waved it around for extra effect.

He looked at my sink. So much for missing it. "You have a party here last night?"

"Just a few friends." *I am so going to hell for all the lies I've been telling lately.* Maybe Ma could put in a good word with her buddy Peta' at the pearly gates. "I'm ready." *And this concludes the apartment tour.* Not waiting for a response, I went back to the entryway. "Did you drive something besides your truck? I didn't see it out front."

"I parked at the harbor. Thought we could walk from here since the lot fills up early. You don't mind, do you?"

How early did he get here? Had he seen me go up

the street to Darla's? Out on the sidewalk I noticed Gus staring through the window of the bakery. How sad he couldn't smell the wonderful aroma of fresh bread like I could right now. "Not at all. I go down there a lot to sit on the dock." Should I have told him that?

"Hey, were you there the night before you came to my motha's? My friend's boat got broken into while he slept."

Yup, I should have stayed mum. Gripping the strap over my shoulder, I remained calm. "Hmmmm...that would have been Thursday night, right? I worked on a few chapters then turned in early." No suspicion there. Why don't I give him a detailed itinerary? "Was your friend hurt?"

"No. He woke up and scared the guy off. Didn't look like anything got taken."

That would be because my lookout sucked at his job and didn't give me a chance to search. "Glad to hear it. Did your friend call the police?" Please say *no*. I didn't think to wear gloves to cover fingerprints.

By this time, we'd reached his truck, and he grabbed a bag of his own. "No. Wouldn't've been anything to report anyways."

Car thieves must not have a good rapport with the local cops. I took off toward the boardwalk, and Jake pulled my arm.

"It's this way." He led us to a lower dock with a few small motorboats tied up.

I could've sworn he'd used the word *yacht* when inviting me. He'd also mentioned other people. A crowd wouldn't fit on any of these. "I'd always thought a yacht had a little more size to it."

He grinned. "It does. This is the dinghy. After the

break-in, my friend decided to anchor outside the harbor. Lemme have your bag." Setting both his and mine into the bow of the boat, he offered a hand to help me in.

Gulping, I stepped back.

He mistook my apprehension. "There's a lifejacket on your seat. Are you afraid of the water? You look kinda pale."

A few hundred feet in this thing and I'll be green. "No, I love the water. I thought we were going on a bigger boat. These little ones make me a bit…queasy…and I didn't take anything."

"It's not far. Keep looking at the horizon, and you'll be fine."

Wish I had a dollar for every time someone gave that suggestion. Usually it came while I lay curled in a fetal position on the deck. "I'm sure you're right." I allowed him to help me in then slipped on my life jacket and zipped it tight. At least when I tumbled over the side from leaning too far, I wouldn't drown.

He stepped into the stern and started the motor. We putted past other expensive toys tethered to anchor ropes and bobbing on the water. Bobbing. Not a good visual. Focusing on the horizon, which also jiggled up and down, I hoped for the best.

We left the protected area and motored around the jetty at the mouth. Our path hugged the shore to the right where the current became choppy, and the boat bounced off each wave. He angled toward sea so we could cut through easier. A white ship lay anchored a short distance out. With my stomach churning, I gripped the rail on either side of me.

Ten minutes later, we neared the yacht with Jason

waving from the cockpit. The same deckhand who helped me the other day waited on the stern. Jake cut the motor, and we drifted the last few feet.

Before I could stand, the sea won the battle, and I heaved over the side. Coffee and bagels spewed into the ocean. Water sprayed my face as the waves slapped the dingy. Jake stepped forward and held my hair out of the way like a pro. All I wanted to do was crawl onto the back end of the ship and pass out. From somewhere close I heard Gus laughing. My stomach emptied again.

By this time, Jason had made his way to the stern. Recognition registered in his eyes. Mustering all my strength, I gasped, "Permission to come aboard, sir."

"Permission granted, Marni. I'd say it's a pleasure to see you again, but perhaps we can reassess the thought after some ginger ale." He looked at his deckhand. "Costas, help Ms. Legend to one of the couches in the salon, then get her a cold glass."

I felt Jake's hands slip under my arms and hoist me up. On shaky legs, I stepped onto the deck where Costas scooped me up and carried me inside.

Before we got through the hatchway, I heard Jake ask, "You know Marni?"

The door slammed shut before I could hear Jason's answer. I closed my eyes as Costas gently placed me onto something soft. I sank into the cushions, and he put a pillow under my head. "Rest a moment, miss. I'll get you something to drink."

Before he returned, I'd fallen asleep. When I awoke, a glass of amber liquid awaited on a coffee table in front of me. The remnants of ice cubes floated at the top. I sat up and took a sip—ginger ale. My insides now calm, I drank more. I unzipped the lifejacket and let it drop to the cushions.

"You're up! Feeling better?" Swinging my legs to the floor, I saw Jake drinking a beer near the kitchen.

"Much. Now I'm on the mama boat and not the baby, I'll be fine. Can we go outside?"

"Sure." He rushed over. "You want a beer?"

I wrinkled my nose.

"Maybe you should stick to this for now." He pointed at my glass.

"Good advice." I stood with steadier footing this time. I carried my drink, and we went to a steep stairway past the galley leading to the upper deck. We popped up in the cockpit where Jason, holding a glass of amber liquid, sat on a bench lining the back. I suspected his beverage wasn't the same as mine when a peaty scotch scent wafted my way. He looked dashing in beige trousers and a white polo. All he needed was a smoking jacket to complete the image. On the other end were Murphy with his arm around the redhead from Maestro's the other night. I glanced sideways at my date.

Murphy sported another embarrassingly bright pair of shorts, this time in orange, matched with a red and purple Hawaiian shirt. I searched my pockets for sunglasses. His date wore form-fitting white shorts over her sizable curves and an orange tank top. Had they coordinated outfits, or was it a tragic coincidence?

Jason stood and gave me a one-armed hug. "Marni, glad to see you're better."

"Do I know how to make an entrance, or what?" I clinked my glass to his.

"I must say this is a wonderful surprise. When Jake had asked to bring a guest, I had no idea it would be you." The man sounded like the billionaire from an old sitcom I used to watch. I wondered where he hid his lovely wife. He guided me toward the other couple. "Let me introduce you to my associate, Murphy, and his…guest, Genevieve." The hesitation spoke volumes.

"A pleasure to meet you." I put on my meet-the-author smile and shook hands with both.

Murphy grunted. Genevieve purred, "Pleasure." Her expression didn't display any hint of recognition. Not surprising, given her state of inebriation when we'd *met* the other night. The reek of gin from her glass told me she was on her way to a repeat performance. Despite not achieving the title of girlfriend from Murphy, he appeared to be claiming territory the way his paws groped along her backside.

"Perhaps, after you've had a little more soda, I can interest you in a glass of wine." Jason continued being the perfect host. "I have a lovely bottle of cabernet franc from a small winery in the Paso Robles, California, area, which I believe you'd enjoy."

Right now, the thought of alcohol didn't enthuse me. "Yes, later. Maybe with lunch? Drinking on an empty stomach is never a good plan."

He agreed.

"This is a beautiful ship. Have you had it long?" Could he be the silent partner Jake referred to?

"She's a beauty, isn't she?" He rubbed the steering wheel. "I've only had her a few years."

Scratch that angle of questioning. "Is this a new hobby for you?"

"Oh, no. I've been into boating for decades. Of course, the ones twenty and thirty years ago weren't nearly as luxurious as my recent acquisition. Those were more along the lines of day cruisers for fishing. Business has been good to me over the years, and I've been able to upgrade my surroundings." He tilted his glass toward me then drank.

"When is Diggs supposed to get here? I thought we was goin' swimming on that private stretch of beach by the bluff?" Murphy asked. Drooling over his companion's cleavage, he added, "If nobody else is there, we won't need bathing suits."

Genevieve giggled. It sounded forced coming from a woman her age. My stomach lurched at the thought of ol' Murph going au naturel.

"He's meeting us there in the skiff we left at the bluff. Shall we get underway?" Not waiting for an answer, he went down to the galley. A moment later Costas came up and got into the captain's seat. I guess Jason preferred a chauffeur rather than piloting himself.

Jake took my hand. "Come on, let's ride on the front. There's a couple loungers. We can refill our drinks on the way."

I followed him down the stairs, and we stopped in the galley. He refilled my ginger ale and grabbed another beer for himself. Exiting at the stern, we walked along the outside rail to the bow. The boat moved before I got seated, so I had to hang on.

The breeze felt good, and I didn't mind the light spray of water coming over the bow. It helped drive away any lingering nausea. I hoped on the trip back I could convince them to cruise us all the way to Northport, so we wouldn't have to use the dinghy. My butt felt a vibration when I realized I still had my phone in a back pocket. Checking it, I saw two texts from Darla. Having passed out, I never let her know I'd arrived. She must've been in a panic and sent a second message. Jake looked at my phone but couldn't see the screen. I forced a laugh and turned it away from his gaze. "Just my brother. I'll let him know I'm busy." Typing a quick response, I told her the planned location, and I'd check in later, then pocketed my cell.

"You're close with your family. That's good." He looked off toward the shore. "I wish me and Gus had stayed close."

As if on cue, Gus appeared sitting on the rail in front of us. "We need to go to the rental house, Marni. Something happened there. Something big."

I gave a slight nod of my head. It would have to wait. Looking at Jake, I said, "You seem to have had a change of heart since you first mentioned him to me. Why?"

He crossed his legs and sipped at the beer. "Because of Mom. We hadn't talked about him in a long time. Then when you were there on Friday and asked about the picture, it stirred things up." His head turned to me. "Not in a bad way. I didn't mean it like that. After you left, we talked about the good times we had with him. She really wishes Gus would come home. I guess I do too."

Placing my hand on his arm, I didn't know what to say. To encourage him that Gus might come back would be wrong, knowing what I knew. Jake's conversation confused me, and I regretted thinking the worst of him. The sincerity in his voice sounded real. He placed his hand over mine, and we watched the water zipping past. Even Gus stayed quiet.

Costas maneuvered the boat around the shore until we came to a small inlet with a beautiful white beach surrounded by walls of dirt and rocks. I could see why Murphy described it as private since you could only access it from the water. A skiff, like the one Jake had shuttled me on, lay beached on the shore. A man, I assumed Diggs, slouched in a camp chair under a pop-up.

"Why don't you change into your bathing suit? I put your stuff on the couch you passed out on." Jake smirked. Everyone was amused by my earlier episode except me.

In the salon, I picked up my bag and looked around for a place to change. Jason stood in the galley. "Why don't you change in my quarters, Marni. Straight ahead at the end of the hallway. I believe you know the way."

Forcing a smile, I pointed. "Thanks. This way, right?" He nodded as I left my glass on the counter and went along the passageway. Once inside I forced myself to take several deep breaths. He couldn't have meant what I thought he did. The hallway had been dark. I wanted to lock the door behind me but decided it would seem odd. Nobody would come in anyway, knowing I used the room.

It took only seconds to change into my one-piece and cover-up, leaving a few minutes to search. I started with the built-in night table on one side of the bed. Nothing of use beyond reading glasses and phone chargers. Moving to the dresser, I found the usual men's undergarments and clothing. The man kept it sparse onboard. In the closet I found the same—a minute wardrobe of similar styles as his current outfit in different colors. Pushing aside the clothes I found a wall safe, locked, of course. I needed a way to open it. Too bad my robber training hadn't escalated to safe cracking. Going to the other nightstand, I found a rubber-banded stack of envelopes pushed to the back of the drawer. There looked to be five or six, the edges worn. Addressed to Jason, the postal stamp on the top one had been dated July 31, 1995. I froze when I read the return address. They were from D. Billingsly. Before I could check the others, the door behind me opened, and I straightened, pressing the bundle of envelopes to my body. Why hadn't I locked the door? Better to be thought a prude than caught rifling through your host's belongings.

Chapter 15

"Jason said I could change in here. He didn't think you'd mind sharing." I heard Genevieve close the door.

Glancing over my shoulder, I saw she wasn't looking directly at me so dropped the letters at my feet and covered the noise by coughing.

"Why are you looking in there?" She stared now.

The bed shielded my feet, but she could see the open drawer. "Oh...um...do you think he has any safety pins in here? The seam on my bathing suit has a snag, and I thought I could secure it."

"You might find something in the bathroom." She threw her bag onto the other side of the bed and began to disrobe.

"Good idea." I picked up my own tote, and let it slip to the floor. "I am all thumbs today. Ever have one of those days, Genevieve?"

"I know what ya mean." She'd already pulled off her top and worked at the hooks of her bra. This, I did not need to see. "Some days I can be such a klutz."

Bending to get my bag and slipping the bundle into it, I stood. "You know what? Maybe I should go ask him rather than looking myself. I'll leave you to your privacy."

"No worries, hon. We're both girls, right?"

I turned away before Genevieve and all her glory came bursting out of the released harness. Yes, we're both girls, but I didn't need to bond that intimately. Going to the door, I cracked it wide enough to slip out.

Murphy blocked the way. "You're the dame that fell in the water at the dock. I recognize you now. But you were with another guy. That your husband?"

Drat. "Husband? I wouldn't be here with Jake if I were married."

"Oh, I get it. You got one on the side. Me too. Don't say nothin' to Genevieve. She'll get all pouty and ruin our fun. Maybe me and you can come to some kinda…ya know…agreement to keep each other's secret." His fingertips brushed up and down my shoulder. Revulsion shuddered through my body. "Ya know what I mean, don't ya, doll?"

I took a step backward and bumped into the door. "Jake and I are friends. There's nothing for me to hide." My hands balled into fists. I wanted away from this slimy character. "But I'll keep your secret. Excuse me, I need to get by."

He didn't budge.

Swelling out my chest to give him a blast of my indignation, I realized too late how Murphy's attention dropped to below my chin. Well, that backfired. I shifted my bag to cover as much of my front as possible and broke his concentration.

"No worries. I think I'll see if Genevieve needs a hand." He pushed past me into the bedroom.

He'd need both hands with her chassis. I reached into the sack and made sure my pilfered stash rested on the bottom underneath my clothes. Hopefully, Jason wouldn't miss the letters for a while. I found Jake in the cockpit, already in his bathing suit. At least he hadn't thought I needed assistance getting dressed.

We were anchored about fifty yards offshore. "Hey, Marni. Jason went with Costas to get lunch set up. This man really knows how to set a classy spread. Wait 'til you see it."

I was sure his role would be supervisor as opposed to participant. Jason struck me as a man who expected others to do his bidding.

The man from the beach motored toward us in the other dinghy. I was glad we didn't have to swim for it as I intended to not let the bag out of my sight. We met him on the stern, and Jake helped me into the boat while introducing our latest addition to the party. After Diggs shook my hand accompanied by a leer, I felt in need of a shower. His brown and gray hair, which Gus had described earlier, looked greasy, and he wore it pulled back in a ponytail. He hadn't aged well with a pockmarked complexion and tobacco-stained fingertips.

"Should we wait for Murphy and his broad?" Diggs asked.

Jake shook his head. "He's helping her change, if you know what I mean. It could take a while."

A ghastly grin cracked across our skipper's face. "Think maybe he might need help? I hear that chick's into threesomes."

My body flinched. Please make him stop talking.

"Let him go solo. I think the boss wants help setting up." Jake said.

The boss? Did I wander into a company picnic? I straddled the fence on whether attending this soiree had been a wise idea or not. After finding those letters, assuming D. Billingsly was my new BFF, I regretted my choice of safety buddy. All I'd done was dig myself deeper into a hole with only a ghost on my side. Could she have tipped off Jason about my nightly visit?

On the beach, Costas had erected a second canopy with sidings on the back to block the sun. Another hour or two and the cliffs would offer more shade. A table beneath it had the beginnings of a buffet with elegant plates, napkins, and gold cutlery. He pulled bowls of shrimp cocktail, lobster tails, and cracked crab legs from a cooler and spread them out on the table along with dipping sauces and a few other platters with cheese and crackers. Jake hadn't been kidding about the extravagant luncheon. Other camp chairs had been opened with folding tables scattered near them. Gus sprawled in one. He'd disappeared when I went below to change. I couldn't tell if he was pouting or waiting for something to happen.

On the far end of the food table Jason opened the promised cabernet franc and had two bottles in reserve. Happily, I noticed real wine glasses next to them.

Jason shooed us away when I offered to help, so Jake and I walked the shoreline a short distance. "Marni, I'm real glad you came today. You know, the whole misunderstanding about Genev—"

After the awful proposition from the fat man and comments by our ponytailed friend, I didn't want to think about how things went the other night. "Jake, stop beating yourself up, and let's move on. If you said it was a misunderstanding, then I'm willing to accept it. Truce?"

He laughed. "Truce. You're easy to talk to, ya know that? And smart. A lot of women I meet, well, they probably don't even read books, let alone write them."

"I'm sure some of them read. There are lots of

picture books out there."

"See that? And you're funny too. My mom said you were a keeper and told me not to screw this up."

Having his mother's stamp of approval didn't sway me, since my intentions were no longer romantically motivated. I wasn't sure they ever would be with him, even if he turned out to be the good guy in all this. Well, besides the grand theft auto thing. "I enjoyed chatting with your mother." I almost choked on the words but had to come up with something complimentary.

The blast of an air horn startled me, and we both whipped around in the direction we'd come. On the ship I saw Murphy standing on the bow waving both arms. Did Genevieve tell him about my poking through Jason's nightstand? Would Murphy have known what was supposed to be in there?

"Are you okay?"

"What?" I looked at Jake.

"The horn. It scared you?"

I shook my head. "Is...is something wrong? With Murphy, I mean, the way he's waving?"

"He's calling Diggs for a ride. Cell service doesn't always work here, so we use the air horn when we need to get someone's attention on shore. Ain't you never heard it go off in the harbor?"

I expelled the breath I'd been holding. "Guess I didn't think about it."

Murphy now stood on the stern and waited with his date, who looked naked. Did Genevieve take her man's suggestion at not needing a bathing suit? When she shifted, I saw three tiny patches in hot pink, strategically placed on her body. Even from this distance, the fabric clearly strained on top. The triangle of pink on bottom made me hope she wouldn't turn around. My wish wasn't granted. As she backed onto the skiff, I wanted to bleach my eyes. She wore a thong that disappeared between her heavy cheeks leaving nothing to the imagination. I felt overdressed in my one-piece.

We reached our little encampment the same time as the rest. Jason glanced at the other woman. "Perhaps, Genevieve, you could put on a cover-up while we dine?"

She glared at the man beside her. "Murph told me I didn't need one."

Our host picked up a crisp, white, long-sleeved shirt, which had been draped over a chair. "You may borrow this." He held it out by the shoulders and helped her into it.

"Swell," she snapped, then grabbed the tails and tied them into a knot just above her navel. At least when she sat, it might cover part of her lap.

Jason picked up the open wine. "Marni, would you care for a glass?"

"That would be lovely." Did I just use the word *lovely*? Present company drew out my inner snob. At least he only offered me wine and not more clothing.

After handing me a glass, he asked, "Anyone else?"

"I'll have a gin and tonic," Genevieve spouted while studying her nails. Ouch. Can we say *pouty*?

"My apologies, dear," Jason mewed. "We only brought wine, beer, and water. Would you care for a bottled water?"

Both her eyes and mouth opened wide as if he'd

stabbed her in the heart.

"Why don't you try the cabernet. It's quite delicious."

"No thanks." Back to the pouting. "That stuff makes me fart. I'll have a be-ah."

Costas quickly picked up three different bottles and held them out for her inspection. He definitely earned his paycheck. She pointed to a Mexican beer, which he opened then stuffed a slice of lime inside the neck. The other men grabbed their own from the cooler.

Jason poured himself a glass of red and held it up in a toast. "To new friends." He echoed my toast from the other night while focusing on me before acknowledging the rest of the crowd.

We all drank. I had to admit, he wasn't wrong about the wine.

Our host declared the meal ready and suggested we help ourselves. Murphy grabbed a plate and dove in first, piling food so high it almost spilled. He sat next to Genevieve, who glared at him. "What, babe? Did I do somethin' wrong?"

"You didn't bring nothin' for me?"

"It's a buffet, not waiter service. Get your tail up and help yourself." Murphy said between inhaling bites of shrimp. Someone should have reminded him to chew.

Costas stepped up. "I would be happy to make you a plate, Miss Genevieve."

With an appreciative smile (*and did she just lick her lips at him?*) she said, "Thanks, Costas, you're a dear." She took aim at Murphy. "But I'll *get my tail up* and help myself." With her nose in the air, she brushed past the crewman closer than necessary as she sauntered to the table.

The rest of us stood back waiting for the tension to subside. Jake looked at me and gestured with his arm. "Ladies first."

When everyone was seated, I asked, "How do you all know each other?"

An awkward silence descended. Maybe I should have started with the weather. Murphy, Genevieve, and Diggs continued eating without acknowledging the question. I caught Jason flashing a slight nod at Jake.

"We know each other from the neighborhood." Jake pointed to the other three.

Again, with the *old friends from the neighborhood* line. It made sense for the four, close to my age, but how did Jason fit in? He would be about thirty years our senior. "How about you Jason? What's your connection?"

He sipped his wine with narrowed eyes. "The boys worked for me years ago, when I owned the crematorium."

"I wondered if there was a connection as I've recently met Charles Dilboy, the current manager." What could Murphy and Diggs have done there? No matter how great my imagination, I couldn't see them gussied up in dark suits with button-up shirts pulling off compassionate expressions. "And Jake, did you work there too?" Gus sat on the buffet table, watching his brother intently.

"No. I knew him through a friend." He didn't look at Jason when he answered. Instead he got up and grabbed another beer, handing Costas his empty.

Gus filled in the details. "He met Jason through Dominique. But you already knew that. You wanted to see what he would say, didn't you?"

Looking directly at him, my lips curved up like a sly cat, just as Jake turned. He hefted his beer toward me, believing the smile was for him.

"Diggs," I attempted to drag the two flunkies into the conversation, "did you like working there?"

His gaze shot to Jason; brows arched.

Jason laughed. "They didn't work at the facility. I employed them in different positions. Marni, have more wine. Costas, refill Ms. Legend's glass please."

"Thank you, but I'd like water. I'm feeling a bit dehydrated."

Costas set down the cabernet he'd poised over my glass and opened a plastic bottle before handing it to me.

During the remainder of the meal, Jason steered the conversation to local beaches, fishing, and a new restaurant opening in town. My line of questioning had been shut down with no hope of resurrection. As refined as the man acted, he apparently liked his guests to be boring or mute.

With our appetites sated and beverages replenished more than a couple of times, Jason encouraged everyone to enjoy the sand and surf while Costas cleared lunch. I'd nursed my first glass of wine intentionally before switching to water. It concerned me how many beers Genevieve had consumed before trudging into the rough current. If she floundered, she could always use Murphy as a flotation device. With his bulk, he'd surface without a problem.

I removed my cover-up and tried sending a quick text to Darla. With no idea whether she was in the enemy's camp, it was vital to keep up the façade of not knowing this recent development. I hit send, and my phone chirped—*delivery failed*. Darn! Jake mentioned cell service wasn't good out here. Why hadn't I thought of this possibility? Hopefully, if Darla was on my side, she didn't panic easily and call out the cavalry when she didn't hear from me on time. I never asked when we'd get back to Northport.

Zipping up my beach bag, a scream broke the silence. Everyone turned to see Murphy standing halfway in the water, holding a bikini top as high as he could reach. Not even trying to conceal herself, Genevieve jumped up and down grabbing for her swimsuit. If she stood a little closer, she'd probably blacken his eyes from the bounce. I turned away and noticed the rest of our crew, including Gus, practically salivating at the scene. Even Jason's cover cracked into a leer as he enjoyed the entertainment.

"I believe I'll have that second glass of wine now." I helped myself, then flopped into one of the camp chairs. Were there any men on this trip who hadn't had a personal encounter with the redhead prancing in the water?

When Genevieve retrieved her toddler-sized top and strapped it back on, Diggs joined in splashing around. Jake suggested we go for a swim, but I begged off feigning too much sun. He shrugged and dashed for the water.

Jason poured himself another glass and sat next to me. "No swimming for you, my dear?"

"I prefer the shade. Thank you so much for inviting me. This place is a hidden gem I didn't know existed. Have you been coming here long?"

"For years. You'd never know it was here if you

didn't have a boat. Now, what's going on between you and Jake? Please tell me he wasn't the one who ditched you the night we met."

I chuckled. "Unfortunately, he was. He's not the usual guy I go for, but he possesses a few interesting qualities. How about you? No lucky lady in your life?"

His face broke into a smile, yet sadness exuded from the expression. "Alas, the love of my life passed away eight years ago. We were married fifty-five years. I don't have the heart to find someone else. It wouldn't be fair; another woman would never get the best of me."

Wow. What would it be like to find a love like he and his wife shared? I thought I'd found it in Tim. Wait a minute. The letters I'd found from D. Billingsly were twenty-seven years old. If they were from Darla, and of a romantic nature, then he'd been stepping out on the love of his life. I couldn't wait to get home and see what they said.

"Ask him about Dominique." Gus remained on the table. I'd almost forgotten he still listened. He had a good point.

"Is the boat named after her? Dominique is a beautiful name."

His shoulders tensed, and his fingers turned white as he gripped the stem of his wine glass. "No. My wife's name was Rose. She truly had been a delicate flower, and the name fit her perfectly. Can I top off your glass?"

Why did he try to ply me with wine whenever he wanted to change the subject? The ruse became obvious the second time around. "No, thank you, this is plenty." I waited for him to continue.

"You gotta push him, Marni. He ain't gonna tell you about her unless you do. Look at the old fool. I can't believe my brother got involved with him. Whenever he saw me and Dominique together, he treated me like garbage and said I'd never be good enough for her."

If Jake returned while we talked about Dominique, it could get awkward. Rubbing a finger along the rim of my glass, I said, "I can see you miss her a lot. Where did the name on the boat come from then?"

He winced, and I expected another diversionary tactic. "Dominique was my great-niece." Jason poured himself another glass. This line of questioning pained him, and I felt awful bringing up the tragedy. Gus must believe his answers were important. Maybe Jason would say something that might trigger more memories for my lost tow truck driver.

"She must've been tickled you named the yacht after her. Does she live around here?" I glanced at Gus who looked away from me. His mother had made it sound like he loved the girl, and she wasn't just a friend with benefits.

"Costas, please prepare the dessert table. I believe our swimmers will have worked up an appetite by the time they return." Jason returned to his seat beside me. "I apologize, but I'm not comfortable speaking about her. You see, she was found murdered shortly after her twenty-sixth birthday."

With a hand over my mouth, I whispered, "No. Oh, Jason, I am so sorry. How awful. Did they ever find who'd done it?"

He shook his head, placing a hand on my arm. "It was a long time ago. There had been a suspect, but the police were never able to locate him. Now, let's talk of happier times, shall we?"

"You bastard! He thinks I killed her." Gus raged as he jumped off the table and landed directly in front of Jason. "How could you think that about me, you stupid old man? You knew nothin' about me, except I was never good enough for your precious Dominique. You're probably the one who convinced her father not to let her marry me. She told me her father would never let her."

A gasp escaped my lips. Gus did love Dominique. Enough to propose. His confession made me reconsider what I believed about him. Did Dominique love him? Or had she said her father wouldn't concede in order to get out of the proposal? With so many people around, I'd have to wait until Jake dropped me off to quiz Gus.

"Is something wrong, my dear?" Jason still touched my arm.

I looked at Gus, then focused my vision beyond him where Costas prepared the last course. Pointing at a glass bowl on the table, I asked, "Is that tiramisu?"

"Yes, do you like it?"

"It's one of my favorites. I can't wait to try it!" Good recovery.

"What is?" Jake walked up with a towel around his shoulders.

"Did you enjoy your swim?" Why did he have to look so gorgeous with the sun glistening off the droplets of water clinging to his tanned chest. A warm rush to my nether regions reminded me how much fun it could be questioning him in private. When he dropped me off tonight, my better judgment might abandon me.

"The water's great. You should've joined us."

"Maybe next time. Meanwhile, I enjoyed chatting with our host, who isn't done spoiling us." I gestured to the table. Beside the Tiramisu sat a marble cheesecake and a bowl of mixed berries.

Genevieve arrived with a towel tied around her waist, thankfully covering her derriere. Murphy and Diggs trailed along behind her, deep in conversation. My guess would be they expounded on the size of the woman's assets.

"Ladies and gentlemen, dessert is served." Jason could have been in a ballroom rather than on a beach with his proper manners.

"Ohhh," Genevieve squealed. "It all looks so good. I better be careful, or my ass might get fat." Nobody would ever accuse her of graduating from charm school.

"You mean fat-*ter*, don't ya, babe?" Murphy had zero survival skills when it came to the opposite sex. He cupped one of her cheeks under the towel and squeezed. "You know I'm joking, right?"

From the murderous look in her eyes, she'd missed the humor. After today, I'd be surprised if she didn't move on to the next guy in line. Genevieve asked, "Diggs, could you get me a little of each on a plate? I am *so* tired after all that swimming." She dropped into the nearest chair. I waited for her to lay an arm across her forehead.

Like a dog responding to a bell, Diggs perked up and grabbed a plate. "Of course, baby. Anything for you." He glanced at Murphy, who wore an amused grin. "Costas, throw some of everything on here for the lady, and don't be stingy. She looks like she could use a pound or two."

Genevieve gloated at Murphy. Could this story of lust on the beach spiral any lower? I hoped it would wrap up in one act. Having used the Italian dessert as a cover when Gus had his outburst, I felt obligated to eat a healthy portion. Not a sacrifice.

Within the hour we'd all eaten our fill, and the buffet and canopies had been broken down. Costas, Diggs, and Jake worked to shuttle everything back to the boat. Murphy dragged a pouting Genevieve behind some rocks a ways down the beach. Ten minutes later we heard moaning, and I volunteered to hop the next skiff to help Costas in the kitchen. Jason scowled in their direction, then insisted I didn't need to help, but thought it best I return to the yacht. I resisted the urge to plug my ears until we'd left the shore far enough behind.

Once aboard, I sent Darla a quick text, and it didn't fail. I told her we were done with lunch and thought I might get to shore within the hour. Now all I had to do was convince Jason to motor the big boat all the way to the harbor. While waiting for the others, I slipped into Jason's bedroom to change. This time I locked the door and did another quick search with no results, before returning to the deck.

The indiscreet couple boarded last. Murphy sauntered around with a smug look on his face. The pout on Genevieve's lips had disappeared, as well as one of the straps to her top This forced her to hold up the minute spec of clothing with her fingers. Within minutes she had a gin and tonic in her hand as she went off to change. Murphy didn't offer to assist this time.

Jake found me in the kitchen, helping Costas put

food away. "Hey, Marni, we need to make a little detour on the way home. I hope that's okay."

"What kind of detour?" I pasted on a smile.

"We'll ride with Diggs to the bluff." He put up his hands when he saw the smile slip from my face. "It's a lot shorter ride, I promise. You won't have time to get sick."

"Can't Jason take us back on the yacht?"

"He's heading into Nassau County with the boat. Got a business meeting or something."

I quelled my anxiety. Did Jason suspect anything from our conversation on the beach? "How will we get to Northport?"

"Diggs's car. We gotta stop at his place on the way. Don't worry, it'll only take a coupla' minutes. Promise. You cool with that?"

Even if I wasn't *cool* with that, I didn't see other options. "Sure. No problem. How far is his place?"

"Not far." He wrapped a protective arm around my shoulders. "What's with all the questions. You gotta be somewhere?"

"Not at all." I hoped Diggs didn't think I was into threesomes like our other female shipmate.

Chapter 16

Jake had been right about one thing—the ride in the skiff took only a few minutes. My innards didn't have time to lodge a complaint. I couldn't believe how close the private cove had been to the bluff without my ever discovering it. The dock and boat launch sat at the far end of the beach, and we didn't have to traverse the zig zag of staircases like on our fishing date.

With the boat secured, we walked to the lower parking lot. There were a few sports utility vehicles and a cherry red muscle car in the far corner, parked at an angle between two spots. I'd hoped to be riding in comfort but knew Diggs was too much of a cliché to be driving anything else. For once, a lack of height worked in my favor.

Jake opened the passenger door and flipped the seat forward. He offered to hold my bag, but I wouldn't surrender custody, even for a moment. Crawling into the rear compartment, my foot caught on the door frame, landing me face first on the seat. So much for graceful. I pulled myself upright and plopped my butt on the bench. When the front got flipped back into place, it rested against my knees. At least the cramped space eliminated Diggs using it for any hanky panky, assuring nothing disgusting would be left on the vinyl.

A half mile from the bluff, we turned right onto a residential street. Houses were large with enough property and stockade fencing to give plenty of privacy. The well-manicured lawns implied professional landscapers frequented the area. At the end of the street, we turned again, heading back toward the shore on a road riddled with potholes. Good thing I had my seatbelt on, otherwise I would have bounced my head off the ceiling.

With another left, we were off what passed for pavement and followed a dirt driveway. Knots twisted in my stomach. Had Jason and Jake discussed my curiosity and decided I asked too many questions? Through the trees, a one-story brick home became visible. Patches of grass and brown spots peppered the front lawn with overgrown bushes partially blocking the windows of the house. While the property overlooked the ocean, with the trees full of leaves, you could only catch a glimpse of the water. The view in winter must be great after the foliage dropped.

The road curved around the left side of the house, ending at a large wooden structure set back from the residence. Jake helped extricate me from the rear seat. My shoe stuck to the floor mat then released as I wiggled my way out. The fresh air felt good in my lungs after breathing in the unidentifiable odor wafting from beneath the seats.

"Welcome to my humble abode." Diggs spread his arms wide. He reminded me of a carnival barker about to introduce the bearded lady. "You guys got time for a brew?"

"Sure. We got time, don't we, Marni?" Jake asked.

"I guess we could stay for one." I followed them to the entry, which Diggs opened without unlocking. Jake held the screen door, and I stepped inside. It reeked of stale cigarettes and fried chicken. If the rest of the house looked and smelled the same, I understood why he didn't bother securing the place. The brown and beige plaid couch, at least I hoped those were the original colors, had fraying cushions covered with stains. A scuffed wooden coffee table sat before it.

Diggs returned from the kitchen with three green bottles. He gave us each one, then Jake slipped mine from my hands and opened the cap before handing it back.

"Oops," Diggs said. "I always miss that one."

"Don't worry about it." Thankful he hadn't touched the mouth of the bottle with his grimy hands, I refrained from wiping the whole thing down with the edge of my shirt. "Did you decorate the place yourself, Diggs?" The clutter around us couldn't be classified as decor, but if he showed us around, I wouldn't have to sit on anything. It didn't look like he owned a vacuum, let alone a dust rag. The sooner we downed our drinks the sooner we could get out of here—I hoped.

"Nah. The furniture was here when I moved in. It used to be Jake's."

"You used to live here?" I couldn't picture Jake living in such a pigsty.

"This is the place me and Jake rented." Gus sat on the couch. I cringed, but since he was already dead, anything still alive on the cushions couldn't hurt him. "It looked a lot better then. This guy destroyed the place."

"Yes." Jake looked around. "Gus and me rented it before…before he left. I moved out after so I could be closer to the garage in Northport." He looked away. "This place was too long of a drive."

I looked at Diggs. "So, you rent it now?"

"Not exactly. I know the owner, and he lets me stay here in exchange for taking care of things."

"Oh, is it a summer home for someone from the city?"

"You sure are a nosy broad." Diggs pulled on his beer and drained half the bottle.

"Marni didn't mean nothin' by that," Jake said. "Let's take care of business so we can get outta here."

My grip on the bottle tightened in case I needed to use it as a weapon. Diggs wouldn't be a problem, but Jake could snap me in half with his little finger. Casually backing toward the door as if I were looking around the room, I braced for action.

"Me and Diggs need to handle something in the barn out back. Why don't you wait here?"

"Sur…Sure." I stopped moving.

Jake chugged his beer as they walked into the kitchen. I saw him open the refrigerator, then heard the clinking of bottles as he pulled out two more and gave one to our host. Out of my view, a door opened, and their footsteps faded. Before it slammed shut, I heard Diggs telling him, "You're gonna love this one. It's a real beauty and…"

"Okay, Gus, spill. This is the house you wanted me to break into the other night, isn't it? Who owns the place, and what's in the barn?"

He slowly turned, taking the room in with squinted eyes. Was he concentrating on something?

Giving him a minute, I walked into the kitchen and dumped my beer down the sink. Peering through the dirty window, I guessed the barn to be about twenty-five yards away and three times the size of this place.

The woods nestling in on both sides of it obscured any of the surrounding homes. Diggs opened a padlock hanging from a chain securing the double doors, and the men slipped inside. The backyard foliage didn't fare any better than the front lawn.

At one time this place must've been beautiful. Rose bushes lined the side of the yard opposite the drive but were overgrown and wild. Weeds poked up through the shaggy grass. The whole place had an unkempt and deserted air. I couldn't imagine anyone living here now.

Gus stood beside me. I asked, "Who owns this place?"

His eyes clear again, he quietly said, "Dominique's great-uncle."

"Jason?"

"Yeah. He let us stay here cheap, and we took care of the place."

"Why did you want to come here?"

He shook his head. "I can't remember. It's like having…this big boulder in front of me. I know there's something beyond it, but I can't get past. Marni, why can't I remember what happened to me?"

"I think you're blocking it out. Something horrific happened to you, and it's holding you back. As much as you want to remember, a part of you doesn't want to know. It's that part we need to unlock, otherwise you'll be stuck here and not able to move on." Grandma had told me I would run into this eventually. As she got older, the circumstances of the lost souls she helped got tougher. She never mentioned anything about solving murders. Leave it to me to take the gift to a new level.

Since the men were still inside the barn, I suggested, "Let's take a quick look around the place. It might jog something loose in that brain of yours."

Beyond the living room, the house didn't have much in the way of furnishings. We found two small bedrooms with the doors open. One had a twin bed and the other a full size with soiled bedding and filthy carpeting. The one with the larger bed had a couple of faded and curling movie posters tacked to the wall.

"This was my room. Jake had the master at the end of the hall." He stood in front of a poster from a surfing movie. "This was one of my favorites."

"Leave it to you to pick a story about a bunch of surfers who robbed banks." I laughed. "Would the film be considered vocational training for you?"

"Vo what?"

"Never mind. This other one from the same decade is another classic felon movie."

"The dark-haired chick in that one was *hot*. I wouldn't have minded bein' her bodyguard."

He acted like the twenty-seven-year-old stud he should have been. "Down, boy. You realize the woman is my age now, right?"

"What a party killer, lady."

"There you are. I thought I'd lost you back in the kitchen. Does any of this inspire you? Do you remember what it was like living here with your brother? Did something happen between the two of you?"

"I get flashes. We had some rockin' parties in this place. Ones that would've killed our old man had we thrown them at his home."

His bedroom sat in the front of the house facing east. I could picture the morning sun streaming through the white curtains, now yellowed. "Did you bring

Dominique here?"

He looked toward the bed. "Sometimes. She talked about moving in with me. Said we'd be set for life after she finished dealing with her great-uncle. I guess Jason was gonna give her a chunk of cash."

"You mean an inheritance after he died?"

"No. She talked about making a sweet deal with him for something. I don't think she told me why he was gonna give her a bunch of dough, but she was sure he would."

"Did Dominique know about you stealing cars?"

"Of course. She helped distract the marks sometimes and got a cut. The girl's family was rich, so she didn't need the money. She did it for the rush. You know how some guys go parachuting to feel what it's like to fall from way up in the sky? It was like that for her when she helped steal cars." The grin on his face telegraphed admiration.

"You did love her."

His jaw grew taut, then softened. "Okay, I'll admit it. I loved her! Happy?"

"Maybe admitting your feelings for her out loud will help break down the boulder. Remember anything else?"

"Hey, Marni, where'd you wander off to?" Jake yelled from the living room.

"Shit! Gus…" I whispered. He'd left again. We shouldn't have spent so much time in here and explored the rest of the house. I popped my head outside the room. "I was looking for the bathroom."

"You passed it," Diggs said. "First door on the left." He pointed at the open doorway closest to the living room.

"Oh, guess I was distracted. Thanks." I stopped at the threshold as I stared at the mold encrusted tiles. The toilet seat was up, and the water in the bowl a yellowish-brown. I shuddered, "On second thought, I can hold it until we get back."

Diggs sidled up beside me. "Ya know, if you wanted a tour, I could show you around. The master bedroom is at the end. We could start there."

I looked at Jake, signaling an SOS with my eyes.

"Hey, she came with me, remember?" Shoving the small man out of the way, he threw his arm around my shoulders and led me to the front door. "We're done. Diggs'll give us a ride back to Northport."

Our chauffeur blasted classic rock on the radio the whole way back, eliminating any chance of conversation, which worked for me. I shot off a text to Darla letting her know I'd survived the outing and would be home shortly. Once Diggs deposited us beside Jake's truck, he gunned the engine and took off. Shocker the man didn't have a wife or girlfriend.

Jake invited me out for a drink, but I feigned fatigue, saying it had been a long day. He took my hand and said he'd walk me home. The suspense of wanting to read the letters in my bag distracted me. When we'd reached my place, Jake led me up the stairs. I'd planned to say goodbye on the sidewalk. Before I knew it, we were at my apartment, and his lips were on mine. His body pressed me against the door, and I didn't want him to stop. All the reasons I'd come up with to end this before it got physical abandoned me. My traitorous libido took over, and all the other body parts fell into allegiance. The brain hadn't been invited.

My arms wrapped around his waist, and my hands

clutched at his back. The tingle scorching through my body felt too good. I didn't have the willpower to stop him. I didn't want to stop him. The zipper opening on my bag forced me to pull back. "What are you doing?"

He moved in and kissed me deeply. "Looking for your keys."

Panic set in as my heart pumped. I grabbed his arm and said, "Let me."

He pulled his hand from the sack and let me fish for the keyring. Finding the keys, I turned and unlocked the door, his body now pressing into my back. I leaned my head against his chest, and his hand moved up, curling around my face. He slipped a finger into my mouth. Sucking it, I pushed the door open, and we almost fell into the entry. My bag dropped to the floor as he swept me off my feet, kicked the door closed, and carried me to the bedroom.

****

An hour later, we both lay naked under a sheet panting. Well, I panted. He looked ready for a marathon.

"Guess you weren't as tired as you thought." He rolled onto his side, propping his head with his hand.

"Must've gotten my second wind." Closing my eyes, I felt his thumb gently trace my lips. I kissed it.

"Ready for round two?" He replaced the finger with his lips, then slipped his tongue inside my mouth and started to slide on top of me.

I put my hand against his chest and gently pushed him back. "Whoa there, cowboy. I need a breather in between courses. You want some water?"

He rolled onto his side. "Sure."

"Be right back." Getting out of bed, I found a long-sleeve button-up on the floor next to the hamper and slipped it on. Nudity didn't bother me, but I couldn't remember if the front window shades were lowered. With a satisfied grin on my face, I waltzed into the kitchen and pulled the shade closed. My unbuttoned shirt drifted open. As I went toward the fridge, a loud screech emanated from the other side of the room.

I spun around. Mom sat at the table, her hands on her cheeks. "Put some clothes on! Why are you walking around naked? What if the neighbors saw you through the window?"

Her appearance left me speechless and motionless.

"Are you going to stand there with everything hanging out?"

"Ohhh, Ma…bad timing," I whispered as I wrapped the meager garment around me. "You need to go. Now!"

"Go get dressed. We need to talk." She crossed her arms and leaned back. "I'll wait."

I glanced down the hallway then stepped closer. "This is not a good time. Really. You have to leave; I'm not kidding."

"Why? What's so important you can't take a few minutes to talk with your dead mother? You got a hot date?"

Footsteps came our way. "Hey, babe, you got anything stronger than water?"

My mother bolted up straight in her chair. "Oh. My. God."

Glimpsing behind me revealed Jake standing in the doorway in all his glory, with a certain body part standing at attention.

"Look at that thing! Is he on steroids? Your father

never looked like that. Not that I'm complaining." She swatted a hand in the air. "He took care of me just fine. He must've, right? After all, I gave birth to you three kids. And believe me, it took more than once for each baby to happen. But he never looked like that." She fanned her face.

Lord, just kill me now! I did not want to hear this. How could I go for round two with visions of what she just said lingering in my head? *I finally get a live one, and we have a voyeur*.

"Is something wrong?" Jake turned me around and kissed my neck as he tugged at my shirt.

I pushed away. "I thought I saw a cockroach." Then spun back toward the table and pointed at my mother. "Over there." Pulling my hand back so my body blocked it, I made a shooing motion and mouthed the words, "You need to go."

"You know what you're doing is a sin. Not that I blame you, after leaving Timothy all those years ago. I know women these days have needs. I did too, it's just…"

I still faced her, scissoring my hands back and forth trying to get her to stop talking. And leave. Her leaving was also very important.

"I don't see nothin'." Jake rested his chin on the top of my head. "It must've crawled away."

"Yeah, it's probably gone." I clenched my jaw and signaled with my eyes for her to scram. Turning back to Jake, and blocking his…extremity…I offered, "I don't have any beer, and I know you don't drink wine. How about whiskey? I've got a good bottle of rye."

He kissed me on the nose. "Perfect."

"I'll bring it into the bedroom." I scooted to the

cupboard to get glasses. Mom still sat at the table. "Do you like it neat or on ice?"

"Ice would be good." He walked into the hallway.

Mom still sat at the table. She bit her upper lip, her eyes glued to his backside.

"Don't be long…" His voice trailed away.

I put ice into both glasses and poured two double shots. Gulping one down, I refilled it and started for the bedroom. Returning to the kitchen, I snagged the bottle under my arm and left.

"I hope you're using protection," she yelled after me.

Chapter 17

We ordered pizza for dinner and ate in bed. I let Jake answer when the delivery guy knocked. If Mom still waited at the table, I didn't want to know. The stress of the last few weeks faded as my body relaxed and enjoyed the experience. When Jake ran out to move his truck from the harbor parking lot to the street out front, I put on a shirt, buttoned this time, and found my panties rolled up on the floor. I braved the hallway and peered into the kitchen. Thankfully, it was empty.

My beach bag lay in the entry where it had landed next to the table. I carried it to the bedroom, retrieved the letters, and stowed them in my nightstand drawer. The irony of someone finding them there made me move the packet to a dresser drawer instead. No sense tempting fate.

"You get those on the boat?"

Gasping, I looked up, expecting Jake. "Gus, you scared the hell out of me! You and your brother sound too much alike."

"Nice outfit." He smirked.

Luckily I'd secured my cover-up. "We'll need to continue this tomorrow. And yes, I found them in Jason's cabin. The room that was supposed to be *empty* the first time I'd boarded his boat."

"You gonna nag me about that until the end of time? I screwed up. Give it a rest."

I prayed he wouldn't be around that long. "Got to get my digs in when I can."

"So, what was in them?"

"I haven't had time to look. You need to evaporate."

"You've been home for hours. What've you been doing?" He looked at the bed with the crumpled sheets, and the blankets lying on the floor. "Bring back a little company, did you? I told you he wanted to get into your pants."

"What makes you think it's Jake? I do have other men interested in me." Well, one other man anyway.

"Yeah, I'm sure your little black book is bursting with possibilities. He leave already? A little dancing between the sheets, and he bolted?"

Crossing my arms and pulling myself up to my full five-foot-three stature, I realized too late this move pulled my shirt up higher too.

Gus put his hands over his eyes. "Geez, lady, I don't need to see your granny panties."

My breasts shriveled. I hunched back down, and my face grew hot. I attempted to sound stern but had lost my momentum and weakly said, "Please have the decency to come back tomorrow."

He vanished as the front door closed. "Did I hear you talking to somebody?" Jake, holding a plastic grocery bag, stood where his brother had a moment earlier.

"No." I nudged the dresser drawer closed with my hip. "I wondered what took you so long."

"Thought we could use more refreshments. The liquor store was still open, so I picked up pilsner for me, and I found a bottle of that wine Jason had at lunch."

He really wanted to outdo himself. The voice in the back of my head nagged, reminding me he might be a crook. A damn good looking one. "How sweet. Thank you. Let's take these to the kitchen."

"You stay put. They need to go in the fridge a few minutes. You can help me work up a thirst when I get back." He swaggered.

I sat on the bed, leaning back on my hands and thrusting out my chest.

"Told you it was my brother." Gus blipped in, grinned, then waved as he disappeared again.

"Bastard!" I muttered.

****

The next morning's activities continued as the night before. We'd woken up early, enjoyed each other, then Jake said he needed to get to work.

Donning the same outfit I'd worn for both my supernatural visitors, I went to the kitchen, loaded up the coffee maker, and set two mugs on the counter. I checked to see if I had any milk for his coffee. Nope. Who buys milk when they don't have kids? I rooted around in my cupboards and came up with powdered creamer. It would have to do. Good thing his mother was among the living, otherwise she'd haunt me for not having real cream.

While the java dripped, I heard Jake in the shower, so I threw on my pajama bottoms and flip-flops. The bakery would already be open, but Bart would still toss me a bag with a couple of rolls. No dress code would be enforced. I slipped in the door, and the place hummed with the morning work crowd picking up breakfast. Three girls worked the counter, calling numbers. Bart came from the back carrying a tray of steaming pumpernickel and slid it onto the shelf. As he turned, he saw me and held up two fingers. I countered with four and mouthed the word *please*. He shook his head and wagged his finger at me before throwing four rolls into a bag and bringing it around the side of the counter.

"This guy better be worth my rolls, Marni," he chastised.

"You've set the bar pretty high, Bart. He may not measure up." I laughed. "Thanks! Tell Sally *hi* for me."

"Always do." He hurried back to his ovens.

Out on the sidewalk, I stopped short. Kendall stood by the door to my staircase holding a drink carrier with three cups of coffee. His other hand grasped a white bakery bag. I hadn't seen him inside the shop. He must've slipped out while I spoke to Bart.

"I thought I'd surprise you with breakfast and convince you to join me at the pier, but I see you've already gotten something. Maybe we could mix and match." He grinned.

"Wow, Kendall, this *is* a surprise." I moved closer to him.

"A good one, I hope?" Doubt colored his voice. "Maybe I should have called first."

Karma had shown up to bite me in the ass. Maybe the old lady at the cemetery I blew off at Mom's interment had connections. "Normally, it wouldn't be a problem. But I'm not really dressed for the pier. I'm not really dressed for the bakery either, but sometimes I take liberties and hope the fashion police aren't on duty."

He laughed. "I would suggest a wardrobe change if you're able to join me."

The door opened in front of him, and Jake came out fully clothed. "There you are, Marni. Hey, I gotta get to work." He halted and looked me up and down. "Why are you outside in your pajamas?"

"I was just asking her the same thing?" Kendall stepped forward. "Kendall Kramer. I'd offer to shake, but I'm out of hands. And you are?"

Jake looked between Kendall and me before answering in a gruff voice. "A friend of Marni's."

Oh good. Male testosterone being thrown about. If they'd had horns, they'd be butting heads like big horn sheep. I assumed Jake had read the card on the flowers Kendall left last week and connected the initials KK.

"This is getting good." Gus leaned against the building. "You should sell tickets."

I glared at Gus.

He shrugged. "What? You told me to come back in the morning. It's morning, so, here I am."

I noticed both men staring at me. Maybe I should be wearing a black and white striped shirt with a whistle around my neck. "Jake, I came down to grab a couple rolls." I held up the bag. "And Kendall happened to stop by offering breakfast."

"Swell, I'm starved." Jake grabbed the bag from my hand. "I'll eat it on the go." Turning to Kendall, he took one of the coffees from the carrier. "Thanks, man." Kissing me on the lips, he added, "I'll call ya later, babe." He strode to his truck parked four slots away.

Dumfounded, I watched him go. Remembering I wasn't alone, I opened my mouth to say something, and Kendall chuckled before I got a word out.

"Well, it appears you're free and in need of breakfast since yours just sauntered down the block.

Care to change and join me?"

"I'd love to. Come on up. There's a whole pot of fresh brew upstairs. We can start with it while I change."

****

We sat on the pier in the same spot as last time. Conversation meandered through work and family before Kendall finally asked about Jake. "What's the deal with you and him?"

"Would you feel better if I told you I picked him up at the bar last night?" I munched on a bear claw. What a sad world this would be if they'd never invented almond paste.

He tilted his head, "Did you?"

"No."

"Oh." He pouted. My answer couldn't have been a surprise, could it? "Am I too late to the party to ask you to dinner tomorrow night?"

Sleeping with more than one man had never been my style—or endurance level. If I moved forward with Kendall, I'd need to cut Jake loose. While last night had been fun, and much needed, I didn't see a relationship blooming with him. If I were lucky, he'd carve a notch on his belt and move on, saving me from making any decisions. And if I spent the night at Kendall's place, the odds of my having additional guests might go down considerably. Getting it on with Mom down the hall wasn't a performance I wanted to repeat.

A whole conversation rattled around in my head, but I'd yet to answer Kendall. "I'd love to have dinner with you tomorrow."

He expelled a breath. I didn't realize his tension over my answer soared so high. "Great! I'll pick you up at six. Have you eaten at Maestro's?"

"It's one of my favorites. Park at my place, and I'll dig out sensible shoes so we can walk."

"Do you own any shoes that aren't sensible?"

He knew me too well. "Once, but they turned on me and threatened to inflict twisted ankles. I was forced to return them to polite society."

Standing, I went to the end of the boardwalk. A boat cruised our way, and it looked like *Dominque's Dream* but was too far out to know for sure. I needed to wrap things up with Gus and Jake before I could devote myself to a second try with Kendall. Arms wrapped around my waist from behind, returning me to the moment.

"You shouldn't stand so close to the edge. There isn't a handy deckhand to fish you out this time. And if I showed up to work dripping wet, Mrs. B might give me a stern look." He pulled me backward a couple of steps.

"She's really good at those. Do you think she practices in the mirror?" I sipped my coffee and enjoyed the warmth of his body.

"Ever wonder what would've happened if we'd stayed together?" His voice remained low.

I turned in his arms. "Kendall, let's not go there. Life is full of 'what ifs.' We need to move forward from this point."

He brushed my lips with his, then let go. Crumpling the remains of the bag and napkins, he said, "You're right. We were different people then with a lifetime of experiences yet to discover."

"We're not done, you know. Everything doesn't happen in your twenties and thirties." For instance, in my forties, I discovered I make a pretty good detective. Not so much in the breaking and entering department, but there were new skills to be learned.

Kendall walked me back to my apartment. When we got to the door, I turned to thank him for breakfast, but he kissed me instead. As he walked away, I noticed Bart standing in the bakery window smiling. He mouthed the word, *again*, and raised his arms. He and Sally knew us when we were an item in high school. When I told them I needed an apartment, they offered to rent me the one upstairs. Being landlords wasn't their favorite part of owning the building, so they only rented to people they knew. Lucky for me, the last tenant needed to relocate for his job, and I only had to live with my mother for a month before the place was mine.

I expected to find Gus in my apartment, but he didn't appear. My schedule had been full between his brother and Kendall showing up. With time to myself, I took out the letters and spread the five white envelopes out on the kitchen table. All were from D. Billingsly. I began with the earliest date. Guilt washed over me at reading someone's personal mail, but it didn't last long. I had two murders to solve.

The first letter, dated February 5, 1993, read:

Dearest J,

I've always believed I had a happy marriage. The loving partner who's spent years by my side has always completed every segment of my life. Until now. A chance meeting in a little café changed me forever. When we ran into each other last December and shared a table out of convenience, how could I know it would turn into a need. A desperate need.

Our Thursday afternoons together have become the

highlight of my week, and I never want them to end. While discretion is of the utmost importance, and I appreciate your sacrifice to willingly give them up if I were to ask, I am asking you to continue. Not seeing you would end me. I look forward to next Thursday.

Yours,

D

The letter was more of a note, handwritten in rough cursive. Knowing Darla, she didn't strike me as someone with delicate or artsy penmanship. Everything about the woman shouted tough and straightforward. It surprised me she'd had an affair. It didn't surprise me Jason had cheated on his wife. While he looked all polished and shiny on the outside, his human flaws slipped out occasionally.

The next envelope bore the date October 31, 1993:

My dearest J,

I find it fitting to write this on Halloween, the day everyone is expected to wear a mask. This is how I feel every day when I am not with you. The face I present to the world is not my true self. Only being with you allows me to rejoice in who I am and how you make me feel.

When you were unable to meet me last week, it drove home how much I've come to depend on you—to depend on us. Thoughts of the joy you send resonating through my body will have to sustain me until our next meeting.

I long for your touch and wait patiently for us to be together again.

Yours,

D

This woman wrote way more eloquently than she

spoke. Her double life sounded completely fictitious, yet I held the proof in my hand. The next two letters were dated April 1, 1994 and August 31, 1994. Both were brief and in the same flowery vein as the first two. I opened the last one dated July 31, 1995. This one held promise for more than a lurid affair.

My dearest J,

My heart is broken for you at the loss of your great-niece. I can't stop thinking about the timing of her death. With it coming so suddenly, you probably were not able to resolve things with her. Her anger at discovering us together two weeks before her disappearance frightened me. Do you think she told my daughter or your wife like she'd threatened? I have not been confronted about our actions and believe we are safe.

It shatters my heart to say this, but our time together must end. I will always love you, but the wellbeing of my family must come first. Please understand this is best for both of us.

Forever yours,

D

What a gutsy move on Darla's part. Having seen her gritty determination, I believed she did end it. Jason must have loved her to have kept those letters all these years.

Chapter 18

After spending the morning working on *Treasures of the Yukon*, I found a missed call from the general manager at the crematorium. His voicemail asked if I would reconsider signing the papers for exhumation. The other family, who buried their relative at the military cemetery, gave permission and found they had the correct one. Dilboy still hadn't heard from France, and the original family with the incorrect ashes grew anxious to have the situation rectified. He'd reached out to Gloria and Calvin but hadn't heard from either.

Rather than call him back, I drove to Roseview. The same red-taloned receptionist greeted me. She announced my arrival, and her boss scurried out and escorted me to his office. I aimed to wrap this up before my mother swooped in for another battle.

"Please sit down, Ms. Legend. I know why you came, and I regret you've wasted the trip." He gestured to a chair across from his desk.

"What do you mean? I came to sign papers and end the confusion. You only need one signature from the family, correct?"

"Well, yes. I thought perhaps he'd consulted with you first, but…perhaps not." He shifted in his chair and folded his hands on the desk. Was he about to pray?

I leaned forward. "Who?"

"Your brother, of course." He fidgeted with a pen.

"Since I left messages over three hours ago, I'd assumed you all knew."

If he didn't make a point soon, I'd have to beat it out of him. "Mr. Dilboy, what in the hell are you talking about? I came to authorize the exhumation of my mother's ashes. Are you telling me my brother blocked the option?"

"Please, lower your voice, madam." He splayed his fingers on the desk as if bracing for rebuttal. "I guess I didn't explain this very well. Mr. Legend left a few minutes before you arrived. You had intended to meet him here, correct?"

"No. Neither of my siblings knew I was on my way."

"Oh, I see. Well, since your brother took care of things, I won't be needing your signature."

I crossed my legs and settled back into my chair. There had to be a way to fight this. Gloria must've browbeat Calvin into submission, and he signed papers blocking further action. "How do I get the order reversed?"

Dilboy snapped his body upright, as if shocked with a taser. "Re…reversed? Didn't you say you came with the intent of allowing us to proceed?"

"Yes. And now Calvin has signed papers blocking me from giving consent. How could you allow him to do that without checking with the rest of the family? What kind of incompetent boobs do you have working here?"

"Ms. Legend, I know how upsetting this ordeal has been for you and your family, but you're misunderstanding me."

Jumping to my feet, I pounded a fist on his desk. "I

understand perfectly. You cannot let my brother and sister keep this from happening. Now, are you going to give me the paperwork to sign or not?"

With shaking fingers, he opened a folder sitting on the corner of his desk. Laying it flat, he slid the file in front of me, quickly withdrawing his hand. "There's no need. As you can see from the signature at the bottom, your brother has already granted permission for us to examine your mother's ashes."

"Oh." I stepped back from his desk, the heat rising in my face. Forcing a smile, I glanced up, and said, "Thank you so much for your time, Mr. Dingbat...I...I mean Mr. Dilboy. No, don't get up. I'll show myself out." I scooped up my purse on the way out of his office. My pace remained a fast clip until I reached the car. Getting in, I rested my head on the wheel. Did I really call him Dingbat to his face?

****

It took me the rest of the afternoon to calm down. Under the circumstances, I owed Dilboy an apology. He wouldn't get one. His crematorium caused this whole brouhaha, and he had to take ownership—even if it meant a dressing down by a woman a foot shorter than him. But I did call him Dingbat.

Dinner consisted of homemade taco salad and the other half of the wine Jake bought. I thought about going to Chorizo but wasn't sure if the new hostess would be on duty. If she remembered me, I'd probably get a table by the kitchen's swinging door.

After admiring my artistic placement of the guacamole and sour cream, I dug in.

"So, what was in them letters?" Gus asked.

"Do you purposely show up when there's food so

you can drool?" My fork poised in the air.

"I didn't bother you at breakfast. Besides, Mr. Cheapskate is a real snooze."

"You've mentioned it a time or two. Believe it or not, I like him. We used to date in high school. Maybe I'd like to start seeing him again."

He leaned back in his chair. "Let me get this straight. You do the wild thing with my brother, then you want to two-time him and see this other guy?"

"Kendall. The other guy's name is Kendall. If I remember correctly, you tried to warn me off from your brother. You can't have it both ways."

"You do."

"That's not fair. I'm with your brother so I can help you." I shoveled salad into my mouth with such force I poked the inside of my cheek.

"Yeah." He leaned toward me. "How much info did you get last night rolling around under the blankets?" He had a point.

"The letters were personal notes written to Jason."

"Then why take them, unless they said somethin' about me?" He straightened. "Did they?"

"No. I didn't have time to read them on the ship. Did Dominique ever say anything about Jason having an affair with Darla Billingsly?"

His laughter filled the room. "Are you kidding me? No way! Not Adriana's frigid mother."

I told Gus what I'd read. "From the dates, the affair lasted a couple of years. Dominique never told you about catching her great-uncle cheating?"

"She never said a word. What would it have to do with me anyways?"

"Maybe nothing. Maybe everything." I added my

dirty dishes to the stack in the sink. "The last letter said Dominique went missing two weeks after she'd found out." I sat down to finish my wine. "Didn't you tell me she expected money from Jason?"

His head shot up. "You think she was blackmailing him?"

"Would she do something like that to her own relative?" I thought *my* family had issues.

"I wouldn't put it past her. The woman could be a real *bitch* sometimes. Jake told her she couldn't help steal cars no more when she got too cocky with the marks. Dom said keeping them distracted didn't give her the rush like at first. She wanted to see their face as the car got taken."

"Did she quit helping?"

"Not like she had a choice. She got mad and threatened Jake. Told him if he kept leaving her out, she'd tip off the police."

"How did she expect to squeal without getting arrested herself?"

He shrugged. "Her old man would've greased a few palms and gotten her off. If not him, her great-uncle had connections."

The right amount of money could buy silence. "Did you still see her, even after she got nixed from the team?"

"What difference does it make?"

"Did you, Gus?" I drummed my nails on the table.

"I thought you didn't want to know about this stuff?"

The smell from the taco meat lingered in the kitchen. I opened the window to let in fresh air. "You don't need to give me all the carnal details. Stop avoiding the question. Did you and Dominique continue to see each other after Jake excluded her from the heists?"

"All right. Yes. We still did the wild thing. Happy?"

"And she never told you about Jason's affair?" I leaned on the sill enjoying the soft breeze fluttering in.

"You really suck as an interrogator, ya know that? I already told you she didn't say nothin' about it."

Raising my hands in the air, I said, "Gus, calm down. Why does this line of questioning make you angry? We're both working to solve your case, and I have to know everything you remember."

My phone chirped. Darla sent me a text asking if I'd like to meet for lunch tomorrow at the café on Maple. Her ears must've been burning. I responded with a yes, and we agreed on a time. When I looked up from my phone, my visitor had gone. Would confronting Darla about her relationship with Jason help or hinder my search?

****

Darla sat at a table on the patio when I arrived. On my way over, a server passed me carrying a tray of Reuben sandwiches. Whiffs of corned beef made me drool. This time I knew the sauerkraut wouldn't taste or smell like kimchee.

"Hi, Darla. What a nice surprise getting your text." The chair scraped as I scooted it closer to the table.

"I'm glad you were free. I thought it might be nice to sit out in public like real people." She smirked.

"Have you already ordered?" I asked.

She picked up her menu. "No, I got seated right before you arrived. How did your sea excursion go on

Sunday? I thought you might've stopped in, but you probably had work to do."

"Sorry, I should have come by." The letters rode in my purse.

"So," she leaned in, "what was it like spending the day with felons?"

Stranger than you could ever imagine. Before I answered, the waitress came by, and we placed our orders. "It was quite the cast of characters. Everyone I expected showed up plus a main squeeze of one of the car thieves. I don't know if she's aware of her beau's occupation or not."

"Did you find anything?" She sipped her iced tea then placed a napkin under the glass, absorbing the condensation forming on the acrylic table.

My fingertips brushed my purse where it hung from the chair back. How would she react if I slapped the packet down on the table in front of her? Would she come clean if I asked her whether she'd stayed in touch with Jason all these years? "Not much. Only the two car thieves from the other night are greasy characters, seriously in need of a wardrobe consultant. A large-bellied man should never wear neon colors."

She cringed at my description of what Murphy wore, both times I'd seen him. "Do you think Jake is involved?"

"Well, he did call Jason 'the boss,' and he and Diggs had *business to attend to* on the way home." I filled her in on the stop at the house with the large barn.

"Interesting. Jason is the owner, and he'd also rented it to the Zuckerman boys. The dots are starting to connect, but you still don't know where they lead. A little too coincidental, the psych center Dominique had been found at isn't far from there."

A shiver went through my body at the mention of the abandoned facility. I don't believe going there would solve anything, but what if Gus's body got dumped there also and never found?

"Marni?" Darla placed a hand on my arm.

Shaking my head, I apologized. "Got lost in thought. What did you say?"

She waved at a young man and woman walking across the patio. "I want to introduce you to my godson. He and his wife must've been eating inside."

The couple walked up and exchanged greetings with my dining companion. "Marni, I'd like you to meet Ray and Wanda."

Looking into the man's familiar face, I blurted, "Officer Talbott." How much smaller could this town get?

"I see you two have met before. Not in an official capacity I hope." Darla tilted her head.

"Ms. Legend had gotten herself turned around. I simply aided her in the right direction." He winked at me.

"Wait, you're Marni Legend? The author?" Wanda asked.

"Guilty as charged," I said, regretting my choice of words.

She stuck out her hand. "It truly is a pleasure. I love reading your books and can't wait for the next one. When will it be released?"

"Not until after the first of the year, I'm afraid." My fan club grew with leaps and bounds. Maybe Jake's mother could start a local chapter.

"Well, we won't keep you. Enjoy the rest of your

meal," Ray said. "Nice running into you, Darla."

After they walked away, she looked at me. "Okay, spill. Where did he find you?"

"Parked in front of Beach Street Psych Center. Glad he didn't arrest me for trespassing, otherwise this would have been an awkward conversation."

"What are the odds?" Darla chuckled. "They do have a bit of trouble with teenagers sneaking into the place. You must've thrown him for a loop."

"He did infer I was a bit *older* than the usual delinquents, all the while with his hand on the butt of his pistol." I grimaced at the memory.

"I'm glad he judged you to be harmless." She sipped her tea. "Back to your boating expedition. Anything else of interest crop up?"

"Beyond Jason serving up an amazing lunch complete with lobster tails and good wine? No." I chose to keep the letters secret for now. My gut told me I could trust Darla, and rarely did it fail me. Her affair would have to stay off the discussion roster until I learned more. I needed to get a look inside the barn, though I had a good idea of what I'd find.

Chapter 19

Choosing an outfit for my date with Kendall proved more difficult than the first one with Jake. I sifted through my paltry choices. Plans to go shopping this afternoon fell through when lunch with Darla ran late. Once we'd covered all my discoveries pertaining to Gus, the conversation turned to family. Before I knew it, three o'clock had rolled around.

Since I hadn't seen Mom in a few days, I hoped Saint Peter had taken pity on me and retrieved her. For that matter, I hadn't heard from Gloria either. Did she know Calvin gave authorization? Could be the topic of discussion this Saturday. Sylvie had sent a text earlier asking me to dinner at their house. She didn't include a guest list, but I'd bet my sister and her husband received an invite too.

I narrowed my selection to two dresses for dinner.

"Wear the red one. You look good in red."

"I'm confused, Gus. Now you want to *help* with my date tonight?" I hung the black one in the closet and took the other off its hanger.

He leaned on the door jamb. "You like him a lot, don't you?"

"I did when we were teenagers. Don't know how I feel now." Liar. I rooted around the bottom of my closet for matching shoes. Settling on a cream pair of low heels, I tossed them onto the bed.

"Watching you fuss over what to wear, I'm sure you more than *like* this guy." He shifted position, remaining in the doorway.

Getting a fresh pair of stockings from my dresser, I went into the bathroom to change.

"Marni," he yelled, "I remembered who I saw Dominique with before I died."

With pantyhose midway up my legs, I poked my head out the door. "What?" Struggling, I pulled them to my waist. Slipping the A-Line dress over my head, I went back into the bedroom, fumbling with the zipper. "Who?"

"Jake." He hung his head.

"You caught her with your brother? Are you sure?" Kendall would have to eat alone tonight. This huge breakthrough might lead to more.

His eyes glowered. "He had her naked on his bed. Yeah, I'm sure."

That's gotta hurt. "Did you confront them?"

"That's all I got. The image of her on his bed."

Now I understood his change of heart about my date tonight. The buzzer sounded. Too late to cancel. Gus looked over his shoulder, then back at me.

"Gus, I have to go. I'd stay, but he's already here. Can we talk later?"

"Sure you won't be doing the horizontal mambo?" He vanished.

How is this my fault? The buzzer rang again.

****

At the restaurant, we were seated at the same table I had last time. If fate was in a sparring mood, I'd see Jake at the bar with Genevieve. Conversation on the way here remained safely on our high school years. An unspoken agreement steered us clear of talking about exes.

"Tell me about your grandchildren. Do you see them much?" I asked.

He poured more wine into both of our glasses. "A few times a year. I love all three and prefer to see them in short visits as opposed to week-long marathons."

"Can't keep up, old man?"

"I'll admit it; they wear me out. Did I see you having lunch at the café today?"

Our server landed heavy plates on the table with a thud. Heavenly scents of garlicky pesto steamed off mine. "Yes. I've made a new friend, after a misunderstanding the first time we met."

"Care to elaborate?"

"I prefer not to incriminate myself." The bowtie pasta melted in my mouth. Why couldn't I cook like this at home? Oh yeah, the regular procurement of groceries got in the way. "Her name is Darla. Very down-to-earth senior citizen, who's lived in the area all her life. She's about ninety, and all her faculties remain intact. Feisty is the best way to describe the woman."

He swallowed. "I bet she knows an incredible amount of old facts on this town. Do you think you could introduce me?"

"I thought I was the history buff." I sipped my wine detecting subtle hints of tobacco and chocolate.

"You are the queen of historical information on several locations, but I'm interested in Northport. I'm working up a display about the town's past and would love to meet older locals. She might be able to put me in touch with others who've been here since the early nineteen-twenties and thirties. Great choice on the vino, by the way."

I tilted my glass in salute. "She'd probably be up for it. I don't know how many of her compadres are still among the living, but I can ask. If she's game, we'll come by the library, and I can make introductions."

"Sounds good. Now, how about dessert?"

"Not if you want me to explode." I placed my hands over my full belly.

"I have a plan B. Let's walk off these carbs, then stop for ice cream by the pier." He motioned for the waiter to bring the check.

We walked hand in hand along the sidewalk. Stopping in a little antique store, we trolled their collection of nautical items and old furniture. I picked up a ship in a bottle from the front window display to get a closer look at the detail of the vessel inside. Jake's work truck rolled to a stop at a traffic light across the street with a sporty red car in tow. The tinted windows prevented me from seeing who drove.

"Marni, come see this old roll-top desk. Isn't it amazing?" Kendall said from behind me.

I turned and found him running his hand over the polished wood. Returning my gaze outside, I found the truck had gone. It could have been a legit towing job. A warm pair of lips pressed against the back of my neck.

"Are you ignoring me?" he whispered. Spinning me his way, Kendall covered my mouth with his.

I pulled back. "How about that ice cream you promised me?"

"I thought you'd never ask." He led me to the door.

We arrived at the shop ten minutes after it closed. "Darn," he said. "I thought they stayed open until ten."

I read the sign in the window. "Looks like

weekends only. That's okay. I should be heading home anyway."

"We could have a nightcap somewhere?" He squeezed my hand.

The desperation in his eyes saddened me. I should be dragging him home and to the bedroom, but something held me back—maybe the thought of Mom being there? I shook my head. "Another time. Walk me home?"

"Sure." His shoulders slumped.

Outside my door, he rallied one more time. Kissing me passionately, he murmured, "Let me tuck you in."

Breathing deeply, I placed my hand on his chest. He covered it with his own. "Kendall, if this is right, it'll happen. Let's take it slow. Forcing the situation might send everything tumbling into ruin."

"Marni, I…" He stopped as his gaze met mine. "It's the other guy, isn't it?"

No. Yes. Maybe? "I'll be honest. You and I have history together, and I don't know if we're riding off of old times or beginning fresh ones."

He held my gaze a moment longer. "You're right. How about dinner on Friday? You still like Mexican? Chorizo makes a great margarita."

So I've heard. "Six o'clock? Sensible shoes?" You're going to love the seating hostess.

"I'll see you then." One more peck, and he strolled off toward his car with less bounce in his step than earlier.

"Why'd you give him the brush-off? I thought you liked this one." Gus stood in between me and the staircase.

"Gus, it's complicated. Please move."

He didn't budge, so I walked through him. "Ooohhh, I like it when you do that."

"Now you've had your cheap thrill for the night. Remember anything more after you discovered your brother and Dominique together?"

He followed me into the apartment. "Nope. What did old Mrs. Billingsly do when you asked her about the letters?"

I filled a glass with wine and took it to the couch in the living room. Kicking off my shoes, I curled my legs beneath me as I sat. "I didn't tell her I had them."

"Why not?" He lounged on the other end facing me.

"It didn't feel right. Besides, my instincts say *trust her*. Showing her those old notes, and her realizing I'd read them, might break down communication between us. Right now, she's given me more information than Jake has about you and what events happened around the time you died."

"I don't trust her."

"You don't have to. I do. Concentrate on catching your brother with your fiancée. Did you argue with him about it? Have a fight with her?"

"Fiancée. That's rich." He snorted. "I never officially proposed. Just told her I would marry her, but she said her dad would never allow it. She'd asked him about it."

I sipped my wine. "Do you think she really spoke with her father? Would she have lied to you?"

"She wouldn't lie to me." He bolted up and walked across the room.

"You caught her with your brother." I left all emotion out of my voice. "Don't get angry and disappear. We need to talk this through."

His hands balled into fists.

"Gus, get past it. Things happened, and your life got destroyed. If you bolt each time I bring it up, you'll be stuck here forever. God knows I can't handle you hanging around for years criticizing my dating habits. We need to focus on getting this resolved. Can you do that?"

He slammed a fist into the wall. It didn't make a sound or a mark. He spun on his heel. "Marni, the more I think about Jake and…and…Dom, the more it hurts. Why would she do that to me? She said she loved me. She said she wanted to spend her life with me. Then she threw it away for a jerk who looked like me. Why?"

Setting my glass on the coffee table, I went to him. "I don't know. People do stupid things. People do hurtful things. Most times there's no rhyme or reason. Maybe she got coerced."

His eyes burned. "You think Jake forced her?"

"I can't say. But maybe there had been more to the situation than simply cheating on you."

"Like what?"

I held my arms up in the air. "I don't know."

He looked at the floor.

"But I'm willing…hey, Gus, look at me."

His half-lidded eyes angled up.

"I'm willing to help you find out."

He crossed his arms. "Ya know, if you'd a been twenty years younger, I would've fallen for you."

Again, with the old jokes. "Ya know, had you lived, we would be about the same age right now."

He mugged. "At least I get to look like this forever."

"Touché. How about we go exploring?" I drained the last sip of wine and set the glass on the coffee table.

"Where to?"

I filled him in on seeing his brother's tow truck pulling a vehicle. "I want to drive by his shop and make sure it arrived there."

"You think you should be driving after all the booze you drank?" Concern colored his eyes.

"I'm fine. Look, I only had one glass." I pointed to the table.

He followed me out and asked, "What about earlier? You had nothin' to drink for dinner?"

"Calm down, Gus. You sound like my mother. I ate dinner a couple of hours ago where I had two. Driving will be fine, but if you'd rather wait here, be my guest."

Despite his apprehensions over my sobriety, Gus sat in the passenger seat as I took off down Main Street. When we passed Ozzie's, Kendall exited the bar and stopped cold. I snapped my face forward, but he'd already seen me. Glancing in my rearview mirror, his reflection stepped into the street where he watched after my SUV. Friday night would involve damage control. I'd better have a good story to tell him.

At the next light, I punched up the address for Jake's Towing on the map application and set my phone to dictate directions. The moment the electronic female voice spoke, Gus jumped.

"Who is that?" He looked at my cell in the cup holder.

"Phones can talk now. I'm using the GPS feature to give me directions."

He screwed up his face and wrinkled his nose.

"GPS. It stands for Global Positioning System. Just

207

a fancy way to say *map*. You can punch in any address, and it tells you how to get there."

"That's cool," he nodded. "But you don't need a map. I can tell you how to go."

I silenced my phone. "As long as you stick around for the whole ride."

He guided me to his brother's shop. When we arrived, I drove by as slowly as I could without appearing obvious. Lights were off in the garage, but the office remained lit. Nobody worked the counter. Whoever might be there must be in a rear office. I'd have to park down the road and sneak back on foot.

Two blocks away, the street turned residential. I pulled over to the curb between two properties. If anybody noticed a strange car, they would think their neighbor had company. We strolled past dark office buildings, then a brightly lit mini mart and a sandwich shop. Passing another unlit structure, I slowed before reaching Jake's. A couple of cars, which could have belonged to customers, sat in the parking lot. No mistaking the cherry red vehicle closest to the door. Diggs must've arrived in the last ten minutes as it hadn't been there when we drove by.

"Looks like the gang's all here." I indicated Diggs's car. "Why don't you zap into the office and check who all is in there. I'll peek into the garage."

"There you go with the *zapping* again. I told you, I ain't a lightning bolt."

I threw my head back, looking skyward. "You know what I mean. Can you please just go inside and explore?"

He chuckled. "It's so easy to rattle you. I got this. Don't get caught."

Skirting the parking lot, I crept up to the garage doors. With complete darkness on the inside and a bright streetlight behind me, I had to cup my hands against the glass as I peered through. Two of the three bays housed SUVs and the third sat empty. It didn't look good for the owner of the sports car.

"Hey, why you creeping around here?" Murphy's putrid breath snaked up the back of my neck. Think he'd be insulted if I offered him a breath mint?

He stood directly in front of me when I turned around. With no room behind, I stepped to the right and put space between me and the halitosis-inflicted man. At least tonight he wore muted clothing in dark hues. Good thing since I'd left my sunglasses at home. Mustering a smile, I said, "Hey, Murph, how's it going?"

"You? What are you doing here?"

"Isn't it obvious?" I opened my arms and shrugged.

"No, it ain't. Why you looking in there? This place closes at seven. Your car in there or something?" He edged nearer.

"My car?" I glanced at the garage, then back to him. "No, my car's not in there. I thought I'd stop by and surprise Jake. Is he around?" Please say, *no*. Please say, *no*.

"No."

I let out the breath I'd been holding.

"He's on his way. Maybe five minutes out. You wanna wait in the office?" Murphy sidled closer. "I could keep you…ya know…entertained until he got here." If his eyes shone any brighter, they'd rival halogens.

Gus stood behind Murphy waving me off and

mouthing the word *no*. Like I'd really consider the gracious offer before me? "Aw, Murphy, that's awful sweet of you. But I can see he's got business, and I don't want to interrupt." I retreated. "Just tell him I stopped by." I spun and walked toward the sidewalk, then turned back. "You know what, don't say anything. I wouldn't want him to be disappointed at missing me. Understand?" I winked and inwardly cringed.

"Sure, doll. I get it. Me and you should grab drinks sometime." He licked his lips.

"Sounds delightful. Gotta go." I waved and sped off.

"Hey, you walk here?" he yelled.

I didn't stop moving. "I'm parked near the sandwich shop. Picking up a late dinner. See you around." My speed didn't allow for more conversation. Given his bulk, coming up on me the first time probably maxed out his step count for the day. My ghostly friend sauntered beside me. "Why didn't you warn me about him?"

"I didn't notice he'd left. Diggs sat at the desk counting dough. He must've had two hundred grand in there. Guess I didn't hear Murphy leave."

My jaw hung open. "Are you kidding me? Didn't hear him leave? The man weighs three hundred pounds. Elephants in the wild would be quieter."

"You could've flirted your way out. Murphy would've gone for that."

"Without hurling? I don't think so. He fell for the sandwich shop scenario. Come on, let's get out of here before Jake sees me." Back inside my SUV, I said, "The car wasn't in the garage. Is there a lot out back?"

He shook his head. "Not for customer cars. If they

stole it, they wouldn't bring it here anyways." Gus sat up straight and opened his mouth to say more then stopped.

"What? What is it? You remember something?" I would nudge him, but he wouldn't feel it. Snapping my fingers before his face, I said, "Gus. Hello?"

Shaking it off, he said, "I know where they took it. You ain't gonna like it."

Chapter 20

My shoulders slumped. "The barn behind your old house. Right?"

"Hey, you're gettin' good at this. Let's go." He pressed his lips together expectantly.

"I don't know, Gus. It's one thing to poke around someplace in town. But out by the bluff? At this time of night? Not a good plan. We'll have to find another way."

He slammed his back against the seat. "There *is* no other way, Marni. Besides, it's the perfect time to go. With Diggs here, we know the place is empty. If we hurry, we can be there and back before they finish. Besides, they'll probably hit the bar afterward. We always did when we…you know…finished a job."

Against my better judgement, I shifted the car into gear and pulled a U-turn. A block after the garage, Jake passed me in his tow truck with his window open. I drove faster.

Once inside the neighborhood near the bluff, I didn't want to risk parking at the house in case Diggs came back early. Using the same tactic, I parked curbside between two houses. These residences were much larger than the neighborhood we'd parked in earlier, but it would have to do. I tucked my purse under the seat, locked the car, and stuck my phone in a back pocket. The chilly ocean air made me glad I'd changed into jeans before leaving the apartment.

The moon shone brightly enough for me to navigate my way without tripping in one of the many potholes plaguing the road leading to the dirt driveway. When I'd gone far enough down the wooded drive and couldn't be seen by neighbors, I switched on my phone's flashlight. My shoulders relaxed when I reached the end and no lights were on in the home or barn. The padlock remained secure on the chain hanging from the double doors. I should have gotten a lock-pick kit. Working my way around the side, I found a window, about two feet above my head. I needed something to stand on. On the back porch, an old metal bucket with more rust than silver showing, sat in the corner. Tetanus, anyone? With the sleeve of my shirt pulled over my hand, I gingerly picked up the pail by its rough handle.

Dead leaves crunched beneath my feet. This place hadn't seen a rake in years and reeked of mulch. I flipped the bucket upside down and stood on tiptoes, shining my light inside. While my perch wasn't high enough to see down to the floor, I did catch the roof of something red sitting inside.

"It's an expensive one all right."

Gus's voice startled me, and I lost my balance as my make-shift step stool toppled over. I landed on my rear with the snap of a branch breaking beneath me. "Ow!" I pulled the sharp stick from under my butt.

"Sorry, Marni. I would've caught you, but…you know. Why didn't you just ask me to zap in there?"

Good question. "After coming all this way, I guess I wanted to see it for myself." Standing up and rubbing my backside, I brushed the dirt and leaves off my pants.

"Do you know if they hide a key around here?"

"Not when I lived here. Jake had the key. Always kept it on him. Like he didn't trust nobody."

"You think maybe because you were all thieves?" We walked toward the back door.

He grinned. "Nah. That couldn't be it."

"Now we've confirmed the car is here, I don't know what else to do. If I go to the police, they'll want to know how I found it." Glancing back at the driveway, the road remained dark. "We better get out of here."

"I wanna see Jake's old bedroom."

"Are you nuts? We've already stayed too long. Last thing I need is Diggs finding me here."

"Marni, I gotta go in there. It'll only take a minute."

I shook my head. "Tell me what you find. I need to leave."

He remained frozen, his eyes wide as saucers. "Two minutes, then we're outta here. Come on. Like you keep saying, maybe I'll remember somethin'."

Placing my hands over my face, I shook my head, knowing I'd regret going inside. The back door opened easily, and the kitchen smelled worse than last time. Adding to the previous stench, bacon grease took a prominent role. With my flashlight app switched on, I stumbled to the living room and down the hall. "Are you sure you want to go in there? It won't look anything like it did when you lived here."

"Open it."

Diggs's bedroom looked nothing like the rest of the house. While everything else smelled musty and had a look of dilapidated disrepair, this master could have been in a respectable home. Well, maybe *respectable* didn't quite categorize the furnishings, but Diggs took care of this space. A dated burgundy shag carpet covered the floor and looked close to clean. The king-sized bed had a massive four-poster frame made from deep, rich wood and a leopard print bedspread. Black satin-covered pillows sat fluffed and stacked. Behind the headboard the wallpaper had a jungle motif, complementing the other three walls painted a creamy ochre color.

Gus turned slowly, taking it all in. "Yeah, this don't look nothin' like when Jake lived here. Those handcuffs definitely weren't here." He pointed to either side of the pillows.

Noticing them for the first time, I tried hard to curb my imagination. No way did I want to picture what the creep played at in here. "That's disgusting."

"Hey, some chicks dig it. Check inside the drawers."

"I'd rather not." I shivered with repulsion at what might be in the nightstands. "Gus, we're not going to find anything useful. Does standing in here help you at all?"

He gazed at the bed. "The covers were blue. Dom slept in the middle, face down. She liked sleeping on her stomach. Her black hair looked all tangled and messy, like she'd just...you know...with him."

My voice quiet, I asked, "Did you walk in on them?"

Going to the back window, he looked out. "No."

"Then how..."

"I came home from my shift. The chain hung unlocked from the barn out back. It was weird 'cause

Jake never left it open. We didn't have no jobs in the past couple weeks, so there'd be no reason to go in there. Then I got mad, thinking he'd pulled a heist without me, and that's why he told me to drive the rig home instead of my car."

Unconsciously, I eased onto the bed, then immediately jumped up. I'd be showering as soon as I got home. "Did you always work the jobs together?"

"Most times. We traded off driving the tow truck and always split things even."

"Was there anything inside the barn?"

He turned and held my gaze. "Dom's car. Now I remember. Her dad's convertible was parked inside, which didn't make sense. She said she didn't want to see me for a while. Wanted a break. I looked at the house and saw Jake through the window and knew she had to be there too." His voice grew louder, anger raced across his face. "I walked to his window and looked inside. He couldn't see me with the light on and his back to me. That's when I saw Dom naked on his bed sleeping. My fist hit the window. I think it cracked. He spun around, then took off into the hallway. I ran inside. Got as far as the living room and took a swing at him. Smashed him in the face."

A car door shut out front. Too late to turn off the light. Maybe Diggs would think he left it on. The master suite ran the width of the house with a window in both back and front. As I bolted into Gus's old bedroom, the front door opened. I'd have a better chance of going unnoticed hiding here in the dark behind the open door. A woman cackled. Genevieve. Did Murphy come with them?

"I got beer in the fridge," Diggs said from the

living room. "You want a cold one?"

"Sure," she slurred. "Let me wrap my warm hands around it." More cackling.

"Yeah, baby. Can't wait for you to wrap your hands around it."

She squealed. Heavy footsteps walked toward the kitchen. No mistaking a woman her size in hooker high heels. They drowned out any noise her companion made. Straining for other voices, I could only detect the pair. As I pressed myself against the wall, thankful the darkness hid whatever I touched, I peered through the crack in the door jamb. Only part of the hallway was visible. Why hadn't I let Gus explore by himself?

Sticking my head out from behind the door, I considered the window as my only escape. If I risked the front, they might see me from the kitchen. Where did Gus go? I needed him to make sure nobody waited outside. "Gus," I whispered. "Gus?" No answer.

Movement in the hall forced me to duck back into my hiding spot. Genevieve came into view wearing a red halter top and skintight black leggings. Did I time travel back to the eighties? Teetering on four-inch heels, she towered over her host. He'd need a step ladder to do what I assumed he had in mind.

Diggs pushed her against the wall, eliciting another high-pitched noise from the woman. He took a swig of beer then grabbed her by the back of the neck and dragged her mouth down to his. Beer dribbled down their chins, while bile rose in my throat. Ewww.

"There's lots more where that came from, baby." He led her beyond my sight.

"You sure Murphy didn't see us leave together?" She clomped down the hall with all the grace of a lumbering bison.

"Relax. He was too busy sniffing around that Cathy broad. A real crime he left you on your own. If you was my woman, I'd always be at your side."

"Really, Diggs? You *are* a prince." A thud landed against the wall next to where I hid. Musky perfume swallowed my sinuses, threating to eliminate any trace of fresh air. "I guess I'm a little tipsy. Maybe I can take off these shoes and get comfortable."

"Don't you worry. I'll get you nice and comfy." Light shone into the hallway when the door opened.

"Ohhhh, Diggs. How beautiful. This is your room?"

"Welcome to my boudoir. And I got a pair of bracelets you're gonna love."

"Jewelry on our first date?" She giggled. Another thud, this time on the floor. "Diggs, I'm so sorry. Let me clean it up."

If he would close the door, I could bolt for freedom and not mess with the window. For all I knew, it hadn't been opened in ages and would make more noise if I had to pry it.

"Don't worry about the beer, baby. You can clean it up later. To make it up to me, you can wear those special bracelets I told you about. And nothing else."

"Hee, hee. You are soooo naughty."

The light partially doused but not completely. A sliver still glimmered on the floor outside my refuge.

"You don't know the half of it. Good thing we don't got neighbors close by 'cause..."

His voice fading spared me from more of their banal conversation. Forget the shower. I'd need an hour-long soak in the tub to remove the grime. "Gus?"

No answer. Risking a look into the hallway, I noted Diggs's door stood ajar. My hand reached for the cell in my back pocket, so I could use the light once outside. It wasn't there. Checking the other side, I remembered setting the phone on the dresser. A vein throbbed in my forehead. I'd have to wait for an opportunity to sneak in and get it or else he'd know for sure I'd been inside. Sinking to the floor, I settled in for a long night. With any luck at all, the walls would be thick enough to dampen their noise.

Gus appeared, sitting on his bed. "What are you doin' there? The coast is clear. You need to scram."

"I left my phone in the bedroom," I whispered. "If we leave it, he'll know someone was here. Go in there, and make sure it's still on the dresser."

His head shot up. "Ain't no way I want to see them rolling around naked. Well, I could stand to take a gander at her. But not Diggs."

He'd suddenly grown a conscience? "Keep your eyes closed. I don't care. We need to know if he noticed it."

"How am I going to look for it if my eyes are closed."

Breathing in deep, I slowly released the air. "Slip in there, don't look at the bed, and see if my phone is on the dresser. You don't need to look around. I'd hate for your delicate sensibilities to get offended."

"Don't talk down to me in your big writer's lingo."

"Gus, I'm sorry. The situation is a tad stressful. It's not every day I might get caught breaking and entering. If you go check, I promise to keep all speech for the next hour down to words of two syllables or less. Deal?"

"All right. I'll go. You really should be more careful with your stuff."

Opening my mouth to fling another snarky remark, instead I said, "Thank you. I will remember that next time we burgle someone's home."

He disappeared for a few moments and came back with his hands over his ears. "It's there. I didn't turn around, but I could hear them. The mattress squeaking, the handcuffs rattling against the headboard. And the moaning. I don't know if it was him or her, but it sounded like…"

I snapped both hands up into the air. "Stop. Just stop. No more details."

"Okay. Maybe you could…"

The strip of light in the hallway grew wider. Light feet padded along, then Diggs called, "I guarantee the second time will be even better with that blindfold on, baby. You just lay there and think about who's your daddy while I get my bag outta the car. Can't believe I forgot it."

"Hurry back! I can't wait to…feel you," Genevieve yelled.

Gus and I looked at each other. Not an ideal situation, but the universe had thrown me a bone. When the front door closed, I tiptoed to the other bedroom. Glancing through the doorway, I looked toward the headboard, hoping to avoid seeing her body from the neck down. With arms spread wide, the woman lay shackled to the bedposts by her wrists. Her head rested on a pillow with a leopard print scarf tied around her eyes. Adding eye bleach to tonight's regimen.

I crept into the room and reached for my phone. The theme from the movie murder scene came out of its speaker. Why would my sister even be up this late, let alone calling me?

"Ohhhh," Genevieve cooed. "What's that kinky music you got there?"

In one fell swoop, I snatched my cell off the surface while hitting the silence button on the side. Slipping behind the door once more, I waited for Diggs to return for his encore performance.

Ten minutes later, he came back. "I told ya, I don't know where Genevieve went. She was there when I left." He stopped talking a few moments. "Maybe Jake gave her a ride home." More silence. "Yeah, Cathy is *hot*." Cackling. "Hey, Murph, how's about when you finish with her, you send her my way?" Snorting. "Okay. I gotta go do something. Catch ya later."

Who needs dating sites? These guys catch a woman then pass her around like a used pair of shoes. While I braced for my bolt to freedom, the light came on. I pressed closer into the wall, fingering the grit. The air now stank of beer and cigarettes. Footsteps went toward the closet, and then, with a soft thud, something landed inside of it. Diggs turned out the light and, I assumed, went back to his entertainment.

"Hey, baby, you miss me?" This time the door slammed shut.

Risking precious minutes, I hurried to find what he'd left. A brown leather satchel sat on a shelf in the far upper corner. Inside I found bundles of cash, ten in all, made up of hundred-dollar bills. My guess would be about fifty thousand dollars. His take of the heist? Before wasting any more time, I hurried out the front door.

Scooting around Diggs's car, my heart pounded as

I half-walked half-ran in the dark to the paved road. When I made it to the residential street without pursuit, my body relaxed. I should have been elated to see my SUV. The police car with flashing lights parked behind it banished my rising mood.

Chapter 21

The officer swung a flashlight back and forth, scanning my car through the windshield. I didn't need to read his name tag this time. "Good evening, Officer Talbott."

He looked up at my approach. "Good evening, Ms. Legend. Lost again?"

"No."

"Visiting someone around here?" He turned the light off and strolled closer.

The lost kitty scenario wouldn't work in this instance either. "Yes, but they weren't answering the door."

Officer Talbott looked the way I'd come. "There's only one house back there owned by Jason Dilboy. He's got a renter staying in it right now. You know his tenant, Ms. Legend?" *The next time I run into him out of uniform, will I be Marni again?*

"Yes. I knocked, but nobody answered." I pulled my phone from my pocket. "Holy cow, look at the time. I didn't realize it had gotten so late."

"Could be why he didn't answer." His face remained a blank slate. "Why did you leave your vehicle here? It's a long walk?"

I looked back at the road I'd come from. "Potholes."

"Potholes?"

"Yeah. The road is chock full of potholes, and I didn't want to damage my car." I smiled.

He examined my SUV. "You've got a pretty high clearance on your vehicle. Probably wouldn't have any problems if you drove slow."

Stepping closer, I put my hand on the door handle. "If there's nothing else, mind if I go?" I scrunched in my shoulders. "The air's a bit chilly, and I forgot a sweater."

The policeman tilted his head and scowled. "Have you been drinking tonight, Ms. Legend?"

His formality made me wish for Kendall's abbreviations. At least then I'd be Ms. L. "Ummm...drinking?" I never knew whether to lie in these instances. It had been a couple of hours.

"Yes. I detect liquor on your breath. Wine?"

"Oh, right. I did have wine with dinner earlier." I nodded. "*Much* earlier."

"Ma'am, I'd like you to take a Field Sobriety Test. You have the right to refuse. However, if you drive away and I feel you're impaired, I can pull you over." His warmth faded faster than the last time we had a roadside chat.

Gus sat on the hood of my car, holding his sides and shaking. I failed to see the humor and glared at him.

"Does the look mean you're refusing?"

"No. No, Officer Talbott. I've never taken one before and don't know what to do."

"Step over by the curb in front of your car."

I did as instructed.

"Now, walking in a straight line, take nine steps putting your heel in front of your toe. Once you've done that, you will turn and repeat the steps back this way. Any questions?"

"Not a one." I performed the dance, adding a curtsy at the end, which didn't elicit so much as a smile from the man. "Did I pass?"

"With flying colors. You're free to go."

Hurrying to my car, I mumbled a good night.

"And Ms. Legend?"

I hesitated, halfway into the driver's seat. "Yes, Officer Talbott?"

"Please don't go for a hat trick in this neighborhood."

"Don't plan on it." I slipped all the way inside and closed the door. Not being much of a sports fan, I still knew the reference. If he caught me out here a third time, he might not be as personable.

****

I slept until eight o'clock. After my nocturnal visit to Diggs's place, I hadn't gotten home until midnight. Before crawling into bed, I stripped off everything I wore and stood under a hot shower for fifteen minutes. The clothes would need to be burned.

As I listened to the voicemail my sister had left the night before, I received a text from Jake. My sister's message simply asked me to call her. Jake's message had a little more meat to it. He'd heard from Murphy I stopped by. Apologizing for not being there, he asked me to meet him for drinks tonight at Ozzie's. So much for my buddy Murph keeping his mouth shut.

I responded with an explanation about how I'd been in the neighborhood and wanted to say hello. No need to apologize. Drinks tonight would be great. A flutter went through me. If I thought I might cool it with

Jake, my body transmitted otherwise. Could this be why I refused Kendall?

Since Gus and I were interrupted the night before, I wanted to hear the rest of what happened between him and his brother. True to form, he'd disappeared after my drunk test and hadn't come back since. Time to bring Darla into the loop of what I'd discovered. With her godson on the force, who also happened to be my new personal escort, maybe she could give me direction.

Before locking the front door, I went back inside and put the letters in my purse. They'd been stowed in my dresser drawer since our lunch, but I needed to come clean with her about knowing of the affair. I don't like having secrets, and this one proved too much of a burden for me.

As I approached Darla's house, a blue two-seater convertible sat in the driveway. Could it belong to her? I hadn't seen what kind of car she drove but expected something more practical. She might have company, and I didn't want to drop in unannounced again. Instead, I went to the ice cream shop Kendall and I missed the other night. Besides treats, they served a delicious Kona coffee.

With a steaming paper cup in hand, I sat at one of the outdoor tables reading emails on my phone. A flash of blue turned the corner across the way. Jason drove the sportster I'd seen at Darla's. Could they have picked up with their affair again? Nobody would be hurt since they'd each lost their spouse. Glad I'd refrained from interrupting.

Not wanting to show up empty-handed, I bought a second coffee and walked to Darla's house. She answered almost immediately, pronouncing my timing to be perfect and admitted the Kona was one of her favorite brews. We went through the kitchen and out onto her patio, which overlooked the bay. Her view beat mine from the apartment. When I grew tired of my tiny space, I might consider a home along this road.

Before I could broach the subject, Darla said, "You just missed Jason."

"Does he stop by often?"

She shook her head. "Once in a great while. My husband and I used to get together with him and his wife, Rose. She and I had been friends since high school. I miss her dearly, sometimes. Such a wonderful person."

I shifted uncomfortably in my lawn chair.

"How goes the investigation?" She sounded almost chipper. Out of character for the woman I'd come to know.

"Things have gotten a bit dicey, and I don't know what to do next." I explained the previous night's escapades, omitting the phone retrieval portion. If she felt my books to be a bit racy, she'd keel over from shock at the visual I'd paint of Diggs's bedroom. Wrapping it up with my running into her favorite officer, I asked, "What should I do about the car theft?"

She removed the lid on her cup and sipped. "You really don't have proof. Other than the stolen car on the property, but how would you explain finding it?"

"I can't, without incriminating myself. At the end of the day, I was trespassing. And if your godson finds me in the area a third time, he's likely to throw me in jail."

"He won't, or he'd have me to reckon with." She

scowled, then chuckled. "You do seem to get yourself into odd situations."

"No doubt. Now I'm in another one."

She shook her head. "You stay out of the car theft thing. Let the authorities handle it. I'm sure they already have an ongoing investigation."

Avoiding her gaze, I plucked up the nerve to confess. "That's not what I meant." I leaned down and pulled the packet of letters from my bag. "That day on Jason's boat, I took these from his nightstand. Genevieve almost caught me snooping, and I had no choice but to slip them into my sack. I read them. I'm sorry."

She took them from my outstretched hand. Tears welled in her eyes.

"I wanted to return them to you when we had lunch, but it didn't seem appropriate in a public place. Please believe me, I felt awful invading your privacy, but I did it hoping to help Gus."

Darla removed the rubber band and leafed through the envelopes.

I mentioned coming earlier and seeing the car in her drive. "When I realized it belonged to Jason, I knew I had to come back and give you those. Guess with both of your partners gone, you deserve to be happy. Please, give me time to resolve the case with Gus. Don't let Jason know I'm on to him. So far, I haven't found him to be involved in the heists."

"Oh, Marni." Tears leaked down her cheeks. She clutched the letters in her hand.

"I'll let myself out. Let me know if you'd like to talk. Or don't want me to come back." Getting up, I went through the house and left. Of all the things in my life I'd regretted, reading her letters ranked among the top five.

Still carrying the paper cup in my hand, I dropped it in a neighbor's trash can as I trudged home. Having surrendered the letters later than planned, I'd probably lost an ally. With her and Jason still in contact, had our alliance been a farce to begin with?

****

After lunch, I returned Gloria's call, but it went to voice mail. "Tag, you're it," I said.

I sent Sylvie a text asking what I could bring for dinner on Saturday. Her response told me dinner would be steak, maybe I should bring a bottle of white wine? Adding her to the family blew in a breath of fresh air. Nobody could accuse her of taking anything too seriously.

When four o'clock rolled around, I stopped working for the day and prepped for drinks with Jake. He wanted to meet at five, so I assumed dinner would ensue. Instead of obsessing over what to wear, I put on the first thing I grabbed from the closet—a yellow summer skirt and white top.

He already sat at the bar with a beer in front of him when I strolled into Ozzie's. Jake kissed me on the cheek and signaled to Derby, who brought a glass of red wine.

"Please tell me you two aren't conspiring, are you?"

"Maybe." Derby dragged out the pronunciation of the word.

Jake lifted his glass in a toast. "To discovering new things."

We clinked glasses, and I sipped an amazing red

blend. "This is delicious. Well done to both of you."

Derby nodded and moved on to his other customers.

"Where did this come from?" I asked.

He grinned. "I asked him for something from Paso Robles, like the other wine you had on the boat. You like it?"

"Love it. How thoughtful of you."

"You're welcome. It's the least I could do. I felt bad not calling you after, well, ya know, you and I…" He looked down. "I got busy with work, and then when you stopped by, I thought I'd dropped the ball and you were mad." Quite an unexpected reaction from such a player.

"Not at all. I happened to be in the neighborhood and noticed your garage. Thought I'd take a chance you'd be there. I much prefer this setting, anyway."

He laughed. "Me too. Guess I felt a little…threatened when the other guy turned up. He's the one who sent you flowers, isn't he?"

So much for an enjoyable, stress-free evening. "Yes."

"So, are you and he…ya know…" He sipped his beer. I didn't expect the tension in his jaw and yearning in his gaze. Could this man be expressing a true feeling?

"I don't know. That's an honest answer. He and I had been high school sweethearts. College got in the way, and life took us in different directions. Now we live in the same town again. And so do you. Still want to see me, or would you rather cut your losses?" Don't know where I got the courage to pull those lines from, but after dealing Darla a low blow, I wanted no dishonesty with Jake. Other than investigating him and his friends for thievery. And talking to his dead brother.

"Fancy meeting you two here." We turned and found Jason standing behind us.

"Hey, man," Jake said. "Wanna join us for a drink?"

"As much as I'd love to, business calls. I just wanted to come over and say hello." He took my hand and kissed the back. "Marni, a pleasure as always. I hear you and I have another friend in common. Darla Billingsly. Lovely lady; known her for years."

No response came to me. Trying to sneak around and be discreet, my secrets flowed from another's lips. Mustering a voice, I said, "Yes. We've met recently and hit it off."

He nodded and put a hand on Jake's shoulder. "Jake, you treat this woman right. She's a gem."

"Don't I know it." He gazed at me. "Don't I know it."

Those butterflies kicked it up a notch and went into overtime bouncing around my tummy.

"See you around, kids. Maybe another boating expedition soon, eh?" He walked away without waiting for an answer.

Jake picked up the hand Jason had held. "In answer to your question"—he kissed the back as well—"I think I'll stick around. If that's okay with you?"

I leaned in and kissed his lips. Drinks led to dinner, and dinner led to another night in the sack at my place. This time, sans my mother.

When he left for work, I toyed with the idea of canceling dinner with Kendall. I didn't have it in me to juggle two men. And the man I wanted came in the form of a possible felon owning a towing company and garage. This wouldn't end well. I didn't care.

****

Gus came to visit Friday morning, right after Kendall sent a text canceling our date. Something about having to head out of town for the weekend. Would it be heartless to say I wasn't disappointed?

I sipped my coffee. "Are you going to finish what happened when you confronted Jake?"

"No." He slouched in the chair across from me.

"What do you mean *no*?"

He shook his clenched fists. "I don't know how to explain it. When we heard the car door shut at Diggs's place, my brain shut off. I knew what happened, and then I didn't. Does that make any sense?"

"In my world? Yes." At least we got farther than Dom sleeping in Jake's bed. They had a confrontation. Could it have been the final straw when Gus's life ended?

I sent Darla a text asking if she'd like to meet me for lunch. She didn't answer. Who could blame her for being angry? After invading her privacy and withholding personal belongings, why would she want to see me again?

Chapter 22

Dinner at Calvin's and Sylvie's loomed before me like a storm cloud. I expected Gloria to be in fighting form. While I backed my brother one-hundred percent, his actions surprised me.

When Sylvie answered the door, I handed her a bottle of chardonnay and a box of rum balls. Gloria and her husband hadn't shown yet.

I cornered my brother at the barbecue. "You want to explain?"

He didn't bother feigning ignorance. "When Gloria arrives, it'll be confession time. Okay?" He flipped the ribeye steaks on the grill. "Until then, why don't you help Sylvie with the girl stuff."

My brows arched.

He sipped his beer. "You know, salad, condiments? Girl stuff."

"Got it." No chauvinism there. His fiancée had everything handled, so I poured myself a drink and settled into a lawn chair waiting for the fireworks to begin. My sister came outside with a glass already in her hand. I stifled a laugh seeing she drank the chardonnay I'd brought. She must really be pissed ignoring her red meat beverage etiquette. I blew air kisses her way. "The boys joining us?"

"No." Her voice seethed with controlled anger.

Sylvie sat next to me. "What a nice afternoon. How

have the two of you been?"

"Fine." Gloria sipped from her glass. Why do people use the word *fine* when they really aren't?

"I've been busy on my next book. My deadline is approaching at warp speed."

"I don't know how you keep coming up with new ideas," Sylvie said. "In high school, I couldn't even write a good short story."

"My inspiration comes from many places. The slightest notion can set off a whole tale. Like the other day, when I visited a friend's mother. She had a picture of herself and her husband at Coney Island in the early sixties. Could be a great era for my next book. Of course, she'd asked if she would get credit and royalties."

Sylvie studied me a moment. "Who is this man in your life? If you're already meeting his mother, it must be serious."

How can she not be psychic? I leaned back against the headrest. "What makes you think the friend's a man?"

"Notion confirmed." She smiled impishly.

Gotta work on my poker face. My brother waved his finger in a circle, signaling the steaks were cooked. Once we'd all filled our plates and took seats at the picnic table, the only sounds were cutlery scraping on china.

Midway through the meal, Gloria rested her fork on the edge of her plate. "You had to go behind my back, didn't you?" She glared at me.

I bolted upright. "Me? What are you talking about?"

"Calvin never would have done this on his own.

Would you?" She cast her eyes his way.

"No. No, I wouldn't." Did he smirk?

Sylvie pressed her lips together. I stopped eating. Gloria swung her gaze back to me. The inferno blazing behind her retinas could've incinerated half the neighborhood.

Gripping my fork like a weapon in case of a frontal assault, I waited for Calvin to intervene. He didn't. "Are you going to step in, Cal, or are you waiting until there's gun play?"

"I can't keep a straight face any longer." He looked at our sister. "Marni had nothing to do with it. But I didn't act alone."

Gloria slammed her hand on the table. "Dragging Sylvie into this is inappropriate. How can you be so smug? We were supposed to agree before taking any action."

Robert wrapped an arm around his wife and squeezed. "Calm down, honey. Let him explain."

"You know we were never going to agree," I said. "But I won't lie. I'd gone to Roseview to authorize the exhumation myself, except it had already been done. What gives, Cal? Why did you do it?"

"Because I told him to." Mom stood behind my sister.

"You told him to?" I placed both hands flat on the table.

My sister jolted up in her seat. "I did *not* tell him to sign the papers. Why would you think that?"

"Not you, Gloria. Mom."

She swiveled her head around. "Is she here?"

"Behind you." I pointed over her head.

"It's true," Calvin said. "Mom, you want me to fill

them in?"

"No, let's wait for the brawl to start," she snapped. "Of course, I want you to tell them what I said."

"Mom knew we would continue arguing, and Marni would eventually do what she thought best. And Gloria would do what she felt to be right. In the end, my signing kept both of you from giving in or making the decision. This was her way of neutralizing the situation."

Didn't see that one coming. "Mom, why didn't you tell us you'd changed your mind about the exhumation?"

"It wouldn't have mattered. What matters is you and Gloria are sisters and need to quit bickering over everything. You've turned it into an Olympic sport. Besides, I'm not gonna be around forever." One could only hope.

"Does this mean you're free and will move on?" I crossed my fingers.

"Nah." She swatted the air. "I got too much to do still."

"What did she say?" Gloria asked.

I gulped my drink. "She's not leaving."

"No," Gloria said. "About changing her mind."

Calvin answered. "Mom wants you two to stop fighting. And until you do, she won't leave."

My hand shot out. "Truce?"

Gloria looked at me with knitted brows. Picking up her fork, she stabbed a piece of meat.

Withdrawing my hand, I did the same. Swallowing a bite, I said, "Ma, you've got nothing left to resolve. Gloria and I will play nice, so you can move into the light."

"What are you talking about? There is no light. All that stuff is a bunch of horse hockey." Mom reclined in one of the loungers.

Calvin said, "Mom, Marni's right. We'll handle things from here. You need to go."

She crossed her arms. "I'm staying."

Holy mother of God. Saint Peter has *got* to have a price. Whatever it is, I'll do it—short of murder. I'd get haunted. "Gloria, you and me, lunch Monday at the Northport Café. What do you say?"

She set her jaw and squared her shoulders. Robert put his hand on her arm and squeezed. Gloria said, "Does one work for you?"

"Perfect. Mom, we've reached our first agreement. Adios time." I looked her way. The lounger sat empty. Had she really left, or would I find her at my kitchen table again?

"I didn't hear an answer," Calvin said.

"Because she disappeared."

"For good?" Gloria asked.

"Jury's out on that one. We'll see," I said.

The air thinned as tension eased. Nobody mentioned anything more about papers, exhumations, or Mom.

****

On my drive home, I received a text from Jake inviting me out for a nightcap. Parking the car in front of my building, I walked to The Corner Bar. The clientele had a rough edge to it, not my usual haunt. I kept an open mind.

Jake signaled me from the back of the bar, where he stood with a pool cue in his hand. As I wove through the crowd across the sticky wooden floor, hard rock blared from the speakers at ear-bleeding volume. Jake leaned over and smacked the cue ball against a stripe, which went into a corner pocket. He banked his next shot, sinking another, and his final hit sank the eight ball.

"Pay up, Murph!"

"Yeah, yeah." Murphy slapped a bill into Jake's palm.

By this time, I'd worked my way around the table. "This place is busy. I don't usually come here on a weekend. Thanks for the invite."

We kissed, then he hung his cue stick in a rack on the wall. "What'cha drinking?"

"Bourbon and diet, please." I spoke into his ear, trying to be heard over the music.

"Got it. Wait here with Murphy and Diggs. You remember Genevieve from the boat, right?" He winked.

"How could I forget?" I tried to banish the vision of her blindfolded and handcuffed to Diggs's bed. Some things you can never un-see. Jake needed a better class of friends. He waved to the bartender as he struggled through bodies to get closer. I exchanged pleasantries with Genevieve, which consisted of us yelling "hi." The blare of a lead guitar made speech impossible unless you could lip read.

Jake returned with my drink and a beer for himself. The music switched to a jazzy song; the mellower tune made it easier to talk. "How was dinner at your brother's?" he asked.

"The usual circus."

His snort made me believe he understood the complications of family.

"You gonna give me a chance to win back my

twenty?" Murphy brushed against me as he stepped closer to speak with Jake. His idea of aftershave must've been inspired by a gasoline commercial.

I searched my purse for a match.

"Why don't we play doubles? Me and Marni against you and Genevieve." He threw an arm around my shoulders.

Murphy laughed. "You're on! Hope you didn't spend that cash already." To his date he yelled, "Babe, get off your ass and grab a stick. We're playing these clowns." His thumb jerked in our direction.

Jake hugged me close. "You can play, right?"

During my last attempt at this game, I banged a guy in the crotch with my pool stick, then launched the white ball across the bar. It nearly took out our waitress carrying a full tray of drinks. "Like a pro."

"That's my girl. I knew we could take 'em."

Take them where? I wanted to have one drink and escape this crew. Selecting a stick from the rack, I rubbed the tip with a cube of blue chalk. No idea what this did for my game, but I'd take any help.

"You wanna break?" Jake asked me.

"Why don't you take care of the first shot." I stepped away and planted the back end of my cue firmly on the floor.

He knocked in two stripes and a solid. Calling stripes, he aimed for another and missed. Murphy took his turn, and we continued in a round-robin. Genevieve played a respectable game and contributed to her team, her cleavage nearly spilling out of her skimpy top as she leaned over. My only achievement sank the white ball on my first shot. The game continued until it came down to one solid and the eight ball on the table. And it was my turn.

Downing the rest of my drink, I set up for the shot. As I bit my lip and took aim, Murphy sauntered over to the table and stood opposite me.

"You're never gonna make this, doll. Don't embarrass yourself. Give up, and I'll buy you a drink with my winnings," he smirked.

"Don't listen to him, Marni. You got this," Jake countered. "Wanna double the bet, Murph?"

No pressure.

"You're on!" He leaned on the edge of the table with one hand, holding a fresh drink in the other.

As I pulled back the stick, Genevieve squealed like she'd gotten her finger caught in a vise. Slamming the white ball, I propelled it across the table and over the edge, hitting Murphy square in the nuts. As a bonus, his drink spilled down the front of his shirt. Worth losing the forty bucks in my book. Would it be in poor taste to take a selfie with him bending over holding his privates?

While the large man cussed a blue streak, the surrounding patrons roared with laughter. I would have apologized, but he wouldn't have heard me over the noise.

Jake whispered in my ear. "Nice shot, babe."

"Thank you. Maybe we should take this as our *cue* to leave."

Laughing, he took forty dollars from his pocket and set it in front of Murphy. Patting him on the shoulder, Jake said, "Nice game, Murph. Let's do it again real soon."

"Get that bitch away from me," he sputtered. "She's crazy!"

Anger flashed across my partner's face. He opened his mouth in what would surely be a protest.

Tugging at his arm, I said, "It's okay. I've been called worse. And probably deserved it."

His good humor returned, and he nodded his head. "That was a damn good shot."

"I doubt Murphy would agree."

He maneuvered us through the bar, dodging drunks along the way. The fresh air outside did nothing to erase the stench of cigarette smoke on my clothes. Strolling hand in hand, Jake led us onto the pier, our footsteps echoing across the water. From behind came heavy footfalls on the boards, and we turned. Diggs hung onto Genevieve's arm as she stumbled along. Three-inch heels in her inebriated condition probably weren't the best footwear, coupled with her teetering close to the edge.

"Hey, guys, wait up," Diggs called. "We're comin' with ya."

"Yeah, wait up," Genevieve slurred.

Swell. The gang's all here. What's next? Bonding over stolen hubcaps? We stopped walking while they staggered along.

"Murphy coming too?" Jake asked.

Diggs snorted. "Nah. He's too busy holding his balls. That was freakin' hilarious!"

"You should apologize, Marni. He's really mad," Genevieve said, then burst out laughing, ending in a hiccup. "Guess he won't be using those for a while." More squeals.

I feared my eyeballs would burst if she shrieked again. "Maybe we should call it a night, Jake."

"So early? But I got a surprise for you."

Tell me we're not partner swapping. "A surprise?"

He tugged my hand. "This way." At the end of the of the dock, *Dominique's Dream* bobbed and tugged against its tethers. "Jason invited us for a night cruise. You game?"

"Ah…sure. But I didn't bring a jacket. It'll be chilly on the water. Maybe I could run home and grab one quick." What I really needed to do was text Darla. She may be angry with me, but someone needed to know I was setting off to sea again with Jason and his merry band of car thieves.

"No need. I got a coupla sweatshirts in my truck, and it's closer. You go on board." Without waiting for a reply, he hurried away.

Diggs went past me with his drunk lady friend in tow. He'd have his hands full trying to get her onto the boat without landing them both in the water. This gave me the chance to send a quick text. Darla would be in bed by this time, but she'd see it in the morning. My fingers flew across the screen, hit send, then I tucked the cell back in my purse.

Jason watched me from the stern, a sly grin on his face. Looking over his shoulder toward the hatchway, he called, "Costas, come help Genevieve on board before she ends up going for an evening swim."

The deckhand appeared from below and moved to where Diggs attempted to get Genevieve onto the ship, while she giggled nonstop. She outweighed Diggs by at least fifty pounds, so his trying to ease her onto the deck failed miserably. Costas reached them in time to catch her from falling to her knees as she dragged Diggs down with her. The scrawny man hit the floor, causing her to cackle even louder. Hanging out with this crowd made my family get-togethers appear tame.

"Perhaps coffee would be in order," Jason said to his drunken guest.

"Coffee? Don't you got any gin?" Genevieve asked.

Recovered from his spill, Diggs tucked up under her arm and said, "Don't worry, babe. He was kidding. Let's get you another drink." He led her through the open hatch.

Jason held out a hand. "Won't you join us, Marni?"

I accepted his assistance and stepped onto the deck, glad to land with more grace than the other two. "Thank you. What a nice surprise. I can't remember the last time I went out on the water at night."

"Glad you could make it. Where did Jake go off to?" He eyed the empty pier.

"He ran back to his truck to get sweatshirts for us, since I didn't come prepared to be out in the chilly air tonight. Shouldn't take him long."

Jason gestured toward the interior. "Then let's keep you warm. I've got a lovely bottle of red open. Why don't we retire to the salon with the rest and get you a pour?"

Down the steps and into the brightly lit seating area, my feet froze to the floor. Darla sat on one of the couches. She lifted her wine glass in the air acknowledging me. Fear coursed up and down my spine. With my safety buddy on the guest list, this might end up being my final cruise.

Chapter 23

"Is something wrong, dear?" Jason asked from behind me.

I stepped aside from where I blocked the doorway. "Not at all. Adjusting my eyes after being outside in the dark."

"I believe you know our other shipmate."

"Yes. Hello, Darla. This night is full of surprises." I trotted out my fake smile. It would get quite a workout tonight.

She stood. "It's good to see you again, Marni. I've been meaning to call you for lunch. Would one day next week work for you?"

"Of…of course. Any day except Monday. My sister and I are getting together. We're going to hash things out and try to abstain from swapping blows. We'll be at the Northport Café if you want a ringside seat."

"I'm not a sports fan, thanks. How does Wednesday sound? Same place?" she asked.

"It's a date." I crossed my fingers and hoped I'd be around come mid-week.

"Look who I convinced to join us," Jake said from the hatchway.

Murphy sauntered in, scowled at me, then went to the galley and took a beer from the refrigerator. He walked upright but couldn't hide a slight limp. "What,

Genevieve and Diggs ditch us?"

"Miss Genevieve wanted to lie down for a few minutes." Costas pointed toward the hallway.

Passed out would be closer to the truth. Diggs must've decided to tuck her in. If Murphy walked in on them, things could get ugly.

"Jason, I'd love a glass of the wine you offered," I said.

"Coming right up. Costas, pour Marni a glass of the cabernet." He sat beside Darla on the couch and retrieved his martini from the coffee table. "Jake, what would you like?"

"I'll grab a brew." He tossed the sweatshirts onto an empty chair. "Marni, help yourself to either one of those if you get cold. They'll be big but will keep you warm enough." Jake got a bottle, and we eased onto a couch across from the other two. He moved his lips closer to my ear and whispered, "Or I can keep you warm."

Darla raised an eyebrow at me, and I gave a small shrug.

After handing me a glass, Costas asked, "Boss, should I get us underway?"

"Everyone's on board. Let's go." Raising his glass, Jason toasted. "Here's to an evening cruise with good friends."

We motored through the harbor at a low speed. Once past the breakwater, Costas opened up the engine, and we sliced through the waves at a faster clip.

"Jason, what's our destination tonight?" I asked.

"We're heading out into the sound, then will anchor. With no cloud cover, it'll be a beautiful night to view the stars."

245

I sipped my wine. "Sounds wonderful. Darla, have you been out on *Dominique's Dream* before?"

"No, this is my first time. When Jason came over the other day for coffee, he suggested I join in the fun. I had no idea you'd be on board as well." She pressed her lips together for only a second, then broke into a smile again.

Her expression did nothing to ease my mind. Was she confused by my presence or conveying a warning?

Murphy stood in the galley popping cooked shrimp into his mouth. "Hey, this stuff is great."

Jason narrowed his eyes. "Murphy, we'll be setting out a late supper, and you're single-handedly devouring the appetizer. Perhaps you might wait until we anchor, and everyone can enjoy it."

The large man stopped mid-bite, with half a shrimp hanging from his lips. "Oh, sorry, boss. I didn't know." Sucking it in like a piece of spaghetti, he swallowed then stuck the bowl in the refrigerator. "Maybe I'll go check on Genevieve." He lumbered down the hall, only to return a few moments later.

"Everything okay with her?" Jason asked.

Murphy chuckled. "Yeah, she and Diggs is passed out on the bed."

Fully clothed, I hoped, and without special bracelets. Surely Murphy would have blown a gasket, had they been found otherwise. He drained his beer and took another, then sat at the dinette facing the rest of us.

Jason described a meteor shower he'd witnessed last year while out at night. I tried to follow the conversation, but my head grew fuzzy, and the room spun. His voice drifted away, and next thing I knew, someone called my name. Loudly.

"Marni. Marni! Wake up. You gotta wake up."

My lids weighed like anvils as I forced them open. A pair of hands crisscrossed in front of my face, blurry at first, but then my focus sharpened. I dragged the back of my hand across my mouth, removing drool from the corner. Who fed me cotton balls? Clearing my throat, the action turned into a dry cough. "Gus, what's going on?"

"You gotta get outta here. I heard Murphy telling Jason about you getting 'mouthy' and asking questions about jobs. He also told him he saw you talkin' to a cop."

Pushing myself into a sitting position, my vision swirled. A sweatshirt fell off my shoulders and onto the floor. I couldn't tell if I needed to throw up or drink something. The half glass of wine sat on the table before me. Not what I wanted. "What did Jason say?"

Gus looked around, as if someone might overhear him. "He told Murphy to take care of it. You'd become a liability, and it was his responsibility. Marni, you gotta get off the boat."

"In case you hadn't noticed, we're not near land, unless we docked while I slept. Do you know where we are?"

He sat next to me. "Somewhere in the Long Island Sound."

"That rules out bolting for the dock. How long have I been asleep?"

"Dunno. I got here a while ago and heard them talking. Must've been trying to wake you up for an hour. You drink too much?"

"No, I did not. Last thing I remember was sipping wine and sitting next to your brother." My gaze shot to his face. "Did Jake hear what they said? Is he in on it too?"

Gus shook his head. "He and Diggs are hanging out on the loungers in front. Jason and Murphy were in the cockpit."

"Tell me exactly what you heard."

"When I first got there, Jason said, 'She's gotten entirely too nosey about our affairs.' Then Murph said, 'Yeah, she's gotten mouthy too.' "

"They said *she*? Did either one say my name?"

"Nah. Who else would they be talkin' about? You are pretty nosey."

"Wait." I bolted up, then slid back onto the cushion. Big mistake. Holding my forehead, I asked, "Where's Darla?"

"Mrs. Billingsly? Why would she be here?"

"Jason invited her. She was onboard when I arrived. In fact, she said this was the first time she'd been on the boat. Could they have been talking about her?" Panic set in as I gripped the edge of the couch, fearing more for Darla than myself. I might have a fighting shot but a frail old woman like her? Not a chance. Gently pushing myself up, I took a tentative step and a deep breath. My head began to clear, so I hobbled to the galley for a bottle of water. The cool liquid flowed down my throat helping to center my sense of balance.

Footsteps sounded on the stairs leading from the cockpit. "There you are, Marni. I thought we'd lost you for the night." Jason rubbed my arm. "Feeling better after your nap?"

The bottle crinkled under my grip. I forced my hand to relax and ease the hold. "Yes, thank you."

Murphy pushed past him, nudging my other arm. "What's wrong? Can't hold your liquor?" He roared louder than necessary and continued out the rear hatchway. A couple moments later I heard the engine on the small skiff ignite.

I grinned at Jason. "I didn't realize how tired I'd become. Where's Darla?"

"She took a cue from you and wanted a catnap herself before supper. I don't imagine she's used to staying up this late. May I pour you more wine?"

The wine. "No. Thank you. I'll stick with water for now. Wouldn't want to fall asleep during dinner." I forced a grin. "Are we eating soon? I could go wake her. Which cabin is she in?"

"No need to bother yourself. Why don't you join Jake on the bow? I'm sure he's tired of Diggs keeping him company." The only way to the loungers on the front would be via the stern.

If I didn't go, Jason would get suspicious. "Maybe I had better put on something warm first. I'm sure the air temperature has dropped quite a few degrees by now."

He studied me a beat too long, fraying my nerves.

Walking to the couch I'd slept on I scooped the sweatshirt from the floor and pretended to fumble with the zipper. Footsteps behind me moved along the hallway where the cabins were located. Sneaking a glance, I caught sight of Jason as he entered the one on the left. As soon as the door closed, I flew back to the galley. Furiously pulling open drawers and cabinets, I rifled through the contents.

"What are you looking for?" Gus leaned on the other side of the counter.

Shifting my eyes toward the hallway, I whispered, "Anything I can use as a weapon. Short of beating someone with a frying pan, there isn't anything here."

"What about the knives." He pointed behind me.

"What?" A wooden block with four large handles and eight smaller ones sticking out sat on the counter.

"You really suck at this, you know that?"

I snorted. "Don't remind me. Where can I hide one of those short ones?" I patted my pockets. There wasn't one large enough to conceal even the smallest blade.

"Put it in your sock," he said.

"Are you kidding me? I'll stab myself in the foot." Continuing to search my clothing, I realized it would be the only place feasible. Pulling one from the block, I carefully slipped the blade inside my sock and down into my shoe. Fixing my pants leg over it, I stood. The denim should be thick enough to hide the bulge, especially if we were outside in the dark, providing I could reach it in time if needed.

"Marni, I thought you'd gone outside." Jason stood at the corner of the galley.

Scanning the kitchen, I said, "Just wanted to grab my water bottle, but I don't remember where I set it down." How long had he been watching me?

He pointed to the coffee table near where I'd picked up the sweatshirt.

Smacking my forehead with my palm, I said, "For heaven's sake. How could I have missed it?"

"You sure you're all right, Marni?" Jason narrowed his eyes.

"Fine. Why?" I took my water and went up through the rear hatchway. As my vision adjusted to the darkness, I found myself alone. Wherever Murphy went to, he hadn't returned yet. "Gus?" I whispered.

He appeared, sitting on the back rail of the boat. "Over here."

"Do you think he saw me?"

He shrugged. "How should I know? You didn't ask me to stand lookout."

I tiptoed to where he sat. "And you say I need to get better at this. Where's Murphy? I heard a motor start after he left." I scanned the ocean. Nothing resembled a large, badly dressed man in a dinghy.

"Who knows? I thought you said Mrs. Billingsly was on board."

"She was when we started. Didn't you hear Jason say she took a nap in one of the cabins? He even went to her cabin as if to wake her. I hope she's okay."

"They had a thing going. Why would he hurt her? I still think it was you they talked about." He peered through the darkness toward the front. "Maybe you should stick with my brother. He can be a jerk, but he'd never hurt a woman."

I maneuvered onto the side of the boat and made my way to the bow. Cigarette smoke cut through the fresh sea air.

"Hey, sleeping beauty. You sure crashed fast," Jake said.

"Don't know what happened. Must've hit my wall." I tucked a stray hair behind my ear.

He moved his legs aside and gestured for me to sit. I cuddled up as the warmth of his arms encircled me. "I know it's later than you'd planned to stay out, but how can you beat this view?" His arm swept across the sky.

The stars were brilliant. This night would've been perfect had Gus's words not echoed through my mind, saying how Murphy needed to *take care of me*. I shifted my leg so as not to jar the hidden weapon and sever an artery.

"You warm enough? You're shaking," Jake murmured into my ear.

"I'm good. Maybe food will help."

Diggs tossed his cigarette into the water and stood. "I'll leave you two lovebirds alone. No rocking the boat now." He gave a guttural guffaw at his own joke as he scooted toward the stern. "Don't rock the boat. I crack myself up."

"Is he having a conversation with himself?" I asked once Diggs moved out of earshot.

"I don't think he ever gave up his imaginary friend from childhood. He was always a weird kid." Jake shook his head.

"Still is." We laughed as I snugged my head underneath his chin.

Sitting this way with Jake, feeling protected in his embrace, made me discount Gus's warning. Jake's hand cupped my face and tilted it upward as he gently kissed me. My body stirred, and I wished we had the boat to ourselves. Away from the other passengers, it felt as if we did. Almost.

"Ewwww. I said hang with my brother, not molest each other. Do you have to do that in front of me?" Gus lounged on the other chair, both arms and legs crossed.

Should we pull up another chair in case my mother showed and wanted to get in on the act too? With a sigh, I pulled away from Jake and tucked my body against his chest. "It's a bit chilly out here, even with a jacket." From this position I glared at Gus, who smiled back. Asshole.

Jake tightened his grip as he massaged my arms, creating heat. "You want to go in? Dinner should be ready soon anyway."

"Probably a good idea. I love being out here with you, but it's too cold for me. You mind?" I looked up at him.

"Whatever makes you happy." He kissed me again, then led me by the hand along the side rail.

In the salon, the kitchen counter lay filled with plates of lobster tails, little neck clams, mussels, and shrimp. Condiment dishes containing melted butter, cocktail sauce, and tartar sauce were set out too. Raw oysters had been shucked and served with a mix of tartar sauce and horseradish.

Jason offered beverages, but I declined and stuck with water. I had my suspicions about why I crashed so quickly.

Diggs already had a plate filled and sat at the dinette with a beer.

"Is Darla joining us?" The tension in my shoulders returned upon finding her absent.

"She begged off. The late hour was too much for her," Jason said. "I promised to save her a lobster tail and steamed clams. Please, help yourselves."

My appetite disappeared along with my comfort. "Why don't I go check on her, to make sure she's okay." I moved to walk down the hall, but Jason stepped in front of me.

"No need. As I said, she wanted to sleep. It's best if we let her do so." He gestured for me to get food. "You're worrying like a mother hen. Do you fear something is wrong?"

I smiled and shook my head. Admitting defeat, I

picked up a plate and sampled the seafood. As Jake and I settled onto a couch, we heard a motor approaching. It pulled up to the boat and stopped. I crinkled my brow at Jake.

Jason took notice and said, "That would be Murphy. I sent him on an errand to handle something that came up while you slept. Not to worry. We aren't being boarded by pirates." Everyone wore an amused expression but me.

Coming through the doorway, Murphy had a scratch on his cheek leaking blood. Even from ten feet away, he reeked of perspiration. Jason touched his own cheek, as he caught the big man's eye. Without stopping, Murphy went straight through the salon, and a door opened and closed near the front.

My eyes wide, I watched after him. It occurred to me we were missing another guest. "Will Genevieve be eating with us?"

Diggs answered. "Nah, she didn't want to eat. Surprised the hell outta me; she's always up for a meal." He howled at his own joke. Sadly, his humor appealed to an audience of one.

"Shut the hell up, Diggs." Murphy lumbered back into the room, the blood from the scratch cleaned away.

"I was just sayin'—"

"Well don't!" Murphy grabbed a plate and threw three lobster tails and a hand full of shrimp onto it, then dumped cocktail sauce over the shrimp. Snatching a fork off the counter, he sank into the seat across from Diggs.

"We have napkins, Murphy." Jason indicated a stack of folded cloth on the counter.

"I don't need one." He shoveled food into his

mouth. "This tastes really good."

The women on this crew didn't make the grade at keeping such late hours. What else had I missed while asleep? I picked at my food, making a half-hearted attempt to swallow. Even the aroma of garlic sauce on the clams couldn't entice me to eat.

"Not hungry, babe?" Jake asked.

"Guess not. It all tastes delicious, but I'm not used to eating so late." I placed my fork on my plate and set it on the table. "Jason, what time are we returning to shore?"

"Tired of our company already?" he joked.

"It's not the company. You know that." I amped up my charm and showed my pearly whites. "Despite my nap, I'm still a bit tired. You understand."

"Of course, my dear. Unfortunately, we'd planned to stay a few more hours. If you're anxious to get back to dry land, I could have Murphy shuttle you over in the dinghy."

Like that was an option. "I don't want to be a bother. I'll tough it out."

Chapter 24

While the meal got cleaned up, Jake and I retired to the cockpit. To my relief, the rest of our shipmates remained below or on the bow. My edginess subsided once we were cocooned alone under the expanse of stars. Beneath a blanket, he and I generated heat of our own.

Gus showed up when Jake went downstairs for another beer. "This is how you're preparing for an attack? Interesting strategy."

"I'm making the most of the situation. What else can I do?" I pulled the blanket around me and leaned over to retrieve the blade. "I better get rid of this before your brother finds it. Where's a good hiding place?"

Gus swiveled his head. "Tuck it behind the seat cushion."

I did as he suggested, then pulled my knees up to my chest for warmth and secured the cover around me. The ocean air gave the fabric a damp, mildewy smell. "Have you seen Darla or Genevieve? I'm concerned neither one has made an appearance since we arrived. Maybe you could…" Noise from the stairs forced me to stop.

When Murphy came up, I wished I hadn't been so quick to ditch the knife. Maybe I could snatch it from behind the cushion if needed? "Where's Jake?" I asked.

"He'll be up in a minute. Him and Jason are having

a conversation. I thought I'd keep you company until he got back." The cushion burped as he sank down beside me. His stench worsened with the proximity.

I held the edge of the blanket over my nose and mouth to block the putrid smell. "Really, that's not necessary. I'm fine by myself."

"I wanted to say there's no hard feelings about what happened at the bar. With your terrible aim, it had to've been an accident." He grimaced.

I played along. "I did mean to apologize. Thanks for understanding." My body scrunched farther into the corner of the seat, gaining a few inches.

"Maybe you could buy me a drink sometime to make up for it." He ran a finger up and down the blanket covering my arm.

Even with the extra layer of fabric between my skin and his touch, my body shook with revulsion.

"You cold? I could warm you up, you know. Nobody would have to know." Murphy slid closer.

I'd run out of bench and couldn't move farther away. "Thanks for your concern, Murph, but I'm good. Jake should be back any time. You don't need to babysit me."

Gus snickered from the driver's seat.

"Hey, I coulda sworn I heard you talking to somebody when I first came up here. You get a phone call or something?"

"She talks to herself sometimes." Jake motioned for Murphy to move over.

I opened my mouth to give an excuse, but Jake put something sweet into it before I could speak. It tasted of minty chocolate and almonds. "Mmmm, what is this?"

"Dessert. Jason put out a bunch of truffles.

257

Thought you might like one." He glanced over his shoulder and back. "What were you and Murph talking about?"

A grin cracked across Murphy's face as if daring me to squeal on him.

"The weather." I snuggled closer to Jake.

The boat jerked as the engine started. I hadn't noticed Costas climb into the driver's seat or Gus's disappearance, but my ghostly friend had vanished We were finally headed for shore, and I prayed there wouldn't be any unscheduled stops along the way.

On our approach to the pier, Jake and I sat in the salon, having abandoned the cold outside when the breeze increased with speed. Murphy followed us as far as the beer stash, then went topside again. Retrieving my purse, I made a renewed effort to see Darla. "We can walk Darla home, Jason. It's not far out of our way."

"Not necessary. She'll sleep here tonight, and I will escort her in the morning. You kids run along to bed." Jason winked. He stationed himself in the hallway blocking access to the forward cabins.

Kissing him on the cheek, I thanked him for the ride and dinner. Jake helped me onto the dock, and I thanked the gods I'd made it back to solid ground unharmed. If he weren't with me, I would have bent down and kissed the boardwalk. We were the only ones to leave the ship, except for Gus, of course. He trailed behind us whistling as if we'd never been concerned about my safety.

At my apartment, Jake followed me inside.

"Where have you been, young lady?" My mother stood in the entry, arms crossed with a scowl on her face. She and Murphy should exchange techniques. While his looked meaner, she had a stronger set to the jaw.

"Hey, Mrs. Legend, good to see you again." Gus waved and went into the kitchen. When did they become buddies?

Strong arms slid around my waist from behind, and lips caressed my neck. Unlike our large shipmate, Jake's aroma had a clean, fresh scent. Closing my eyes, I enjoyed his closeness for a moment.

"Marni, don't ignore your mother," Mom spouted.

My eyes shot open. *Moment's gone*. I pulled out of his embrace and turned, noticing Gus holding his sides pretending to belly laugh. "I really want you to stay, but I am exhausted. Can we do this another time, Jake?" My libido pulsed, voicing its indignation at being denied.

He pulled me in and planted his lips firmly on mine, his tongue searching for an opening.

Putting my hands to his chest, I gently pushed away. "Tonight was a great surprise, but I need sleep. And I know if you stay, I won't get any. Please go."

With a hand, he cupped my face, gave me one more quick peck, then said, "Okay. Another time. I'm holding you to it."

"Thank you."

"Good night, babe. Get some rest." He opened the door then glanced back over his shoulder. "You'll need it for the next time I come over. We'll be up late then also."

My mother exhaled with such force it surprised me the dishes didn't rattle off the shelves.

"Did Marni fool around like this in high school,

Mrs. Legend?" Gus asked.

"Please, call me Angela. I have to admit, she and that Kramer boy needed to be hosed off once in a while. Not like her sister, Gloria. She always acted proper when it came to the boys she dated. One time I caught Marni and him on the couch and..."

I locked the door behind Jake and spun to curtail the conversation going on behind me. "Mom, enough. Gus does not need to hear about my teenage love life."

"I could stand to hear a bit of history. After all, you're always asking me personal questions," Gus said.

"First of all, anything I ask you has to do with solving your murder. Believe me, I have enough going on without knowing personal details not pertinent to your situation."

Mom took in a deep breath, her hand to her chest—one of her favorite stances. We should have erected a statue over her grave holding that pose instead of a headstone. "You were murdered? Oh, you poor boy. How horrible."

"Thanks, Angela," he said.

"Sorry to break up your little ghost support group, but we have bigger fish to fry. I thought you'd moved on."

"You thought wrong." She followed me into the kitchen. "I'm not going until I *see* you and your sister getting along. Besides, those nitwits haven't given an answer about my ashes. Signing the papers isn't enough; I want to know where I'm really buried."

Pulling open the fridge, I grabbed a water and snapped open the lid. "Can't you sense they're your ashes or not?"

"If I could *sense* it, wouldn't I have told you?" She

plopped into a chair opposite Gus. My table filled up fast.

"Not if it meant you could hang around dragging this out. Look, Mom, I've got other problems to solve right now. Can you give me a little space?"

"I'll sit here quietly. You won't hear another peep out of me." Over her lips she made a motion as if turning a key and throwing it away.

My mother, sit quietly? Not likely. "I give up. Stay or go, I don't care. Gus, did you get a look in either of the other cabins to make sure the other women were aboard?"

"Nope. Why didn't you tell me to look?" he asked.

"Because that fat walrus sauntered over when you and I were talking. You couldn't extrapolate from where I stopped speaking?"

He tilted his head. "Extrapo-what? You gotta speak English."

"Gus, you seem like a nice boy, but sometimes I wonder about your education. She means, why didn't you kill them." She looked at me. "Can ghosts do that?"

I leaned my elbows on the table and held my head. Waking up in a stupor on the boat had been preferable to this conversation with the dead. "Mom, that would be *exterminate*. Gus, what I meant was you couldn't figure out what I was going to say?"

"Ghosts aren't psychic, Marni. Who taught you about spirits anyway? You?" He jerked his thumb at my mother.

"Don't put me in the middle of this." Both hands rested in her lap as she sat up straighter. "My mother had the gift, not my generation. And good riddance. Why would I want to talk to the dead? No, not me, because if I had…"

"Mom, let me handle this. Why don't you go visit Calvin? I'm sure he'd love to hear from you," I lied.

"He and Sylvie were asleep hours ago. I wouldn't want to disturb them. With the weird hours you keep, I knew you'd be awake."

If I weren't so exhausted, I would have gotten up and banged my head against the wall. The resulting headache would be the same. "Gus, did you see anyone else leave when we did?"

"Nah. You couldn't see with Jake's arm around you, but by the time we was off the dock, the boat went back out."

"Shit! Why didn't you tell me?" I jumped up and ran to the window, as if I could see *Dominique's Dream* from here. "Gus, can you…" When I turned, he'd gone.

"He comes, he goes. I don't know how you can stand dealing with those crazy spirits," Mom said. "Your sister could never handle it."

"What?" I sat and slammed my hands onto the table.

"It's just he doesn't always stick around. Gus is very young. His mother must've had her hands full with him."

"Not Gus. What did you say about Gloria?"

She shifted in her seat. "Gloria? I was talking about Gus." Mom looked away, not meeting my gaze.

"You said 'My sister could never handle it.' She can't see or hear them. What's not to handle?"

"I meant the way you tormented her. Like when you'd tell her a soul hovered nearby when there wasn't one."

I chuckled. "That one never got old."

"Do you think your friend is in trouble? The old lady?"

"I don't know, Mom. With no way to check on her while the ship is at sea, all I can do is pray she's safe."

Mom sat back. "At least she's lived her life to the fullest if it's over. Look at me. Struck down so young."

"Mom! What an awful thing to say."

She lifted her arms into the air. "What? It's not like she's a spring chicken with her whole life ahead of her."

I leaned back. "No, I meant what you said about being struck down so young. You weren't that young."

She huffed. "Now you're being mean. No wonder you and your sister don't get along. Gloria would *never* say anything like that to me."

"That's the difference between me and her. She strives for perfection. My goal is humor."

"What's funny about calling me old?"

Nothing, but if I piss you off, you might leave. "I dunno. Look, I'm beat. Good night."

"Sleep well." Did her voice crack?

Chapter 25

I called Darla's number at seven a.m. and got voicemail. Every fifteen minutes I tried again with the same result. By nine I couldn't wait any longer. Walking to her house, I rang the bell. No answer. After knocking with the same result, I went around to the backyard. The rear door was locked, so I peered in through the sliding glass doors. Nothing moved inside, and there weren't any lights on.

With no other recourse, I called the local police station and asked for Officer Talbot. He wasn't on duty. I explained who I was and how I needed to talk with him regarding his godmother. The officer on duty said he would pass my message on. Within a half an hour, I got a return call from Ray. He said he'd drive around and check her house. If she hadn't returned by then, he'd contact the Coast Guard.

At ten, I received a call from Darla. The ship had stayed out to sea late, and Jason walked her home when they'd docked. She invited me for coffee, and I hurried to her place, arriving in time to see Ray drive away.

When Darla opened the door, I wrapped her in a hug. "I'm sorry. It's just, I thought you had been...well...you know. Gus told me about a conversation between Jason and Murphy and it sounded like someone had been too nosy. When I made it home okay, I thought—"

"Oh, honey. I didn't mean to worry you. When you fell asleep, I wasn't far behind. Thanks for calling out the cavalry. Ray appreciated you contacting him."

"I didn't know what else to do, short of commandeering a boat and scouring the Sound for your body. You drank the same wine I did, didn't you?" I asked.

"Yes."

"I think they drugged us. Only you and I drank wine."

Darla sipped her coffee. "I hadn't noticed. Were we the only ones having the red?"

"From what I saw. Did Genevieve get off okay?" I asked.

She got up and refilled her mug, then held the pot up toward me. I shook my head.

"She wasn't around when we docked. Wouldn't her boyfriend, Murphy, have driven her home?"

How could I explain the complicated relationship those two had? "You would hope, but he doesn't always treat her well."

"He's an odd bird, isn't he?" Darla laughed.

"More like a dodo. And in serious need of a fashion consultant. Diggs is creepy too." I shuddered.

She nodded. "Why would they drug us? I've known Jason for years, and he has always been a gracious host. Though, he never has asked me onto his boat before. Do you really think something sinister was behind the invitation?'

"Gus convinced me something went on while we slept," I said. "He felt sure they were going to do me in." Her coffee had a mocha flavor that tickled my tongue with chocolate as I sipped. "Still, we need to make sure Genevieve got home safely."

The color drained from Darla's face, as her mug thudded on the table.

"What's wrong?"

She stared over my head with eyes wide. Twisting in my seat, I saw a television mounted to the wall, playing the news on mute. The caption below read, "Woman's body found on Crab Meadow Beach." I knew the place—a private beach for the township of Huntington, east of Northport.

"Turn on the sound," I whimpered.

She swiped the remote from the counter and pressed the button until we heard the announcer's voice, "…washed ashore on Crab Meadow beach. No identification has been confirmed at this time. The woman, standing about five-six and weighing approximately one hundred and fifty pounds, has red hair and a mole on the side of her neck. She does not match any descriptions of currently reported missing persons."

Darla reached out and grasped my hand. "How could I know? I'd assumed she left when you and Jake got off the ship. Nobody said anything to me about her being missing."

"Now you know why we were drugged. I'd only had one drink before boarding, certainly not enough to cause me to pass out after half a glass of wine. There's no other explanation. With us aboard, it validates Jason's claim of a pleasure cruise with friends if the body should get traced back to him."

Covering her mouth, tears rolled down her cheeks. "She died, and we did nothing."

"Darla, we had no idea. Neither you nor I will be

held responsible, but we owe it to Genevieve to bring them to justice. She wasn't the brightest tool in the shed, or the most loyal—don't ask—but she didn't deserve being murdered. Her falling off the boat was *not* an accident. We need to find a way to prove it."

She sat back in her chair. "Can you talk to her?"

If only it were that easy to contact lost souls. "It doesn't work that way. She needs to come to me, providing she hasn't moved on. Even if her spirit is still around, it could take years before she's ready to contact someone who can help her. Look at Gus. He waited two and a half decades."

****

Back at my apartment, I called Jake. When he didn't answer, I left a message saying to please call me.

Had he known what Jason had planned during our late-night cruise? It sickened me to think he'd helped. Gus had said his brother would never hurt a woman, but that was the Jake from twenty-five years ago. Who was the Jake of the present?

I spent the remainder of Sunday watching the news for further developments. An autopsy would be performed before the police could release the body for burial, providing her family was located. Should I step forward and volunteer to identify her? Jake never responded to my text.

****

As much as I wanted to cancel lunch with my sister on Monday, I knew it needed to happen. I arrived at the café first and took a seat on the patio. By the bottom of my second glass of iced tea and no Gloria, I sent her a message, then ordered lunch. She never showed or responded. Could her agreeing to meet have been a show for Mom's sake and nothing more?

Munching on my sandwich and homemade chips, I sensed someone beside my chair.

"May I sit?"

I took in a breath finding Kendall standing there. "Ah...sure."

We faced each other across the table. Gesturing to the second setting, he asked, "Are you expecting someone?"

"Gloria, but she's forty-five minutes late and not answering her phone. My guess is I've been stood up. What are you doing here?"

"Came by for lunch and spotted you on the patio. Rather than scurrying away, I thought I'd man up and talk to you. If you'd rather not, I understand."

Sipping my tea, I didn't know whether to invite him to stay. My good manners got the better of me, and I found myself suggesting he order lunch. "How did your out-of-town trip go last week?"

His cheeks reddened as one corner of his mouth rose. "Yeah, that...I lied."

I chewed slowly. My actions hadn't been upfront either, but I knew I couldn't share information about my supernatural abilities with him. Before he said more, the waitress set his plate on the table and asked if we needed anything else.

His last words hung in the air like a grenade waiting to explode. "Marni, I loved reconnecting with you. Yet I feel we're going through the motions for old time's sake and not necessarily for something real. I got the feeling you wanted to put the brakes on after our last date. You saw me catch you driving down the street after telling me you wanted sleep rather than invite me in. Am I wrong?"

I leaned back and took a breath. "You're not wrong. But you're not completely right either. I don't know how I feel about you—about us." Reaching, I touched his hand. "Maybe we have too much history to start rewriting it."

He grasped my fingers, gave a squeeze, then pulled away. "Part of why I came over here is because I saw you and the other guy at The Corner Bar on Saturday. You looked happy and at ease with him. At least until you blasted the cue ball into that guy's crotch, and the two of you bolted for the front door."

I smiled at the memory. "I'm sorry if you felt jealous, but I was upfront about seeing Jake."

Kendall held up his hand. "That's the thing. Where I should have been hurt seeing you with another man, I felt relieved. If I cared about you in a romantic way, there would have been an emotional sense of loss. Instead, I found myself happy for you and thinking about a different future for me. Does that make sense?"

He'd nailed it.

"I don't know if this is the right answer, but yes, it does. So, where do we go from here?"

"We're not teenagers anymore. And we kinda live in a small town where we'll run into each other from time to time." He gestured to the patio around us. "Let's move forward as friends who've reconnected from high school and go from there."

"I like that. You know, we can still meet sometimes for a meal or a drink," I said.

"Who knows, we might even go on a double date. You game?" He crunched a chip from his plate, the crumbs sticking to his lips.

"Quite a progressive step. Think we're ready for it?" I relaxed, admiring him for coming to my table. It took a lot of moral fiber to begin a conversation like this one.

"Possibly. First, I'd need to find someone as fabulous as you and start dating her."

He paid the bill and walked me to the sidewalk. With a brief hug, he headed back to the library. A sadness swept through my body realizing the possibility of a relationship with Kendall disappeared before it had a chance to begin. Despite agreeing we didn't belong together as a couple, I feared it might taint our ability to have a friendship.

"Two-timing my brother?" Gus walked beside me.

I glared and walked away, rather than taking the bait. Once out of earshot of the other diners, I lit into him. "Why didn't you help Genevieve? She may be a ditz, but she didn't deserve to be murdered."

He stopped walking. "They killed Genevieve? I thought you was the one they were going to off. How could I have known? Or helped? Remember, you're the only one who can enjoy my presence."

As much as I hated to admit it, he had a point. What could he have done with me unconscious? "You're right. But she deserves justice. We need to find a way to prove Jason and crew murdered her." I hesitated a moment. "Do you think your brother helped?"

"I don't know. Even if he didn't, how could he have been on that boat and not known? I always believed my brother couldn't hurt a woman, but who knows what's happened since I died." He raked a hand through his hair. I wasn't sure what bothered him more—Genevieve's death or the possibility his brother had a hand in it.

Reaching my apartment, my phone dinged. Darla had sent a text asking me to come over as soon as I could. Heading straight over to her house, she met me at the door before I could knock.

"It's not her!" Darla exclaimed.

"What?" I stepped inside the entry.

"I didn't know what I should do, and when I called my godson, he suggested I start with identifying the body. When I got there, the woman looked awful, but I could tell it wasn't Genevieve. Ray told me there weren't signs of a struggle, so she may have accidently drowned. They'd know more once all the tests were in and the autopsy complete."

I slipped onto a kitchen chair. She placed a large mug of coffee in front of me, then took a bottle of whiskey from the cabinet and held it up. I gave a nod, and she put a shot into my cup. "Do you know who it might be?"

She shook her head. "I've never seen the woman before, but it definitely wasn't our shipmate."

Sipping my spiked caffeine, the warm liquid tingled down my throat. It helped ease some of the tension, but I still had many unanswered questions. Could the victim be connected to this whole mess?

Gus appeared in one of the empty chairs at the table. "So, it wasn't any of you they was talking about?"

"No. We don't know the identity of the woman on the beach," I said.

Darla's gaze shot up and saw I looked at the chair beside her. "Is Gus…"

I nodded.

"Can he remember anything else they might have said? Any leads at all?" she asked.

Gus shook his head. "I told you everything I heard. They never said who they was talking about. At least not while I stood there."

"He didn't hear anything else," I told her. "I haven't been able to reach Jake since he dropped me at home. Maybe I can drive over to his shop and see if he's there."

Darla stood abruptly. "No, it's too dangerous. This goes way beyond grand theft auto. Now with murder possibly on the menu, you may not be safe if he suspects you know anything. It's time to let the authorities handle the rest. My godson said he'd tell us once the body gets identified and they confirm how she died."

I carried my empty mug to the sink. "Darla, I'll be fine. It wouldn't hurt for me to get a look around his office and see if I spot any clues. He has no reason to think I know about any illegal activities. Nothing will happen, and maybe I can find evidence which might clear him of being part of murder. There's always the possibility he's an unwilling victim in this mess."

She walked me to the door and made me promise to contact her once I'd safely left Jake's garage.

By the time I'd walked home and gotten my car, the clock on the dash read five forty-five. Gus appeared in the passenger seat as I drove along Main Street. "Do you really think my brother didn't know?"

Tucking a loose strand of hair behind my ear, I said, "I don't know what to think."

"But you want him to be innocent, don't you? You

like him." He tilted his head in my direction.

Stopping for a red light, I gripped the wheel. "Yes, I do. When I first got involved with him, it never occurred to me this could go anywhere, as far as a relationship. My focus was to find out what happened to you all those years ago, and why he accused you of embezzlement." I faced his way. "Now I'm not sure what I really want. When we're together, he makes me smile. I never thought I'd say this out loud, but he's got a genuinely caring way about him in the way he treats me. Once we solve your disappearance, I want him to remain in my life."

A horn blast forced my attention back to the stoplight, which had turned green. In my rearview mirror, a man in the car behind us gestured for me to go. I hit the accelerator and drove through the intersection. At the garage, two of the large doors stood open. A mechanic, whom neither of us recognized, worked on a blue SUV in the first space. Jake's tow truck sat parked in front of the third bay. We went into the front office where a girl in leopard print glasses greeted me with a cheerful, "Can I help you?"

She looked too young to be part of his harem of old friends from the neighborhood. "Is Jake here?"

Her bright expression darkened. "Do you have an appointment to drop off your car?" She rested her bony elbow on the counter.

"I hope my brother didn't knock her up. She's way out of his league."

Her loose top betrayed the bulge of her belly. The conversation could turn sticky if the bundle of joy she carried belonged to her boss.

"No. Is he around?"

273

"Why do you want to know?" Her protective instincts could rival the toughest of night club bouncers. Nobody would get past her without a thorough explanation.

Smiling, I leaned against the counter. "Jake's a friend of mine. I wanted to surprise him. Would you mind getting him?" I gestured toward the back-office door.

She assessed me from head to toe. "Sorry to disappoint you." Her taut lips said otherwise. "He's out on a call and won't be back for a while. I'll tell him you stopped by, Miss…"

Rather than filling in the blank, I said, "Oh, but his tow truck is here. Do you think he arrived through a back door and didn't tell you?" I didn't know whether he owned two trucks but took a shot at his only having one.

She straightened, crossed her arms, and rested them on her baby bump. "I told you he's not here. Look, I got a lot of work to do. If you don't mind, I need to get back to it."

I thanked her for the hospitality, at which she blasted air through her teeth then turned back to her computer without another word.

"Marni, you know she was lying. Why didn't you just go into the back office?" Gus asked as we walked to my car.

"Because I can't just barge in without a reason. And I certainly didn't want to get into a power struggle with a pregnant lady. I wish I knew why her talons came up when I asked for him?"

"Maybe he's home. Let's go there." Gus said as we backed out of the parking spot.

I hit the brakes. He hadn't given me his address when he bailed on our fish barbecue date. "He never told me where he lived. Could it have been intentional?"

"What would it matter? All the goods end up at Diggs's place."

We turned left out of the parking lot.

"Where we goin' now?" he asked.

"Home. I'll have to wait for Jake to contact me before making another move."

"What? So, we're just gonna sit around and wait? Marni, we're getting close. I feel it. Let's go to Diggs's place. Last time I got a whole bunch of memory back. Maybe this time I'll remember the final parts of what happened to me."

"There's no point in going out there uninvited. Are you forgetting how things turned out last time I snuck in there? The sights and sounds still haunt my waking hours." I shuddered at the visual of Diggs's boudoir.

"Fine! You don't really want to help me. Do you? All you care about is yourself."

"Gus, that's not fair. I'm sorry this happened to you, but I'm still alive and would like to remain in this state of being. Let's go back to my place and revisit the clues we do have to see if we've missed anything." I looked to his seat expecting to find it empty. For once, he didn't disappear after throwing a tantrum. But the accusatory glare he gave unsettled me more than if he had vanished.

Already regretting what I was about to do, I flipped a U-turn.

His eyes popped wide. "We're going to the bluff?"

"No. Back to your brother's shop. If little Miss

Guard Dog did lie, then I may have a chance at talking to him sooner rather than later." My foot pressed the gas pedal harder than planned as we whipped around the corner and into the parking lot with the tires screeching when I hit the brakes. Hopping out of the driver's seat, I marched into the front office.

Glancing up from her computer, the receptionist asked, "Back so soon?"

"I know Jake's here. And if he's not, and is truly on his way, then I'll wait for him in his office. He won't mind. I'm his girlfriend."

"Way to be aggressive, Marni. Now we're getting somewhere." Gus rubbed his hands together.

Before I advanced more than two steps around the counter, the ferocious little guardian stepped in front of me. She moved fast considering her condition. "This office is private and off limits to anyone but staff." With hands on her hips, she stood in my path staring me down. "And if you really are his *girlfriend*, you would know he doesn't like to be disturbed at work."

While she did her best to intimidate, the girl couldn't have been more than nineteen or twenty. Certainly not in a position to go toe to toe with me.

The door to the garage opened, and the mechanic from earlier stood there wiping his greasy hands on a rag. "Hey, Midge," he said, "call Mrs. Crandell and tell her the car's done."

This was enough of a distraction for me to get around Midge and through the office door. Once inside, I immediately closed and locked it before looking around. Behind the desk sat a surprised Murphy scooping packets of money into a large canvas bag held open by Diggs. The large man's jaw dropped toward the floor as he looked from the cash to me and back.

The amount of money scared me. What lay beside the pile frightened me more, as Murphy snapped out of his trance and wrapped a hand around the grip of a handgun. I didn't know much about firearms beyond the old-fashioned pistols and rifles I'd researched for my books, but I knew I didn't want to be on the receiving side of the bullets.

"Oh, crap," Gus muttered.

The receptionist pounded on the door behind me, yelling for me to open it, or she'd call the police. Somehow, I believed her words to be an empty threat, given what I'd found.

"It's okay, Midge. We got it from here," Diggs yelled.

After a moment of silence, she spoke through the door. "Okay, Uncle Diggs." *Uncle?* The thought of that cute young thing being related to this slimy creature made me feel sorry for her. Almost. She wasn't the one facing the business end of a gun.

"Hey, guys," I stammered. "Thought Jake might be in, but I can see you're busy, so I'll leave you to it." Spinning around, I fumbled with the lock.

Murphy called, "I wouldn't do that if I was you. You better come sit down so we can chat."

"Marni, you gotta get outta here. These guys don't mess around when it comes to business."

"Ya think?" My sarcasm blasted at Gus.

"Yeah, I think," Murphy answered, waving the gun toward one of the two chairs on my side of the desk. "Too bad you had to see this, Marni. Jake really liked you."

Liked? As in past tense. No, no, no, no, no. This

couldn't be happening. *Think, Marni. Stay calm and talk your way out of this. You're good at talking.* Forcing a smile, I asked, "See what? You're counting the day's receipts for the shop. I didn't realize you two helped Jake with the accounting. And Diggs, that's your niece? Wow, what a cutie. How far along is she?"

"You never struck me as dumb." Murphy sneered. "Don't make me change my opinion now. Sit," he commanded.

Gently I sank onto the filthy striped cushion. The fabric had grease spots, making me cringe as I settled onto it, never taking my eyes off the weapon. "Murph, why all the fuss? I'm sure there's a logical explanation for whatever is happening here. Let's not get out of control. Midge said Jake would be back soon. I'm sure he can straighten things out."

With his other hand, Murphy took out his phone and hit a number. "We got a problem. Marni walked in on us here at the office." He listened. "We was stashing the bills." Nodding, like the person he spoke with could see him, he said, "Got it." He ended the call and told Diggs, "Bring my car around to the back door. The three of us is going for a ride."

We waited in silence for Diggs to return. If only there was a way for Gus to get a message to Darla. When the door opened again, a black sedan had been backed up to it with the trunk open. My limo had arrived.

"You sure we should be doing this?" Diggs asked.

"Just do what you're told. We don't call the shots," Murphy said. "Get up and walk ahead of me." He gestured toward me.

I stood on wobbly legs and shuffled toward the

exit. My feet turned into lead weights as I trudged. Murphy snatched my purse and fished through it, retrieving my keys. He handed them to his partner. "Follow us in her car. Finish packing up the take and bring it with you. Throw her purse in too. We can't leave any trace."

Diggs swirled the key ring on his finger, and I heard them jingle together.

Murphy grabbed my arm and forced me onward. Before shoving me into the trunk, his rancid breath crawled over the back of my neck as he whispered, "Guess we'll have time for that *date* after all." Wet, sloppy lips covered my ear, and his tongue slobbered across the lower lobe. *There had better be a bucket in the trunk, otherwise he'll need to clean the carpet liner.* After his moment of victory, he pushed me inside and slammed the lid. The engine roared to life, and the vehicle tore out of the parking lot, fishtailing as it took to the road. My body slammed from side to side until I could brace myself against the back.

This afternoon didn't turn out the way I'd envisioned it. *Why did I let Gus badger me into action?*

Chapter 26

Dissolving into a hopeless puddle wouldn't rectify my current predicament. Instead, I allowed anger to course through my veins. As I rode in darkness, this emotion festered until it escalated into rage. My fingers searched the interior for anything I could use as a weapon. Beyond rags and what felt like an oil funnel, I came up empty.

Think, Marni. Shouldn't there be a jack or tools in case he broke down? He must have something back here. As I felt beneath me, there wasn't any place in the compartment for a spare tire. It had to be under the carpet. Lifting the edge, I hit paydirt. My fingers wrapped around a small screwdriver. This might come in handy, but I needed something with more weight. My head felt woozy with the movement of the car and the dense air in the small space. More searching scored me a tire iron. What more could a girl held hostage hope for?

The last minutes of the trip had me bouncing up and down. He might consider getting the shocks fixed on his vehicle. The change in terrain took me by surprise, and my head slammed against the top. Stars danced before me. I shut my eyes and breathed deep. All the jostling around in this warm, cramped space left me feeling nauseous. The whiskey I'd had earlier probably added to my discomfort.

There was no doubt in my mind where Murphy had taken me. Any hope of screaming for help slipped away since no neighbors lived close enough to hear me. The vehicle jolted to a stop. There'd only be one chance to use my weapon, so I pushed it toward the opening, hidden out of sight. With a chirp of the remote, the trunk popped open, momentarily blinding me with what little sunlight remained in the sky. My hand flew up trying to block the brightness. Squinting, I made out Murphy standing about ten feet away, his hands empty except for a key fob. Damn. I thought he'd be closer.

"Welcome, babe. Looks like we have the place to ourselves for a bit." He licked his lips.

Lucky me.

"Get out nice and slow."

More deep breaths. I pushed the queasiness away as best I could to clear my head. *You can do this*, I muttered in my mind over and over. I swung one leg over the edge, and my foot found the ground. Trying to hold onto the anger so adrenaline would kick in, I pictured smashing his head in. My other leg trailed out, and I grabbed the tire iron with the hand still inside the compartment. The moment my foot securely planted on the ground, I heaved the heavy object with all the strength I could muster. It flew through the air and landed with a dull thud a yard in front of my captor's left shoe. Crap! That thing was heavier than it felt in the car.

We stared at it on the ground, until he erupted in a deep-throated laugh. "That was your big escape plan? Chucking a tire iron at me? Maybe you shoulda told me to step closer first." He shook so hard from cackling at his own joke, I waited for him to reach around and pat himself on the back.

"Marni, run, he's off guard," Gus yelled from beside me.

He was right. If I dove into the woods, it would be a sure bet tubby couldn't keep up with me. I ran two steps before the gun shot made me to freeze in my tracks.

"You only get *one* warning, got it?" Murphy had lost his mirth. His bulk tramped closer until he squeezed my arm and dragged me inside the house.

"Can't we talk about this?" I pleaded. "This is a huge misunderstanding. Call Jake. Please. I know he'll explain it all away. Murphy, you don't have to do this."

"Do what? You did it to yourself. Now, you and me is gonna get cozy over in the bedroom. I'd offer you a beer, but I got other plans for that big mouth of yours."

For once my motion sickness came to my aid as I hurled my lunch down the front of his shirt.

Gus's roaring amusement bounced off the ceiling, at least for my benefit. Too bad Murphy couldn't hear him.

"Wow, Murph." I stifled a sneer. "I'm sorry. Guess the stuffy air in the trunk, and all the bouncing got to me. Kinda like being on a small boat. You might want to—" My cheek stung from his meaty hand making contact.

"You BITCH. You did that on purpose." He raised his fist to give me another blow.

"That will be enough." Jason stood in the kitchen doorway. "Murphy, go clean yourself up. You're beginning to stink up the room even worse, if that's at all possible." He waved a hand in front of his face wafting away the smell.

Murphy stormed off toward the master bedroom.

I palmed the spreading warmth of my skin. There'd be a healthy bruise by morning—if I lived to see the morning. "Jason, there seems to be some mistake. Murphy and Diggs are under the impression I'm a threat."

"Are you, my dear?"

"No. Why would I be? If you don't mind, I'm going to head home. It's getting late, and my family will be wondering why I haven't turned up for dinner." I backed toward the front entry.

The man made a clucking sound with his tongue. "You're not a very good liar, Marni. Why would you be having a family dinner on a Monday night, especially after meeting your sister for lunch?"

I hesitated. He remembered my conversation with Darla. "She and I made up and wanted to celebrate." Inching farther away, I bumped into someone behind me. Spinning round, I found Diggs, then turned back to Jason.

He spoke over my shoulder. "Hey, boss, should I pull her car into the barn?"

Crossing his arms, I noticed Jason held a gun. "Not just yet, Diggs. I may have another use for the vehicle."

"Marni, this looks bad." Gus remained at my side, running his hands through his blond hair. "Maybe my brother can reason with them."

"Where's Jake? Please, let me talk to him." I searched Jason's face for any hint of weakening, but unlike me, he sported a great poker face.

Murphy sauntered down the hall wearing a tight red tee shirt, accentuating his rolls of fat as they jiggled.

"Thanks for the loan, Diggs. This stupid dame blew chunks all over my new Hawaiian shirt. I was gonna wear it on my date with Genevieve."

She should thank me for saving her the horror of staring at it all evening.

Outside a truck sped up the drive and screeched to a halt. The door slammed, and Jake ran into the house. "Marni, I recognized your car. What're you doin' here?" His strong arms wrapped around me, pulling me close. Resting his head atop mine, he asked, "What do you guys think you're doing?" Pulling back, he noticed my cheek, and his face screwed up in anger. "Who did this to you?"

"Don't get your panties in a wad," Murphy said. "She had it coming."

Jake pushed me behind him, strode to Murphy, and took a swing, landing a fist squarely on his jaw. This caused the big man to sway backward. "You bastard. Don't you ever lay a hand on her again, or I'll kill you!"

"Gentlemen, please, settle down. The last thing we need is infighting amongst ourselves."

Murphy held his hands up in defense of Jake's raised fist. "Come on, man. She's just another broad. You gonna let her stand between us?"

Jake backed down and returned to my side. "Marni is a lady. You treat her with respect."

"See, Marni," Gus said. "He's got your back. Told you he wouldn't hurt a woman."

Looking directly at Gus, I said, "I wish my brother could hear you say that."

"What do you mean? Your brother seems like a cool guy, he…right. Your brother."

"If only he could know as much as the crypt keeper," I whispered.

Jake furrowed his brow. "What are you talking about, Marni? Who's the crypt keeper?"

Gus widened his eyes and opened his mouth in understanding. With a nod, he vanished.

I shifted my weight from foot to foot, searching for an explanation to the gibberish I spewed. "You know that old horror show on TV when we were kids? This place kind of reminds me of the setting." I forced a chuckle.

"She's just plain nuts," Diggs said. "That place didn't look anything like this house."

"As delightful as a conversation about your childhood is"—Jason grimaced—"we have business to attend to."

"Well, I believe that would be my cue to leave. Diggs, if you wouldn't mind giving me my car keys, I'll be out of your hair." Planting a kiss on Jake's cheek, I added, "Call me later. Okay?"

Confusion darkened the scrawny man's face. "Boss, are we letting her go?"

"Diggs, why do you have her car keys?" Jake asked. "And why is it Jason's decision about letting her go?"

The exasperation in Jason's voice grew as his patience diminished. "No, we are *not* letting her leave. She's seen too much." He focused on me. "I knew I should have had this matter handled when you broke into my ship."

I gasped. "What are you talking about?" If he knew, why hadn't he said anything before?

"Oh, come, come. I may be old, but my vision is

quite sharp. Enough light spilled into the walkway to see your profile, coupled with the scent of your perfume, when you invaded my cabin. Though, it's beyond me what you were looking for." He turned and walked into the kitchen. "Enough. Bring her along."

"Wait a minute. Are you guys going to fill me in?" Jake asked.

Murphy stepped up and said, "She walked in on us while we was counting the dough in your office. We can't risk her going to the cops."

"You can't be serious?" I glared at Murphy.

Jake turned to Jason. "Marni doesn't know anything about what you were doing. Boss, I'm going to walk her to her car. She's leaving."

Jason stepped back into the room and lifted his weapon. "I don't think that's possible. You knew the risks when you got involved with the woman. Now bring her, or you'll forfeit any rights you have in this situation." He motioned with the gun then led us into the backyard.

The barn door stood open washing light over tufts of crab grass and weeds. A small black convertible sat inside. Probably their latest acquisition. The fading sun gave me an eerie sensation—one of desolation thinking it might be the last time I'd see the bright orb in the sky as a corporeal being. A breeze rustled through the trash and debris littering the unkempt lawn. The faint pounding of the surf on the beach below beat with a slower cadence than my heart. Behind us the door smacked the outside of the house as the other two cronies followed.

"Jake, you don't understand." I gripped his arm. "They're making a terrible mistake. I don't know anything about whatever business you guys are into, and I don't want to know. Let me leave, and I'll forget I ever saw this place."

"Young lady, the situation is way beyond forgetting what you've seen," Jason purred. His smugness exuded confidence and control.

"Marni, I'm sorry," Jake said. "I need time to think."

Gus materialized by my side again. Raising my brows in a question, he nodded. "You need to stall."

I wanted to scream, *Don't you think I've been doing that?*

"Tell me one thing," Jake asked as he took a step away from me. "Why was you so interested in my family? You was always asking questions."

Gulping, I knew there would only be one way to prolong this. "Because your brother wants to know what happened to him."

It was Jake's turn to gape in wonder. "What…what are you talking about? He's…he left. He stole money and left."

"That's what you wanted people to believe. It isn't true, is it?" I accused.

"Stop the charade," Jason said. "We all know how this will end."

Jake shot a gaze toward his boss. "You aren't going to hurt her. She may be nosy, but I won't let you kill another woman."

"What did you think? We would hold her hostage indefinitely?" Jason raised his pistol.

I turned on Jake. "You knew about the woman who washed up on the beach yesterday, didn't you? Did you take part in her murder?"

"The one on the news? I had nothing to do with her. They don't even know who the woman is yet, or if she accidentally drowned. I would never hurt a woman."

"Wouldn't you?" Jason asked. "If I remember correctly, Jake, you were the one to strangle Dominique."

Jake's hands balled into fists at his sides. "You told me I had to, or you would turn Gus over to the police and make him the scapegoat for the robberies. It's your fault she's dead. I was protecting my brother."

"You bastard!" Gus's punches swept through his brother's body unnoticed by everyone except me.

Horror crept down my spine realizing I'd been dating a murderer. "Jake, you were the blond-haired man seen riding in her car the night she disappeared? Your mother showed me the picture when you dyed your hair. You and Gus could have been twins." I stepped back farther and fired off at the old man. "Why would you have your own niece killed? What kind of monster are you?" My situation grew worse by the minute. The floodgates of truth were open, and there would be no shutting them down. But the more they confessed, the chances of my surviving the night diminished.

"What harm would it do now?" Jason shrugged. "As you know, from the letters you stole out of my nightstand, I was having an affair. Word of it getting out would have destroyed my standing in the business community. Dominique found out and tried to blackmail me, coupled with threatening to go to the police about our little car *acquisition* business."

Gus stopped his attack. "That's why she said her

uncle was gonna give her a bunch of cash."

"Having an affair couldn't possibly have been that devastating. It was the nineties for heaven's sake. But why throw Gus under the bus?" Out of the corner of my eye, Gus slumped to the ground.

"It was he who brought Dominique into our business, and he needed to be the one to fix the mistake. She may have jumped into her role wholeheartedly, but she never would have gotten mixed up at all if she weren't enamored with the young hoodlum."

Looking at Jake, my words came out in a gasp. "When Gus found out what you'd done, you killed him too."

"I didn't kill my brother! Wait." He screwed up his brow. "How could you know he found out?"

I knew I had to keep them talking. "Because he told me. He saw Dominque through your bedroom window. She lay naked on your bed. He thought she slept, but really, she was dead, wasn't she?"

"How could you know what my brother saw? You wasn't there the night it happened." His voice escalated as the color drained from his face.

"Because your brother is here now. I have a...a gift...an ability. It allows me to talk with people who have passed on. Gus told me he found her car parked in the barn, so he looked in your bedroom window and saw her sprawled across your bed. What did you do to him?"

Diggs laughed. "Are you saying you see dead people? That's rich." He jerked a thumb in my direction and looked at Murphy. "Is this chick for real?"

"Marni, you're not making sense. How...how could he be here now?" Jake asked as he swiveled his

289

head, searching the yard.

"His ghost is here. Listening to the whole conversation. He's twenty-seven, with blond hair and the same tattoo, except his is red and black. You both got them on a dare."

"You said it yourself. The picture my mom showed you had all that stuff, and I told you about us getting them on a dare."

"Gus, tell me something only you and your brother would know."

He stood, his eyes glowing with desperation. "Tell him…tell him…when we was in grade school, I scratched our dad's car with my bike. My dad didn't know who did it and was gonna whip us both, but Jake…" He stared at his brother. "Jake told him he did it so I wouldn't get beat."

I relayed the story.

Jake's eyes welled with moisture. "He's really here, isn't he?"

My voice cracked as I tried to answer. I could only manage a nod. Swallowing, I said, "He doesn't remember how or where he died. What happened to your brother?"

"Oh, go ahead and tell her," Jason snapped. "We'll never get her to shut up until you do."

With a hollow stare, Jake spoke. "Gus came tearing into the house accusing me of messing around with Dom. He didn't know I'd already killed her and stripped her to make it look as if she'd been attacked. Murphy and Diggs were going to dump her body someplace. Gus took a swing at me. We were fighting right there in the living room when Jason arrived." He held his head with both hands. "Jason shot him."

The old man shrugged. "Can we get on with this now? I've heard enough ghost stories."

Ignoring him, I walked to Jake, placing my hand on his arm. "What did you do with his body?"

He pointed at the patch of rose bushes on the side of the yard. "I buried him there. Jason had me spread the story about the stolen money, so everyone would think Gus left town. It would explain why he disappeared and didn't come back." Jake looked skyward. "Gus, I'm sorry. I was your big brother. I should've protected you, not dragged you into my twisted life of crime. Because of me you're dead, and I lied to keep it a secret and save my own ass."

"I'm over here, dummy. If I was up there, we wouldn't be doing this now." Gus stood beside his brother. "Marni, tell him I forgive him. Tell him he needs to be the man now that he wasn't back then and do the right thing."

"I will." I told Jake what his brother said.

"Well, since Marni has grown so attached to your little brother, perhaps we should bury her in the same plot." Jason raised his gun and cocked it.

"No," Jake yelled and stepped in front of me as three loud bangs sounded.

It was Gus's turn to shriek in agony as he watched his brother fall.

Another shot rang out, and I waited for the hot metal to sear through me. It never did.

Jason slumped over holding his arm. His weapon lay on the ground.

"Freeze! Police! Drop your weapons." Four uniformed officers swooped into the yard from two sides along with a man in plain clothes.

Murphy let go of his gun and raised his arms. Diggs followed suit, and my rescuers grabbed the men and slapped them in handcuffs.

I knelt beside Jake, my tears falling as his breathing shallowed. "Why did you do that?"

"Because I wanted to be the man Gus needed me to be. I needed to save you."

Kissing his forehead, I shushed him from speaking and sapping his strength.

He wouldn't listen. "Guess I'll be seeing him myself, soon."

With the area secured, paramedics rushed in and took Jake. The bullet Jason received hit his shoulder, causing him to lose his gun, but not his life. Jake wasn't as lucky and was gone by the time they'd reached the hospital. I couldn't imagine how tough it would be on his mother learning she'd need to plan a double funeral.

Officer Talbott came over while one of the ambulance crew checked me over. I held an ice pack to my cheek and had a blanket draped around my shoulders. Except for confirming my face would sprout a beautiful bruise by the next day, I remained unharmed—at least physically. My heart wrenched when the paramedic told me the news about Jake. Tears drifted down my cheeks. I wished things could have turned out differently.

"Glad to see you're okay," Talbott said.

"I'd ask how you got here so fast, but I have a hunch your godmother had a hand in it." I wiped the moisture from my cheeks and hopped off the back of the ambulance. We walked toward the rear of the house.

"Darla called me right after you left her place and

told me what you intended. We already had an open investigation into the car theft ring, but we didn't have enough evidence to connect Jason Dilboy. Thanks to your meddling, we do. I arrived at Jake's garage in time to see Diggs drive out in your car. Skeevy little fellow if you ask me."

I snickered. "That's an understatement. How'd Jake get past without spotting your cruiser? There's only one way in and out of here."

Waving an arm over his civilian outfit, he said, "It's my day off, so I drove my personal vehicle. While parked by the last house calling for backup, he shot past me without a second look."

Stammering I asked, "How much of our backyard discussion did you hear?"

He grinned. "All of it."

"Aha." Envisioning national headlines, I wondered how long before every lunatic on the eastern seaboard would come pounding on my door asking me to conjure their loved ones. "Did Darla tell you how this all started for me?"

His head cocked sideways. "Let me compliment you on a wonderful performance. His mother must have told you the story of the scratched car." He winked.

"Thank you."

"By the way, do you remember what I said would happen if I found you up here a third time?" His voice deepened with authority.

I held out my wrists. "Okay, arrest me, officer. I'd hate for you to break your word."

"You get a pass this time, but tread carefully. I'm not known for my leniency."

"Noted. Now, I have things to…ah…wrap up by

the rose bushes. I assume you'll get a crew in here to excavate?"

"It's in the works. Let me know when you're ready, and I'll have one of the officers drive you to the station and take your statement."

I stood beside Gus as he stared at the patch of dirt where his bones would be found. The sea air chilled as dusk fell and the temperature dropped. I wrapped the blanket tighter. "I'm sorry about your brother. They told me he died on the way to the hospital. He saved my life, you know."

"You wouldn't have been in danger if he'd been a better man. Who am I kidding? I might still be alive had I been a better man. When Jason's gun went off, everything came back to me. I remembered being shot."

We remained silent a moment. What could I say? They had both been criminals. "Everyone makes choices about their lives. In the end, Jake turned out to be one of the good guys by sacrificing his life for mine. For what it's worth, I really had fallen for him. Despite knowing it couldn't end well with his being on the wrong side of the law, I wanted him in my life. How sick is that?"

Gus grunted. "What can you expect? You've been hanging around me for the past couple of weeks. I ain't the best influence on people."

My arms ached to give this lost soul a hug.

"Guess you won't be seeing me anymore, huh?"

"That's usually how it works. Your murder's been solved, and your soul is free."

"Thanks, Marni, for everything. You are one cool lady."

"You know…" I stood alone. "Rest in peace, Gus."

Chapter 27

By the time the police cruiser left me at my doorstep, it was after midnight. They wouldn't give my car back until they processed any evidence Diggs left inside. Too tired to argue, I gratefully accepted my apartment key and purse. My cell had a couple missed calls from both Darla and Calvin. Despite the late hour, I shot off a text to both then turned off my phone.

Exhaustion consumed my body, and I couldn't remember my head hitting the pillow but woke up in my own bed wearing pajamas. Turning on my cell, I noted the time read ten thirty. I saw a response from Darla asking me to come visit when I felt ready.

Fortified with a healthy dose of caffeine and a couple rolls from the bakery, I got dressed and went to visit my friend. With all Darla had been through with me, I felt she deserved a full report, though I suspected she'd already grilled her godson for details. This time it was her turn to throw herself at me the moment she opened the door.

"I can't tell you how glad I am to have you back safe. When Ray told me he'd gotten to you in time, I knew I'd done the right thing by not waiting for your text."

She led me to the living room and gestured toward the couch. I really had come up in her world being invited to use the good furniture. I accepted her offer of coffee, and she left to retrieve it.

Placing a steaming mug in my hand, Darla settled into an armchair across from me sipping her own. "Ray told me about Jake. Despite his dark side and poor choice of friends, you were happy when you talked about him."

"Yup. Leave it to me to fall for the bad boy." A smile couldn't quite make it to my lips. What he'd done for me tore at my soul.

"My godson didn't get very chatty. Now it's your turn. Spill."

It took an hour to fill her in on the events of the previous night. She got all the details starting with Diggs's niece, to the nightmare of riding in a trunk, all the way through to Gus leaving. Darla listened without interrupting once.

When I'd finished, she said, "I hope I didn't overstep my bounds, telling Ray how you knew some of the things you did. Don't worry; he won't think you're a kook."

"He hinted at knowing, but I got the distinct impression he'd remain discrete. I'm not worried. What does concern me is what came to light about you and Jason. I feel awful at having pried into your personal letters. Can you forgive me?" I rose my eyebrows at the strange composure covering her face.

She pursed her lips before answering. "Marni, I didn't write those letters."

"But they came from D. Billingsly with your address. Are you saying someone fraudulently used your name and address when they sent them?"

She shook her head, then nodded toward the fireplace where pictures of her family sat on the mantel.

Her gaze rested on a photo at the far end depicting her and her husband—Drake.

My cheeks flushed. "Oh, Darla. It never dawned on me to think…" I covered my mouth for a moment. "If I hadn't given you those letters, you would have never known. You probably didn't want to know. I'm such an idiot."

She put up her hand. "I knew."

"How? Did you catch him?"

"No. He came clean after he broke it off with Jason."

I sat back. "I don't understand. You stayed with him anyway?"

Her smile grew. "Drake was my best friend. We'd had our rough patches over the years. To me, this telegraphed I didn't make him happy. I offered him a divorce if he wanted one, but he didn't. We went to counseling and came out of it with a stronger marriage and were closer than we'd been in years."

"Didn't you hate him for cheating on you?"

"Maybe at first. The more we talked about how we both felt, the more we learned about each other. No relationship is perfect, and there's always work that can be done to improve it. The difference is we both wanted to try. It wouldn't have gotten better any other way."

This woman summed up why my marriage hadn't survived. Only one of us wanted to try.

"Ray also gave me a little inside info, soon to be public, so it's okay for me to share. They've identified the woman found on the beach as Catherine Shelby. I guess the one they call Diggs has been singing like a bird ever since they brought him in, and he pointed the finger at his partner. When you and I went on the cruise, she lay tied up in the dinghy. Once we were far enough out to sea, Murphy took the small boat out, removed her bonds, and drowned her. They'd fed her a lot of alcohol before kidnapping her, hoping her death would look like a drunk passenger falling overboard. They'd found DNA under her fingernails, so she must've been conscious enough to put up a fight."

"The night I'd snuck into Diggs's place I heard him on the phone with Murphy talking about someone named Cathy. It sounded like Murphy was fooling around with her behind Genevieve's back. He must have flapped his gums too much, and she became curious."

After rehashing last night's ordeal, I stood to leave.

Walking me to the door, she asked, "So is Gus—"

"He's gone. I believe he's finally at peace now he's gotten the full scoop on his murder and where his body lay. Jason firing the gun caused his final memories to return."

My footsteps dragged with fatigue as I trudged along the sidewalk. The stress of everything would take a few days to shake off. As I approached my apartment, I found Gloria waiting. Another mystery solved—she hadn't fallen off the planet.

"Can we talk?" she asked.

I didn't see an olive branch in her hand. "Sure. Wanna go for coffee?" I pointed down the street to the ice cream shop.

"It's best if we have this conversation in private."

I thought about frisking her for weapons. She followed me through the door and upstairs. Since I'd moved in, she hadn't once visited me. Probably because I'd never invited her.

Walking in, she said, "This is cute. I can see why you like living here. Simple and close to the pier."

Gloria sat at the kitchen table, her hands clasped in front of her, watching me expectantly as I leaned against the counter. Should I wait her out, or did she expect me to speak first?

I folded. "What's up?"

"I know you're angry."

Raising my arms, I said, "Me angry? Why would you think that? You stood me up for lunch. You didn't answer my texts. How could that make me angry?"

"Marni, please sit down. I need to talk to you about something. And apologize—not just for my actions yesterday."

My foot tapped involuntarily while I remained standing. A car horn blasted on the street below cutting through the silence.

"Please." She gestured to the seat across from her.

Acquiescing, I took a seat and crossed my arms. I should've offered her coffee or tea, but I couldn't muster the ability to be hospitable. She did elevate my curiosity as to why she turned up on my doorstep like a lost kitten.

Letting out a breath, she said, "I'm sorry, Marni."

"For what?"

Placing her hands flat on the table, she held my gaze. "Sorry for not showing up yesterday. Sorry for being angry at you all these years. Most of all, I'm sorry for being jealous of your gift."

Wincing as if she'd slapped me, I asked, "Why would you be jealous of my gift? You've always hated my paranormal abilities. At times you acted like you hated me, even when I felt I didn't deserve your wrath.

299

I'll be honest, sometimes I did deserve it when I knew I'd antagonized you for no reason—other than pure entertainment. It's what I do." I shrugged.

Gloria's lips grew thin. "Having you as a sister can be a...*challenge* sometimes." Her features softened. "But my jealousy stemmed from your skill at handling yourself while dealing with the dead. Something I never mastered."

"How could you master something you don't have the ability to do?"

She rose and walked across the kitchen. After a few moments, she came back to the table. "This isn't easy for me, Marni."

"Gloria, you're officially scaring me. Tell me what's going on in that well-ordered head of yours."

That elicited a smile from her. "When you started *seeing things* as early as you could speak, you took it in stride. Never did you run screaming or act as if it were a big deal. You eased into your role helping lost souls without batting an eye. Sure, Grandma had been there to help you, but it all came to you so naturally. Not like me."

"Wait...what?"

"I've lied to you all these years. Mom and Grandma too. They both knew."

Uncrossing my arms, I leaned forward. "You're saying you've been able to see all the spirits I have?"

"No. At least not after Grandma helped me."

"I'm confused."

"Guess I'm not being very clear. The thing of it is, I began seeing spirits as young as you, but they terrified me. Waking up in the middle of the night to find a stranger standing over my bed sent me screaming. By the time I turned six, I couldn't sleep through the night without having horrible nightmares. No matter how hard Grandma tried to settle me down into accepting my role as a helper to these poor souls, I couldn't handle it. Watching you all these years confront these ghosts with candor, humor, or even bullying when it was or wasn't warranted, I grew jealous. And angry. Why couldn't I have been able to act confidently?"

For the first time in my life, I felt ashamed of the way I'd treated Gloria over the years. Here I thought her to be the perfect daughter, wife, and mother, while all the while she struggled with her own demons. "What did you do?"

"It was what Grandma did. She helped me turn it off."

"I didn't know that was possible."

"Neither did Mom. She said it wasn't common practice, but Grandma's grandmother had taught her how to do it in case it became necessary for future generations. We held hands, Grandma and me, and focused on closing a door. It sounded simple, yet the strength it took wore us both out. But it worked."

"I guess I was too young to remember you could see them too. Why keep it a secret all these years?"

"Grandma made Mom swear never to talk about my having abilities. She feared it might influence Calvin and you. As for me, I didn't ever want to talk about it again."

I got up and poured us each a shot of whiskey. Returning with the glasses, I said, "I know it's early, but exceptions need to be made." I expected her to refuse, but she surprised me by downing the liquid in one gulp, then grimaced. "Why are you telling me now?"

"I might need another before this conversation ends." She giggled before taking on a serious tone. "It's time for you to help me open the door."

Now it was my turn to down a shot. "No. You're not prepared. This isn't something you spring on an adult who's been dodging anything paranormal all her life. Gloria, believe me, you don't want to do this now."

"You don't understand. I have to."

"You're right, I don't understand. Explain it to me." I went to the cupboard, grabbed the bottle, and set it on the table.

"Grandma explained to me, at some point in time, I would have to accept back my abilities and help you. The cases have been getting tougher, haven't they? You're way beyond finding a lost set of keys or discovering where the savings bonds are hidden."

"This is stupid." Exasperation dripped from my tongue. "Fifty-one is not the age to begin a new career. We are not going to be ghost-hunting siblings."

"Honestly, I thought it might happen years earlier. Grandma told me some of your cases couldn't be completed alone. Once you helped the tow truck driver, things would start to get out of hand. Possibly dangerous."

"How did you know Gus drove a tow truck?"

She gave a sheepish grin. "I researched him on the internet. Just like I've investigated other souls you've mentioned. This time I got a hit on a Gus Zuckerman disappearing, and he worked at a garage driving a tow truck."

Pouring and drinking a second whiskey didn't calm my rising anxiety over this news. "How did Grandma know about Gus and what would happen next?"

Gloria reached across the table and placed her hand over mine. "Her mother told her. Our great grandma came back to visit her…you know…after she passed. Once she delivered this message, Grandma never saw her again. It had to be my choice to have them returned. I *want* to do this. If I don't, the consequences could be deadly for you. I can't stand by knowing I had the power to change the outcome and didn't."

Should I tell her this line of work almost took me out with my last case? Silence enveloped the room. Returning her ability to see spirits might send her spiraling down in terror like it did when she was a child. On the selfish side, it would be nice to have someone who understood my life.

"So, how do we do this? Does it involve poking our fingers and making a blood pact? I've always been a bit squeamish around sharp objects."

"I knew I could count on you to turn this into a total farce." She grinned. "No blood-letting involved. Hold my hands and close your eyes." She held out both hers then clasped them with mine. "Now, focus on a door. It's made of wood, solid oak, with a brass handle. There's a matching brass knocker on the other side. On my side. Can you hear it knocking?"

Squeezing my eyes tight, I visualized what she described. The brown wooden door. I stood before it. From the other side, the knocker sounded three times. Mentally wrapping a hand around the knob, I turned. It spun easily, but when I tried to pull the door open, it held fast. "It's stuck."

"Use your mind." Gloria sounded far away. "Pull hard while I push."

I felt the cool metal in my fingers. Placing my other hand on the knob, I yanked. There didn't appear to be any leverage to brace myself against, so I leaned back with my feet planted firmly on the floor and continued to tug. All at once I fell backward as the door swung toward me, and the weight of a body landed atop.

My eyes flew open, and I expected to find myself lying on the kitchen floor with Gloria on top of me. Instead, we remained seated at the table, hands clasped. Her eyes opened, and she laughed.

"Marni, are you okay? I didn't know what to expect."

Letting go my hold, I asked, "Did it work?"

Mom sat between us watching and shaking her head. Before I could say anything, Gloria's jaw dropped toward the floor. She grabbed the edge of the table to steady herself. "Hi, Mom. It's good to see you." Her voice cracked with emotion.

"It's good to be seen."

"I did what Grandma asked. Let's hope I can do her proud," Gloria said.

"You always do," Mom said. Turning my way, she added, "Both my girls always do."

If this were a chick flick, I'd be passing around the tissues about now. "This is the unfinished business you had to stick around for."

"Come on, Marni, keep up. You don't think I stayed just for your brother's wedding, do you? I'm kinda glad I won't be around to see that fashion travesty. There'll probably be swans and pink flamingos wandering the grounds. No, thank you."

"You know there won't be," Gloria said. "I think

Sylvie is partial to ostriches and llamas. Don't you agree, Sis?"

Sis. She'd never called me that before. Things might get better between us.

"You do realize," I said, "your perfectly ordered life is about to tumble into chaos with very little control on your part?"

She nodded. "It's time my life got a bit shaken up. Robert already knows about my picking up a sideline. I can't tell you how excited he is for me to have a new hobby which doesn't involve ordering him around." Had I known resurrecting her abilities forced her to acquire a sense of humor, I would have insisted on this ceremony years ago.

Time to deal with another loose end. "Mom, this would be our final good-bye I take it? You've kept Dad waiting long enough."

"I do miss him." Her lips curved up into a sad smile. "I only have one piece of advice."

There was always a catch.

"Okay, shoot," I said.

"Take care of each other. You may see spirits, but you're not bulletproof. And, Marni, don't think I didn't see what went on by the bluff."

Placing my hand to my chest, I tilted my head feigning innocence.

"Wait. You got shot at?" Gloria asked.

"They missed. Don't worry; there usually isn't gun play. Well, actually, there's never been weapons involved. The future may get interesting. Bye, Mom. My regards to Dad."

Stuttering a moment, Gloria said her final farewell as Mom disappeared.

Sighing, I grabbed the bottle and filled our glasses. Holding mine up, I toasted. "Here's to a brand-new era."

Gloria clinked hers to mine, and we drank.

"Wait a minute." Mom reappeared. "What about my ashes? Am I buried with your father or not?"

"I forgot," Gloria said. "*Dingbat* called me this morning. Your earthly remains rest with Dad."

"Oh, thank God. I couldn't face your father if I had to tell him a stranger shared his grave. What a relief." She sat with her hands folded and resting on the table.

Gloria and I stared at her for a full minute.

I took charge. "*Good-bye*, Mom. Rest in peace."

"Maybe I could stick around a little longer. You two might need my help with Gloria's first case. It couldn't hurt to have reinforcements."

My sister and I crossed our arms, sat back in our chairs, and waited.

"Okay, I can take a hint." She faded from view.

Saint Peter was about to have his hands full.

A word about the author...

Terry Segan currently calls the state of Nevada home. Most weekends she can be found riding backseat on her husband's red Victory motorcycle. While the beach is her happy place, any opportunity to travel soothes her gypsy soul. The musings conjured by her imagination while riding on the back of the bike can be found throughout the pages of her writing.

http://terrysegan.com

Thank you for purchasing
this publication of The Wild Rose Press, Inc.

For questions or more information
contact us at
info@thewildrosepress.com.

The Wild Rose Press, Inc.
www.thewildrosepress.com

www.ingramcontent.com/pod-product-compliance
Lightning Source LLC
Chambersburg PA
CBHW070049030726
47506CB00002B/409